Rebecca's Crossing

KAY D. RIZZO

Pacific Press® Publishing Association
Nampa, Idaho
Oshawa, Ontario, Canada
www.pacificpress.com

Cover design by Gerald Lee Monks
Cover design resources from iStockphoto.com
Inside design by Aaron Troia

Copyright © 2012 by Pacific Press® Publishing Association
Printed in the United States of America

You can obtain additional copies of this book by calling toll-free
1-800-765-6955 or by visiting http://www.adventistbookcenter.com.

The author assumes full responsibility for the accuracy of all facts and
quotations as cited in this book.

Library of Congress Cataloging-in-Publication Data:

Rizzo, Kay D., 1943-
Rebecca's crossing / Kay D. Rizzo.
    p. cm. — (The Serenity Inn ; bk. 8)
ISBN 13: 978-0-8163-2625-9 (pbk.)
ISBN 10: 0-8163-2625-8 (pbk.)
1. Women pioneers I. Title.
PS3568.I836R43 2012
813'.54—dc23

                                        2011044189

12 13 14 15 16 • 5 4 3 2 1

DEDICATION

To Alec:
Thank you for bringing so much sparkle into my life.
You are a solid gold grandson.
Lots of love,
Grandma

Contents

NOT FOR ME!

R EBECCA WOULD ALWAYS REMEMBER that Monday—the Monday that forever changed her life. The morning began like most weekdays during the five years since she had begun working at Joe Masters's Mercantile. Mr. Joe, a sixty-year-old widower with iron-gray hair and a ruddy complexion weathered from years of running supply wagons from Sacramento to Hangtown, as Placerville was called in the early days of the California gold rush, had hired her fresh out of the classroom. On a Friday, Becca, as she was called, completed eighth grade at Placerville's one-room school; and on the following Monday, she reported for work at the mercantile.

The girl thrived on the busyness of life at the general store. She enjoyed working side by side with Joe's two younger sons, seventeen-year-old Jed and twenty-two-year-old Hobie, both of whom had a light crush on her. But Becca's heart was in the high country. If she could spend her days rambling over the rocks and hills along the south fork of the American River with her faithful friend, a black-and-white mongrel named Tag-along, her life would be ideal.

A couple of hours before the cool winter sun crested above the Sierra Nevada range on that fateful February day, the girl fastened the bone buttons on her dusty, gray canvas saddle coat, tucked her waist-length, honey-brown braids under the rim of her newsboy cap, and headed toward the door of her parents' log cabin. Before lifting the bar on the massive oak door, she slipped her hands into a pair of heavy kidskin gloves.

Then she jammed her Colt six-shooter into the leather holster hanging from her belt.

"Is that you, Becca?" her mother called from the partitioned room beneath the loft. "Don't forget your snakebite kit."

"I won't, Mama. See you in a couple of hours." At the thought of facing down a reptile of any kind, Becca instinctively ran her gloved hand over the carved bone handle of the hunting knife she wore in a second leather sheath attached to her belt.

"I dropped a slab of beef jerky in your gunnysack," her mother reminded. Every evening Fay Cunard faithfully wrapped a piece of beef jerky in a corner of the previous day's newspaper and stuck it in Becca's prospector's pack.

"Thank you, Mama." Satisfied she had everything she needed, the girl heaved the lumpy gunnysack containing a collapsible prospecting shovel and pick and other necessary tools over her shoulder and lifted the bar. The iron hinges squeaked in protest as she opened the heavy wooden door.

"Be careful out there," her father, Pastor Eli Cunard, warned. "It may be too cold for rattlers or bears, but last night I spotted cougar tracks in the frozen mud outside the barn. A mite of a girl like you would be a tempting snack to a hungry cat about this time of year."

"Yes, Papa," Becca called as the door slammed shut behind her. The chill in the mountain air slapped her across the face and bit the tip of her upturned nose. The girl grinned and inhaled deeply. It was on mornings like this that she felt most alive.

Tag-along, who'd been sleeping on the stone doorstep, snapped awake. "Come on, boy." She tapped her leg, and the eager black-and-white mongrel fell into step by her side.

Early mornings were her time to do as she pleased. And nothing pleased Rebecca Susanna Cunard more than hiking alone in the peaceful forest above the town. But when the first rays of sunlight glinted off the roof of the Fountain-Tallman Soda Works building, she would sigh and reluctantly return to the parsonage. Once home, she'd shed her prospector's garb for a lacy bodice, a full, ankle-length skirt, and an embroidered crinoline or two—appropriate garments for a day at the mercantile.

Though the large veins of the precious ore that sparked California's famed gold rush had petered out by 1859, and most serious prospectors—along with many of the merchants, gamblers, and soiled doves, as her father called the fancy ladies of the night—had moved on to digs in Nevada, Canada, and Alaska, Becca still found enough chunks of the coveted metal laying about the mountain trails to whet her appetite for her early morning forays. Old Eagle Eyes is what Rebecca's father called her whenever she returned home and dumped her morning's find in the middle of the massive black oak table.

The early morning solitude was also a time when the nineteen-year-old could forget about being Pastor Cunard's darling daughter with the freckled nose and copper-brown eyes or the dimpled clerk in Masters's Mercantile. She could just be—without living up to anyone else's expectations.

Becca kicked at a rock with the toe of her boot. The stone tumbled over the edge of the cliff beside the trail. Tag-along bounded ahead of her, chasing imaginary varmints into the brush. A smile of contentment crept across the face of the five feet, two inch tall Becca as she stopped to gaze at the towering cedars and giant ponderosa pines along the trail.

After several minutes of hiking, the girl climbed onto her favorite rock to watch the sun peek through the treetops on the far side of the valley. Tag-along curled up on the ground beside the rock to catch a few extra minutes of sleep. Becca set her pack on the ground beside the rock and rolled three small chunks of gold ore the size of glass marbles about in her left hand. *Hmm!* she thought. *Not worth much alone, but definitely worth keeping.*

She dropped the ore into her canvas pack and located the strip of beef jerky. Tearing off a small chunk with her teeth, she dangled it in front of Tag-along's nose. The dog gave a grateful yip and wolfed down the meat in one gulp. Becca took longer chewing her portion of the jerky strip as she inhaled the clean mountain air.

Finishing the snack, she stuffed the scrap of yesterday's newspaper into her pack. From a jacket pocket, she removed a silver harmonica her parents had purchased for her while on a trip to San Francisco. After swiping the instrument across the sleeve of her jacket, she began to play a lively rendition of "O for a Thousand Tongues to Sing," an old Wesleyan hymn that she had renamed "Ode to the New Day." The melody echoed across the valley and back. She then switched to a couple of rounds of "Buffalo Gals" and then finished with "Sweet Betsy From Pike."

Becca again wiped the harmonica on her sleeve and stuffed the instrument into her pocket. She hugged her knees to her chest and leaned forward. One of her braids escaped the confines of her newsboy cap and dangled over her left shoulder.

Life isn't fair, she mused. *If I'd been born a boy, I could hike through the hills and prospect for gold to my heart's content with nary a raised eyebrow from my parents or from others in this tiny community.* If she'd been born a boy, her mother wouldn't insist Becca learn how to sew and cook, scrub pots and pans, and make poultices for bee stings and snakebites.

Woven into the morning melody of the wind whistling through the ponderosa branches, the girl could almost hear her mother's stern admonitions. Fay Cunard, a handsome woman in her late fifties with a perceptive eye and an easy smile, knew her own mind and knew exactly the lessons her only daughter needed to learn to grow into a productive wife and mother as well.

"It's time you grow up, my girl. Wearing boys' britches, throwing knives at hay bales, and shooting whiskey bottles off fence posts with the Masters boys are unseemly pastimes for a mature lady of nineteen. By your age I'd given birth to your brother Caleb and was pregnant with Aaron." She'd then turn to her husband. "Tell her, Eli!"

Papa, a pleasant-faced man, as tall and lanky as his wife was short and rounded, would glance up from the sermon notes spread out on the dinner table and grunt, "Your mama's right, Rebecca. Sooner or later, you'll fall in love and marry some young swain, and you'll wish you'd listened to your mother's instructions."

"Not me! And definitely not marry a preacher!" Becca would declare. "Don't be insulted, Papa, nor you, Mama. But I don't want to waste my life washing and cooking for some rube and birthing a new baby every year before turning up my toes!"

At the mention of babies, Mama would gasp. "Rebecca! Don't be sacrilegious! It's a woman's God-given responsibility and a joy to produce children for the heavenly kingdom."

Feeling a twinge of embarrassment, the girl would try to defend herself by pointing to her two older brothers. "Well, look at Caleb and

Serenity. What is it? Two babies now? And Aaron, he and Lilia produced four kids in as many years! They've certainly done their bit and mine for society and for the Creator, don't you think?" The girl warmed to her subject. "And then there's Widow Becker. Her husband gets shot in a barroom brawl, and she's left alone to feed and clothe seven children before she even turned thirty!"

Mama clicked her tongue in indignation. "Rebecca Susanna Cunard! Bearing children is a woman's place in God's plan for this world." Clamping her lips shut, Mama would then give a short nod as if the subject were settled when she'd set her chair to rocking.

From painful experience, Becca knew arguing with her mother after the woman sealed her lips would prove to be futile, but the girl couldn't stop herself. "Birthing is a whole lot of pain if you ask me! I've helped you deliver babies here in Placerville. I've seen the agony the mother goes through! And then, God forbid, when a newborn dies, I've heard the parents' cries. Nope! That grief is not for me."

At this point, her mother would glare across the lamplit room at her husband. "Eli! Say something!"

Slowly Papa would lean back in his chair, his voice measured and consoling. "Rebecca, honey, you're right. Being a parent isn't easy. Raising you and your two brothers had its trials, but there are so many more joys. Losing your little sister Amy in childbirth pains your mother's heart seventeen years thence." He would then pause and cast a compassionate glance toward his wife.

"As for me, saying goodbye to Caleb and Serenity when we left Independence for California was one of the darkest days of my life. And knowing I'll never be able to bounce their precious little ones on my knee pains my heart every day." Slowly, his frown broadened into a smile. "But yet, I thank God every morning for each of my six grandchildren, as I do for you and your brothers. I wouldn't trade one day of my life with anyone. You children truly are the joys of my life, a heritage of the Lord, the handful of arrows in my quiver, as King Solomon wrote in Psalm one-twenty-seven."

At this point Becca would run to her father and throw her arms around his neck. "Oh, Papa, I love you and Mama so much. I didn't mean—oh, I don't know what I mean."

"That's all right, honey. No one wants to grow up faster than necessary.

But Mama and I do want you to be prepared for that day. You take your time. You've a smart head on your shoulders. Sooner or later you'll find your place in God's world."

"Eli! You're encouraging her!" Mama would grit her teeth and take out her frustration with her knitting needles. At that moment, Becca vowed, not only would she never become some man's wife, but she would never become a preacher's wife.

* * * * *

The crunch of a fallen branch snapped the girl out of her reverie. Suddenly alert, Tag-along growled; his ears twitched as he slowly rose to his feet. With an almost imperceptible movement, the girl slid her revolver out of its holster, cocked it, and aimed it in the direction of the intruder.

"Hey, don't shoot! Rebecca, it's me, Bart Stanley." Bart's shrewd hazel eyes narrowed as a cocky grin widened across his face. "You'd better watch it, little girl. When you pull a gun on someone, you'd better be ready to use it."

Bart Stanley had been sweet on Becca since primary school. With her working at Masters's Mercantile, he'd come in several times a day to purchase one trinket or another. At times, Mr. Joe had to force him to leave following his lewd comments about the female shoppers and for telling off-color jokes.

"And you, Bart Stanley, can be grateful I don't shoot first and ask questions later!" With Becca's six-shooter aimed at the crease in the dome of Bart's gray felt hat, the dog pressed against the girl's leg, growled, and bared his teeth. "What are you doing up here on the mountain at this hour?"

The interloper cowered behind a scraggly bush. "Hey, call off your dog!"

"Stay, Tag-along! Stay!" The girl slowly rose to her feet. "Bart, I asked you what you are doing up here at this hour."

"This is public property. I can walk wherever I like." His eyes shifted from the girl to the dog and back again. "Call off your dog or I'll shoot 'im." Bart Stanley, the son of California state senator Bartholomew Stanley, tensed his right hand on the butt of a shiny new rifle.

Becca's eyes narrowed; her finger tightened on the trigger. "You kill Tag-along and it will be the last of God's creatures you'll shoot, I assure you."

He shouldered his weapon. "Rebecca Cunard, you got no cause to act so uppity."

The girl jutted her chin forward and narrowed her gaze. "Did you follow me? How did you know where to find me?"

He tipped the rim of his hat back from his forehead with the barrel of his rifle and flashed her a flirty grin. "So what if I did? What can you do about it?" When he took a step forward, Tag-along growled, causing him to quickly step backward.

"Come any closer and, I assure you, you'll find out! As you know, I do know how to use this thing." Keeping her six-shooter aimed at Bart's hat, she scooped up her gunnysack and draped it over her shoulder. "Come on, Tag-along, something around here stinks to high heavens!"

"Gonna play hard to get, little lady? You should know that sooner or later, Bartholomew Stanley III always gets his man."

"You make me feel grateful I'm a woman," she snorted.

The expression on his face darkened. He shifted his weight from one leg to the other. "Somebody should teach you to hold your tongue, young lady. That mouth of yours is gonna get you in big trouble someday."

"Becca? Becca?" It was the voice of her father.

"Papa! Papa! I'm just up the trail." She uncocked her six-shooter and slid the weapon into her holster. "If you know what's good for you, Bartholomew Stanley III, you'd better hightail it out of here before my father sees you."

Momentarily unnerved, the young man shouldered his rifle and pointed a finger at her. "You . . . you . . . I'll make a proper woman out of you yet. And I don't give up so easy. Just wait; you'll see." He ran his tongue over his lower lip.

As Preacher Cunard appeared over the crest of the hill, Bart disappeared in the opposite direction, but not before Tag-along snarled once more.

"What's bothering the dog?" Papa asked as he approached his daughter. "Did he spot a mountain lion or something?"

"Oh, you know. Tag-along can sniff out varmints of all kinds. So what brought you up here this morning?"

Her father took the gunnysack from Becca and slung it over his shoulder. "When you didn't come home at your regular time, your mama got worried. She sent me out to find you."

The girl tapped her leg. "Come on, Tag-along. Whatever you smelled wasn't worth the chase." After taking a quick nervous look over her shoulder, Becca caught up with her father. "Sorry, Papa. I guess I spent too long woolgathering this morning."

Her father paused and eyed his daughter. "Is something wrong, little girl? You're acting as skittish as a colt around a rattler."

Becca ducked her head to avoid his searching gaze. Lying to her father didn't come easily, but protecting him from any trouble with Senator Stanley and his namesake seemed worth it. "Of course not, Papa. Let's hurry. I'm as hungry as a bear this morning. I can almost smell Mama's flapjacks from up here."

CHAPTER TWO

THE LURKING MENACE

Hobie Masters, the hulking middle son of Joe Masters, greeted Becca with a broad grin as she entered the store. At six feet, four inches tall, the sandy-haired giant with steel-gray eyes and a ready smile towered over the diminutive girl, as well as over most other people in town. Because he seldom spoke, the townspeople believed him to be slow-witted. The girl knew differently. While the man spoke slowly and softly, his mind was like the sharpened teeth of an iron bear trap. Nothing seemed to rile him. Hobie had a knack for memorizing long passages of scripture and recalling them when the need arose.

In elementary school, Becca would spit out her fury at the other children for calling her friend a dolt, a dumbbell, or a dunce. "Fight back," she'd urge. "You need to fight back. You could flatten those bullies with one swipe of your arm."

Hobie's shrug and subsequent grin infuriated her. "Their saying so don't make it so. What good is it to squabble? 'The forcing of wrath bringeth forth strife.' " He quoted Solomon, his favorite author in the Bible.

Hobie had taught her, since she'd begun working at the mercantile, not only how to record her sales and balance the books but also how to shoot a knot out of a fence post at fifty feet, and how to split a bull's-eye with a knife at twenty paces. His presence in the store also kept tipsy prospectors from getting too friendly with Becca after a visit to Godfrey's Saloon. Becca realized the male customers' unwanted advances toward her had more to do with a lack of single women in town than with whatever limited beauty she possessed.

"Here, let me help you," Hobie volunteered as he helped remove the navy-blue, boot-length woolen cape from her shoulders.

The girl unbuttoned the bone button at the neckline. "Hobie! I think I am capable of hanging my own coat on the hook behind the counter."

"I know. I just want to help." He shrugged his shoulders. "Pa says a gentleman always remembers his manners around a lady."

Becca placed her gloved hand on his forearm. "You're right. I'm sorry. Thank you, Hobie." As she untied the ribbons of her poke bonnet, her honey-brown braids tumbled down her back. "Here, take this too." She handed him the hat. "And could you put my gloves in one of the cape's pockets as well?"

Smoothing the part in her hair, the girl strode around the end of the broad butcher-block counter to the cash register. "Did the new shipment of flour come in last night?"

"Sure did, Miss Rebecca. Jed and I helped Quince unload it first thing this morning." At the mention of Andrew "Quince" Quincy, the girl's eyes sparkled. Not that Becca was the only girl in Placerville to find the muscular blond teamster intriguing. Quince had broken the hearts of hopeful young ladies along the entire route from Placerville to Sacramento. Knowing his reputation, Becca managed to keep her "wits about her" as Mama would say, whenever he cast a flirty grin her way.

Becca slipped the white canvas shopkeeper apron over her head and fastened the ties around her waist. "Good. Mrs. Simmons has been checking every day for a week now. She's running low at the bakery. She swears that the flaky light crusts on her apple turnovers come from the fine white flour she purchases from Sacramento."

The shop's bell jangled, interrupting the beginning of a quiet morning. Becca glanced toward the door. Quince and Hobie's younger brother, Jed, strode into the store.

"Good morning, gentlemen," Rebecca tossed her braids over her shoulders. "And how is your day going?" After casting her own smile toward Quince, she hiked her skirts to the tops of her black leather boots, grabbed two metal kerosene lamps, and climbed to the top of the three-step ladder behind the counter.

"Becca!" Hobie ran around the end of the counter. Not knowing where to touch her in order to steady her, he waved his hands helplessly in the air behind her. "Let me do that for you."

"Nonsense! I can do it myself." The stepladder wobbled. The tin kerosene lamps clanged against one another as she grabbed for the shelf, then for the solicitous young man's shoulders. "Hobie! You almost made me fall!"

Ignoring the sad frown on the man's face, she set the kerosene lanterns on the top shelf alongside a row of dusty copper kettles that hadn't sold too well in the pioneer town.

When she urged the ladies of Placerville to purchase one of the pots, one of the women said, "Shiny copper pots just create more work. I prefer enamelware kettles and ironware skillets."

It's because of the copper pots, she thought. Becca's views on marriage and housekeeping became more solidified every time she watched her mother begin baking bread before dawn and was still was scrubbing burned-on food off the bottom of her copper kettles by nightfall. Long after the sun went down each evening, Fay Cunard's hands would be busy repairing her husband's canvas britches, ironing his Sabbath shirts, or piecing together a new quilt for winter. *No man will tie me down like that,* she vowed as she hopped off the ladder and wiped the dust on her fingertips onto her apron.

"Just because I'm short doesn't mean I'm helpless!" Her high-top boots had barely touched the rough wooden floor when she pointed her finger in the face of her employer's son. "Hobie! I know you are only trying to help, but please stop it. Besides, I'm more sure-footed than you ever will be."

The giant of a man with the sandy brown hair averted his eyes and took a step away. "Yes, Miss Rebecca. Sorry." The frown on his face matched Tag-along's whenever she scolded him.

Becca gave a short decisive nod. "Thank you. That's much better. Why don't you and your brother inventory the latest shipment of pickaxes and shovels? Your father will be checking the order slip against the delivery."

Becca felt bad as she watched Hobie, his shoulders slumped, shuffle to the storeroom. Without a word, Jed and Quince followed. *Why do I treat him like that?* she wondered. The half boy–half man never got angry; he never fired back. *He deserves better.*

The bell over the door jangled a second time. Becca smiled at the wives of the owners of Placerville's two largest mines as they sashayed into the store. Lowering her pink ruffled parasol, Mrs. Murphy gave the girl a broad, eager smile. "Hello, Rebecca. I hear Mr. Joe received a new shipment of calico from San Francisco."

Mrs. Pierce added, "My Anna Belle said you also have a bolt of icy-blue taffeta." The second woman's eyes twinkled with eagerness. "I just know that fabric was made for my blond, blue-eyed twelve-year-old!"

Mr. Joe had ordered the expensive fabric from San Francisco especially with the wealthy ladies of the community in mind. "We certainly do." Becca led them toward the fabric display. "I think you'll love the bolt of lavender velvet as well. Add a crisp white collar with tatting along the edge, and your daughter will have a stunning Sunday-go-to-meeting gown."

The women hurried toward the bolts of fabric stacked along the far wall.

Mrs. Pierce got to the fabric display first. "You are so right, Rebecca. I adore this lavender. So springlike!" The woman held the fabric up to her face and asked her friend, "What do you think, Amanda? Is it my color or Anna Belle's?"

Becca turned as the bell over the door jangled again. Three men tromped into the store. "Mornin', Miss Becca. We're here for a game or two of checkers. Fred, here, thinks he can whup me today, but you and I know better, don't we?" Josh Bird chortled and winked at Becca.

The girl laughed. "Mr. Rowe is pretty good. You've got your work cut out for you, Mr. Bird." As Becca picked up a feather duster from behind the counter, her fingers brushed across the cold metal barrel of the tiny derringer Mr. Joe kept loaded in case of an "emergency." Running a general store in gold country had its share of "emergencies."

The checker players set up the board on the large wine barrel designated by Mr. Joe for that purpose. As they sat down on the whiskey kegs, the bell over the door rang again. Feather duster in hand, Becca broadened her best customer-service smile. "Good morn—" She halted midsentence. Her smile turned to ice. Instinctively, she whirled about and headed toward the storeroom. "Jed," she called, "would you please wait on Mr. Stanley?"

"Sure." He stepped from the storeroom into the shop. "Anything I can help you with, Bart?"

"It's not you I came to see, junior!" Bart brushed past the boy and ambled over to the shelves of fancy dinnerware that the girl had been dusting. "You can't avoid me forever, Rebecca Cunard. You're what I'm here for." He flashed a grand, politician-sized grin and caught her wrist. "I'm here to see you. I'm here to invite you to attend the hoedown with me on Saturday night."

Confidence ringed the face of the son of the state senator. Outside of the church service each week and Wednesday evening prayer meetings, the square dance and family game night drew people from as far away as Coloma.

Becca glared at the hand gripping her wrist and then at his smirking face. "Bart Stanley, unhand me this instant!" She jerked free and massaged the wrist with her other hand. "As to your invitation—sorry. I already have a date for Saturday night. Jed is taking me. Isn't that so, Jed?"

The seventeen-year-old gulped and blinked in surprise. "Er, yes, ma'am. Sure enough, ma'am—the hoedown on Saturday night—you, me . . ."

For an instant, Bart's face flushed, and then he tossed his head back and roared with laughter. "You're gonna settle for a little boy when you can have a real man like me?"

"Jed is more of a man than you will ever be, Mr. Stanley!"

A hush fell over the room. The two women froze, clutching bolts of fabric to their chests. The checker players stared at the board as if trying not to listen, yet poised to come to the young woman's aid should they deem it necessary.

Becca sniffed, tilted her freckled nose in the air, and quickly scooted behind the counter. "Bart Stanley! I would date a banana slug before I would date a man like you."

He heaved an exaggerated sigh. "What is it? If you are just playing hard to get, you're going too far. You should feel honored I even asked. Every single gal in town would drool at the chance to be courted by the son of California state senator Stanley."

"Well, let me see. That number comes to ten if you count the three new ladies working at Sadie's Lounge. Please feel free to set those gals a drooling if you'd like, because there are not enough sugar cookies in Mrs. Simmons's Bakery to set me drooling over you. And I love her sugar cookies!"

Bart's eyes narrowed. The man moved around the end of the counter. "You watch your mouth, little girl! When you become my wife—and you will—I'll teach you how to speak to a man." His mouth hardened as he reached out to grab one of her long braids. "I could snap your scrawny neck with one twist."

The two women gasped at the threat. Becca heard but did not see the whiskey kegs slide away from the game table. Encouraged by their support, the girl straightened to her full height and jutted her chin. "Like you do with hapless birds and innocent kittens? I've seen you use God's creatures for target practice."

"Why you little . . ." He slid the fingers of one hand around her neck and took a step closer to intimidate her further. What he failed to see was Becca's hand slide under the counter and her fingers grip the handle of Mr. Masters's derringer. With one slight twist of her left wrist, she jammed the tiny gun against Bart's ribs. "I'd rethink that, if I were you, Mr. Stanley. Now, I advise you to get back on the other side of this counter so I don't have to use this."

Bart's face reddened as he eyed the tiny, but lethal weapon in her hand, as well as the fury in the girl's eyes. He shot a nervous glance at the checker players, who were now standing with their hands on their six-shooters, and then another at the fear in the eyes of the female shoppers. Forcing a weak smile, he raised his hands in surrender. "All right! All right! You got me this time, Rebecca Cunard. But sooner or later, little gal—"

Jed gasped as the girl shoved the derringer into Bart's belly. "If you ever come near me again, I will put a hole straight through you, Mr. Stanley! Don't think I won't! Now git!"

At that moment, Hobie stepped into the mercantile from the storeroom. "Hey! What's going on here?"

"Don't worry, Hobie," Becca insisted. "I have everything under control." She snarled at Bart. "Are you hard of hearing? I said, 'Git'!"

Fire shot from Bart's eyes. A vein in his forehead throbbed. Humiliated at the girl's rejection, the man stormed from the general store. Behind him, the door slammed, rattling the bank of paned windows.

Mr. Bird shook his head. "That boy's so mad, he's heading for trouble. Mark my word. You better watch yourself, Miss Rebecca."

His checkers partner added, "Yup. He's headin' for Godfrey's Saloon. If you want my advice, little lady, you'd better have Hobie walk you home tonight—for your own good."

"I can take care of myself!" Becca snapped, slamming the derringer onto the shelf beneath the countertop.

As customers came and went from the mercantile throughout the rest of the day, the girl tried to erase the morning altercation from her thoughts. And by the way Hobie hovered around the store, she knew it was on his mind as well. When closing time came, Hobie grabbed Becca's cape from the hook behind the door.

"What are you doing, Hobie?" she demanded.

"Walking you home like Mr. Fred said I should."

She placed her poke bonnet on her head and tied the ribbons beneath her chin. "Don't be ridiculous! I don't need someone to walk me home. I'm not a five-year-old, you know. Besides, isn't your father expecting you to keep the store open an extra hour this evening being it's payday at the mines?"

"Jed can do that. I'm walking you home! As Solomon said, 'Discretion shall preserve thee, understanding shall keep thee.' " He gave a nod of finality, much like Rebecca's mother did whenever she considered a subject to be closed.

Becca sighed. "Fine." There was no arguing with Hobie once he'd set his mind on something. "Oh, wait, didn't Jed make a delivery of feed at the stables this afternoon?"

Hobie glanced toward the storeroom.

"Is he back yet? You'd better check. We can't leave the mercantile unattended." Slowly, she slipped her fingers into her gray, wrist-length kidskin gloves. The man nodded, stepped through the door to the storeroom, and called his younger brother's name.

The bell jangled as Becca bounded out the front door and down the street toward the parsonage. She giggled, imagining the look of consternation on Hobie's face when he returned and found her gone.

The afternoon sun had almost disappeared behind the Sierras to the west. The shadows of night had already begun to fill the valley's nooks and crannies. The girl's heart raced as she dashed along Main Street, partly from her escape from Hobie and partly for fear of Bart's all-too-real threat. She ran past the Methodist church and on past the bakery, knowing that she could find refuge in either place should it become necessary.

Home never looked so good as it did when she pushed open the front door, and the aroma of johnnycake baking in the oven accosted her senses. Tag-along, who'd been eagerly awaiting her arrival, gave a welcoming yip and trailed her into the warm, inviting cabin. When the door slammed shut behind her, Becca doubled over to catch her breath.

Her mother looked up from her knitting. "What's wrong, child? Why are you out of breath? Have you been running?"

"It's a long story." The girl staggered over to the table and plopped down onto the nearest chair. Tag-along followed, nestling his head onto her lap. Distracted, she scratched him behind the ears. "You wouldn't believe what a horrid day I've had!" She untied the ribbon to her bonnet.

"Oh, sweetie, I'm so sorry." Mama dropped her yarn and knitting needles into the basket beside her armless kitchen rocker and hurried to her daughter. Gently, she massaged her daughter's shoulders and neck. "Is there anything I can do to help?"

"*Mmm,* that feels so good." Unbidden tears glistened in Becca's eyes.

"Are you crying?" her mother asked in surprise. The girl hadn't cried since she was bitten by a king snake when she was ten years old. "Why, honey? Whatever happened? Why are you crying?"

"No . . . I mean yes . . . oh, I don't know what I mean. It's just been a terribly horrid day—the worst day of my entire life!" Becca flung her hands dramatically in the air. "If only I hadn't been born a girl; nothing like this would have happened!"

"Born a girl? Did you have a little accident?" Her mother tenderly broached a topic reserved for conversations between a mother and her daughter. Since she was twelve, Becca had resisted the inevitable physical changes that came with growing up female.

"No, Mother! I didn't have an 'unexpected visitor,' if that's what you mean!" Both women knew the mere mention of her monthly cycle could send the girl into a tirade.

Mama heaved an exasperated sigh. "Then, tell me, what has you so upset?"

"It's Bart Stanley! The cad's incorrigible. He won't leave me alone."

Mama chuckled. "Aw, so the boy's taken a shine to you."

"Mother! This isn't funny!" Her eyes snapped with irritation. "Not only did he embarrass me in front of a store filled with customers, but he actually threatened to choke me!"

"I'm sure he didn't mean—" the woman began.

"Yes, Mama, he did! I vow I'll shoot him if he doesn't leave me alone! Did you know he followed me up the mountain this morning? If Papa hadn't arrived when he did, I don't know what might have happened. And then, later today, he came into the mercantile and tried to . . . to . . . to . . . I am so thankful that the store was filled with customers."

Before Mama could respond, the cabin door flew open and in strode Papa, his face revealing his concern.

"What in the world have you done?" he asked. "It's all over town that you threatened the life of Bart Stanley. Is that true? Why would you do such a thing?"

"Papa, I can explain." Becca sniffed back her tears.

The man paced in frustration. "I certainly hope so. I still don't think it was a good idea for Hobie to teach you how to use a six-shooter, let alone purchase one with your own earnings; but I figured you might need protection from the varmints you would meet in the hills. Tell me you wouldn't use it on a fellow human being."

"I-I-I don't know." She gulped. "I think I would have shot a hole in Bart's hat this morning if you hadn't arrived when you did."

Like a California brown bear hunched and ready to attack, her father leaned across the table. "What? You didn't tell me that boy was up on the mountain with you this morning."

"He wasn't with me; he followed me."

"Did he threaten you?"

"Well, yes, sort of. And he threatened to kill Tag-along."

"What do you mean 'sort of'?" Before she could reply, her papa straightened to his full six-foot height. He wagged his finger in Becca's face. "That's it!" He thumped his fist on the table. "I forbid you to go up on the mountain alone ever again!"

"Papa," the girl wailed. "You can't mean that."

"Oh, yes, I do!"

"I can take care of myself."

"Obviously not! Don't defy me on this, Rebecca Susanna Cunard."

The girl dropped her head. Whenever her father used her entire given name, she knew he meant business. And she knew he wouldn't change his mind any time soon. But how long could she live without visiting her daily retreat overlooking the American River?

CHAPTER THREE

INTO THE NIGHT

A HEAVY PALL HUNG OVER the Cunard supper table. Papa glowered as he picked up his knife and spread butter on his johnny-cake and ate his favorite dish—New England–style baked beans. As for Becca, her stomach churned. The beans on her plate almost dared her to eat them.

"Come on, honey," Mama coaxed. "You have to eat." She turned to her husband. "Eli, say something."

Papa eyed his wife. "I've said all I intend to say."

"Will you be walking me to work and back each day too?" The moment it came out, the girl regretted her sarcasm.

"If I have to—to keep you safe." By the set of his jaw, both women knew the discussion had ended.

Becca pushed back from the table and dabbed her lips with the blue-and-white checked napkin. "I'm not hungry. Please excuse me." Receiving a nod of permission from her father, she climbed the ladder to her loft bedroom. There she wrapped her red-and-yellow quilt about her shoulders, curled into a ball, and buried her face in her downy pillow. She didn't sleep but strained to hear her parents' conversation in the room below. Perhaps her mother would talk some sense into her father.

"Are you sure you're not being a bit harsh, Eli? You know how much our daughter enjoys her morning outings."

"Harsh? I am trying to protect her. That boy is as dangerous as a rabid polecat. Young Bart has made claims all over town that he will bed our daughter to force her to marry him."

The woman gasped. "I didn't know—"

"His threat is all over town." Her father's voice came out in a feral growl. "Frankly, I don't know how I can adequately protect her. Maybe she should quit her job at the mercantile. If Becca has no place to go—"

"Eli, maybe the first thing we should do is put in our request for a contingency of heavenly bodyguards."

"*Hmmph!* That boy has been nothing but trouble since he reached his majority. He's been in and out of trouble with the law—drunkeness, barroom brawls, even theft, though that was never proved. People believe the senator bribed the witnesses to make it go away." Papa grunted again. "It's going to take ten thousands angels to protect our daughter from the senator's rogue son, I'm afraid. But you are right. Prayer is our first and most powerful defense."

Without looking, Becca knew her parents had linked hands across the supper table and had bowed their heads to pray. But this time they weren't praying for a sick child or for an injured parishioner. This time they were praying for her.

"Dearest Father," Papa began, "the safety of our darling baby girl is heavy on our hearts tonight. She is truly the apple of our eyes, as she is Yours. This time she's stirred up a hornets' nest. Lord, You know how reckless our precious Becca can be. And You also know how much she treasures her freedom. I don't want to frighten her into seclusion, but I don't want her life ruined by this determined young rogue either." He paused to clear his throat. "Please, Lord, give us wisdom. And if it isn't asking too much, surround her with ten thousand of Your burliest angels. Please don't allow any harm to come to our precious little one. Amen."

A cacophony of emotions swirled through Rebecca as she tried to sleep. Below, behind the sheet partition, her parents prepared for bed. Her father extinguished the flame in the table lantern, and darkness filled the cabin. Soon exhaustion overtook her emotional turmoil, and she slipped into a deep, dreamless sleep.

Becca started awake when Tag-along began barking; seconds later, someone banged on the cabin door. Fearful it might be a drunken Bart, she instinctively drew her covers up to her chin.

"Wait a minute! Hold on, I'm coming," her father shouted as he hauled his overalls over his nightshirt.

The door hinges squeaked in protest as the door was opened. A gust of icy wind whipped into the cabin.

"Sheriff Tate, what are you doing here at this time of night?" Becca's father asked. "Is someone sick? Is someone dying? Come in and get warm while I get dressed." Those were the two reasons the sheriff might come knocking at the parson's door at such an hour—death and sickness. They were part of the reason Rebecca vowed never to marry a preacher. "Tag-along, go lie down!" her father ordered. "Is that Joe Masters behind you, Sheriff? What's going on?"

"Eli, we need to have a word with you." The sheriff's lazy Texas drawl held a somber tone. Becca scrambled to the foot of her bed to better view the unfolding drama.

"Of course! Of course!" Papa beckoned the two men inside the cabin.

"What is it, Eli?" Mama called from behind the bedroom partition.

"Sheriff Tate and Joe Masters are here. Go warm your hands by the hot coals in the fireplace, gentlemen." A note of apprehension had entered her father's voice. "That's a brisk north wind blowing up the canyon—a three blanket night, to be sure. Let me brew a pot of tea to warm you."

From behind the partition, Mama called, "I'll make the tea, Eli. I have sugar cookies to go with the tea," she added. "Just give me a minute to fetch my robe."

The sheriff, a short, wiry man from Amarillo, his felt hat in hand, shifted nervously from one foot to the other. "Thank ye kindly, ma'am," he drawled. "But we're here to talk to your daughter."

"Rebecca?" Papa blinked in surprise. "She's asleep in the loft. Becca," he called. "Could you please come down here? The sheriff and Mr. Masters need to speak with you."

Becca sat up in bed and conked the side of her head on a rafter. "Ouch!" she yipped and rubbed her bruise. *I'm going to get a giant goose egg from that one.*

"You're here to see my Rebecca?" Mama swept into the room in her ankle-length wool plaid robe. Her hair, which she usually wore pulled back in a tight bun, flowed about her shoulders. She bustled across the room to the dish cupboard and removed her favorite porcelain teapot from the top shelf.

Becca's hands trembled as she slipped her pink-and-white flowered flannel robe over her nightgown. She tied a knot in the silk cord at her waist and slid her bare feet into her felt bedroom slippers. Having removed the braids from her hair before retiring, the girl's locks cascaded in ripples down her back and shoulders, making her appear ten years younger, something she considered to be a curse.

Don't let me fall. Oh, please don't let me fall. Carefully she made her way down the ladder to where her parents, the sheriff, and Mr. Masters stood around the table. When her foot missed the lowest rung of the ladder, her father caught her by the waist.

He slid an arm about her shoulders and turned her around to face their late-night guests. "And now, Sheriff, whatever is so important that you would need to speak with me and with my daughter at this unearthly hour?" His voice held the no-nonsense tone of a fiery New England preacher. "What could not possibly wait until morning?"

The sheriff cleared his throat. "Sorry, Preacher, but there's been a shooting in town and we need to ask your daughter a few questions."

"Shooting? Questions? Who was shot?" Papa demanded.

The sheriff glanced toward his companion and then back at the girl. "I am sorry, Miss Rebecca, but the people in the store heard you threaten Bart Stanley this morning."

Joe Masters raised a hand in defense. "My sons told me he antagonized you, threatened you, even."

"Huh? Whatever are you talking about?" The girl glanced first from one face to another. "Who was shot?"

"You did threaten to shoot Bart Stanley this morning, did you not?" The sheriff gazed steadily at the girl.

"Only after he cornered me behind the counter and tried to choke me." Her reply came out as little more than a whisper.

"Did he actually touch you?" the sheriff asked.

"Yes." She pointed to her neck. "I honestly believe he would have hurt me if no one had been in the store."

The sheriff shook his head and clicked his tongue. "Someone shot Bart this afternoon and left him for dead in the alleyway behind the brickworks."

"No!" Mama gasped. "That's terrible!"

"And you actually think this tiny little gal could have done such a thing?" Papa asked.

The girl vigorously shook her head. "Honest, I didn't shoot Bart

Stanley. I may have wanted to, but I didn't! Honest!"

"Is he dead?" Papa asked in a strained voice.

"Fortunately, not. Doc Adams removed the bullet from the left side of the boy's head and tried to patch him up. It was from a Colt six-shooter like yours." The sheriff rolled and unrolled the brim of his hat between his hands. "But unfortunately, Bart is in bad shape. He drifts in and out of consciousness, repeating Rebecca's name, making us wonder whether she was the one who shot him."

"Oh, that's terrible!" Mama staggered over to the table and collapsed in a chair. "Rebecca? Are you sure?"

The girl gave an involuntary sigh. "Of course, I'm sure, Mama. I think I would know if I shot a man, any man."

"Then why would he blame you?" Mama's eyes pleaded for a reason, any reason. "You were out of breath when you got home."

"Yeah. That's because his threat scared me. I ran straight home from the store. Ask Hobie. Ask Jed."

Joe raised an eyebrow. "We did—and they both said you tricked Hobie into checking the storeroom to make good your escape."

"Sheriff," Papa tightened his grip on his daughter's shoulders. "If my girl says she didn't shoot the man, she didn't shoot him. You do know Bart harassed her this morning on the mountain?"

The sheriff studied the rim of his hat for a second before answering. "No, but that's all the more motive for her to shoot him."

"I'm not lying!" Becca insisted. "I didn't shoot Bart Stanley!"

The sheriff paused before speaking. "I'm prone to believe you, Rebecca. But the question is, will Senator Stanley? Unfortunately, one of the senator's aides was in town and heard what happened. He left immediately for Humboldt County, where the senator is campaigning. Everyone knows the senator is unreasonably protective when it comes to his only child." The sheriff's brow knitted. "It's rumored that once when Mr. Jaye disciplined the boy at school for misbehaving, the senator sent two thugs to beat up the poor teacher. I don't know what Stanley will do if he thinks Rebecca tried to kill Bart Junior."

Joe Masters cut in, "As I see it, whether she shot the boy or not, we must get Rebecca to a safe place before the senator and his men come looking for revenge."

"Where could she go?" her father asked.

"Your son Aaron and his family live in Sacramento," Joe reminded. "What if she spent a few weeks with Lilia and the children until this gets sorted out?" Joe Masters employed Eli Cunard's son as a purchaser of supplies for the mercantile.

Mama grasped the neckline of her woolen robe. "Sheriff, surely you can protect my baby."

The lawman paused for several seconds before answering. "Ma'am, you know the trouble we've been having with vigilantes, people who think I don't move fast enough to arrest thieves and troublemakers. If the senator and his men ride into town breathing fire, they could incite the vigilante-prone citizens of this county to riot. If that happens, they might string her up before my posse and I could restore order, especially if the boy dies."

Becca's mouth went dry as if she'd swallowed a wad of cotton batting. Spots danced before her eyes. Her father's grip on the girl's shoulder shifted to her waist and tightened. "Buck up, honey! Stay strong," he whispered in her ear.

"I have a suggestion." Joe spoke very slowly. "I have an empty wagon scheduled to return to Sacramento in the morning. It could just as well leave before dawn, with your daughter on board."

"Sounds good to me," the sheriff volunteered. "If she were my daughter, I'd—"

"Who would drive?" Papa demanded. "I certainly won't send my nineteen-year-old girl out alone with one of your teamsters."

"You're right." Joe stroked his chin thoughtfully for a moment. "Quince is scheduled to make the run, but the boy might be tempted if the senator paid him for information as to her whereabouts."

Papa hugged the girl tighter. The merchant eyed Becca and the preacher over the rim of his spectacles. "When my son Hobie learns what is happening, he will insist on driving. The boy's quite protective of your girl."

Mama leaped to her feet. "The only way I will allow my baby girl to go to Sacramento is if I go with her!"

"What?" Papa started at his wife's suggestion.

"It's settled then!" The usually docile woman shifted into a fierce she-bear posture, ready to do battle. "Rebecca and I are going to Sacramento for a few days! Joe, hitch up your team. We'll be ready to leave in fifteen minutes!"

When no one objected, the woman spat out a string of orders. "Becca, stuff as much clothing as possible in my maroon carpetbag." She gestured with her hand. "Wear your hiking clothes. And before you put on your shirt, wrap your bodice with those strips of cotton I store in my steamer trunk. My new quilt can wait!"

The woman shot challenging glances at each of the stunned men. "What? People will be looking for a runaway girl, not a chubby young boy. Well, what are you waiting for, girl? Hurry!" Mama bustled into the partitioned bedroom.

"Fay, if anyone goes with Rebecca, it should be me," Papa sputtered, as Becca skittered up the ladder.

"Let 'em go, Eli," the sheriff urged. "Fay is right. It's the only way you can keep your girl safe until we can sort this out."

From behind the partition, Fay called to her husband. "Eli, pack the leftover beans and corn bread in my tin berry bucket, the one with the lid that fastens closed. Toss in several slices of jerky." There was a slight pause. "Oh, yes, tell Becca to stuff her braids under the brim of one of your felt hats instead of her newsboy cap. It will hide more of her face and keep her braids out of sight. And tell her to bring along several of her crinolines, including her new one. Also, grab my sewing kit."

Caught off guard by the sudden change in the soft-spoken woman, the three men exchanged surprised glances. When no one moved, Mama shouted, "What are you gentlemen waiting for? Time's a wastin'. We've got a wagon to catch."

Joe was the first to respond. "Sheriff, you and I had better get that wagon hitched and awaken Hobie as well." As the shopkeeper opened the door, a blast of cold air swept into the room. "Bundle up. It's mighty cold out there tonight," he called.

The sheriff followed the merchant from the cabin with one parting admonition. "You'd best board the wagon behind the mercantile. Wagons come and go from there all the time. No one will notice."

Papa stared after the two men as they disappeared into the darkness. It took a sudden gust of biting cold air to stir him to action. "Food," he mumbled. "Pack the food."

Becca threw a couple of changes of clothing into the carpetbag, along with her mother's strange request to bring along her crinolines.

She could hear her father murmuring parts of Psalm 91 as he hastened to do his wife's bidding.

"Oh, Father, please deliver my darling wife and my precious baby girl from the fowler and from the pestilence that walketh in the darkness. Give Thine angels charge over them to keep them in all their ways. Let no evil befall them. Bear them up lest they dash their feet against a stone . . ."

As the familiar words drifted up into the loft, Becca gritted her teeth. *If my heavenly Father cares so much about me, why did He let this happen in the first place?*

Fay came out from behind the partition. "I can't forget my medicine bag. Eli, how much cash do we have on hand?"

He strode over to the trunk beside his favorite armchair and opened an oval brass snuffbox. After counting out a handful of silver coins, Eli replied, "About ten dollars, maybe."

"That's not enough! We forgot to ask Joe how much he would charge to take both of us to Sacramento." Fay raced across the room to the blue-and-white porcelain ginger jar displayed on a shelf above the dry sink. She dumped the contents into her hand. "I have another five dollars from this month's egg money. I hope Aaron can—"

"Fay, whatever the cost, I'm sure Joe will extend us credit."

"Mama, I have several gold nuggets," Becca volunteered. "They're bound to be worth something."

"Good idea, honey, bring them along. I'll carry the coins in my purse and pack the nuggets in our carpetbags with our clothing. Rebecca, don't forget to pack your knife, your six-shooter, and extra ammunition— just in case."

Papa recoiled. "Just in case of what?"

"An emergency, of course." The woman clicked her tongue. "We might encounter a dangerous varmint or two along the way."

The man inhaled sharply. "I don't like this! This plan is getting way out of hand."

"We'll do whatever we must do, Eli." Mama firmly planted her hands on her hips. "Remember back in New York state when we had to flee from the Southern bounty hunters to save Caleb's life?"

"But we never needed to shoot anyone!" the man of peace argued.

"Maybe not, but to protect my family, I certainly would have."

* * * * *

The bright, midwinter moon hung low in the sky, lighting the roadway with shades of gray as the Cunard family crept along the back alleys of the town. Pressing close to Becca's ankles, Tag-along's occasional whine indicated that the animal sensed danger.

"Fay, I still think I should be the one to go," Papa hissed as they rounded the corner of the brick mercantile building. Silhouetted in the moonlight were several supply wagons. In the middle of the alleyway sat one lone wagon. Lantern light danced back and forth from the building. "What good will I be here, knowing you might be in danger?" the man insisted.

Fay gripped her husband's arm. "Eli! Think. You are too visible." She cozied closer to his side. "You need to go about business as usual. If someone should ask for me, tell them I'm indisposed."

"You want me to lie?"

"*Shh!* Keep your voice down. Someone will hear you!" Mama scolded. "Darling, say whatever you think best at the moment. Or better yet, pray that no one will need me, and you won't need to lie."

"As if that is likely to happen," Becca interjected. The Cunards' neighbors dropped by the parsonage every day with one problem or another for her mother to solve. "Mama, this is the biggest news since old Gabe Hartman went on a drinking spree and shot holes in Widow Conner's outhouse, with her in it!"

"She's right, Fay." Papa cleared his throat nervously. "By morning every woman in our congregation is going to stop by the house to learn whatever she can about the shooting."

Mama clicked her tongue in disgust. "*Tsk!* Tell them I am so distraught, I don't want to talk with anyone. I am, you know! That would be the gospel truth!"

Becca heaved a ragged breath. A shiver ran the length of her spine. *This is real! I'm not dreaming,* she realized. She clutched the leather straps of her carpetbag and of her smaller leather satchel a bit tighter. The weight of the gun and leather holster hanging from her waist emphasized the danger. *This is really happening!*

No one spoke as the merchant and his youngest son loaded empty wooden produce crates on the back of the wagon and Hobie climbed into the driver's seat. Her friend's face looked drawn and solemn.

Choking back a sob, Papa kissed her goodbye. "Go with God, my child," he whispered. "Take care of your mother. She's not as strong as she thinks she is! Neither are you, in fact. Remember, you are never alone. God promises never to leave you or forsake you."

Becca knelt to kiss Tag-along while Papa drew his wife into his arms. "Kiss my son and his family for me. And, darling, come home soon." Tears streamed down each face as Papa repeated the Mizpah. Becca's mind flashed back to another time her father had prayed the Mizpah. It was like when they bade farewell to Caleb and Serenity outside Independence, Missouri. They all realized they might never again see one another on this earth.

"May the Lord watch between me and thee while we are . . ." Her father's voice broke. He struggled to continue, "Absent one from another." Eli placed an almost savage kiss on the weeping woman's lips. "Come home to me, Fay! Promise you'll come home to me!"

Unable to speak, the woman nodded.

"It may be best that you ladies sit in the back of the wagon in case someone sees us leaving town." Hobie gestured toward the rough-hewn wagon bed. "Wrap up in the quilts there on the floor behind the driver's box. You might want to pull the canvas over your heads, just in case some nosy busybody is looking out her window at this unearthly hour."

Becca climbed on board, and then Joe and the sheriff helped the older woman into the wagon. Once seated, the women covered themselves with the rough canvas tarps. They heard but could not see Tag-along snapping and barking at the wagon wheels as they rolled westward over the frozen ground.

The girl lifted a corner of the tarp to see her father lift the agitated dog into his arms and bury his face in the animal's bristly ruff. Tag-along squirmed to escape, but her distraught father held the whimpering animal fast. She watched until their forms faded into the night.

CHAPTER FOUR

BOLD ESCAPE PLAN

A BOOM OF THUNDER AND a jagged streak of lightning merged into one terrifying jolt, followed by the sound of a splintering tear. Somewhere in the night, a tree branch crashed to the ground. Intent on ignoring the late winter rainstorm raging outside the second-story bedroom window, Rebecca rolled over on the down-filled bed and punched her feather pillow. She started awake at the sound of terrified whimpers as two-year-old Helen's tiny body landed atop Becca's hip. "Auntie Becca! I scared! I scared!"

Before she awakened enough to respond, she was joined by three-year-old Izzy and four-year-old Anne as they tumbled into bed alongside the youngest daughter of the Aaron Cunard clan. The frightened wails of the one-year-old baby Aaron, or A.J., filled the rafters of his parents' room as well as the long hallway separating the bedrooms.

Without opening her eyes to view the eerie black-and-white predawn world, Becca slid her arm around the two-year-old. "*Shh! Shh!* You're safe now, little one. Go back to sleep."

Being an aunt to three noisy, active nieces proved to be hard work, even with her mother taking charge of A.J. Her sister-in-law, Lilia, was pregnant with baby number five and upchucking at all hours of the day and night. Rebecca's vow to never marry and have babies of her own had hardened during this visit.

The three little girls could find more ways to get into trouble than the nineteen-year-old ever could begin to imagine. As the wriggly bodies snuggled close to her, Becca stared at the wooden beams overhead and groaned. Silhouettes of drying lavender, mustard, parsley, oregano, and ropes of garlic hung from the rafters. The mingled aromas set the girl's stomach to growling.

"Auntie Becca," Izzy whispered, "I gotta go potty."

Rebecca sighed. "So go. The chamber pot is at the foot of the bed."

"I'm scared. Can you go with me?"

"Izzy, honey," Rebecca rose up on one elbow. "You don't need me to go to the potty with you. Just climb out of the bed, and I'll be right here watching you."

"You promise?" The little girl sniffed.

"I promise. I won't go back to sleep until you're safely under the covers."

Whatever sleep she'd hoped to enjoy faded when Izzy climbed back into the bed and the two other girls, in succession, announced that they needed to use the chamber pot as well, and would Auntie Becca promise to stay awake for them while they did. The three girls giggled when, after all the talk of needing to use the porcelain pot Auntie Becca could no longer resist the urge either.

The quartet of bodies snuggled beneath the puffy, wedding-ring-pattern quilt Grandma Fay had made for her grandbabies the previous Christmas. Izzy sighed with pleasure. "I sure do love you, Auntie Becca. You are so much fun."

Feeling a twinge of guilt for her attitude, Becca groaned silently. Out loud, she said, "I love you, too, Izzy."

"And I love you, too, Auntie Becca," Anne assured.

"Me loves you too." Two-year-old Helen gave a satisfying wriggle.

"I hope you stay with us forever," Anne added.

"Me too," Izzy seconded.

"Me too." The two-year-old's golden curls tickled Becca's chin.

"All right. We all love everybody." Becca brushed the curls away from her face. "*Shh!* Let's go to sleep, shall we?"

"I'm not sleepy, Auntie Becca." Izzy squeezed up against her aunt's back.

This time Becca could not swallow her groan. "Honey, you have to sleep. The sun won't be up for another two hours."

"But I'm not sleepy," the little girl insisted. "Maybe if you tell us a story about where you and my grandma lived before you came west on the wagon train. That always works for Daddy."

Becca heaved an exaggerated sigh. "All right. One story, but only if you close your eyes and don't talk. Deal?"

Anne, the oldest, spoke first. "Deal!"

"Has your daddy told you about the time your uncle Caleb, auntie Serenity, and I hunted for treasure in a cave beside Lake Cayuga?"

"No," the three girls chorused.

"*Shh!* You promised," Becca reminded.

Anne sat up and leaned across her sister's back. "But Auntie Becca, you asked a question. It would have been impolite not to answer."

"Yes, Anne. You are right." Becca laughed. "Lie back down. I promise not to ask any more questions."

Becca waited until the four-year-old's head hit the pillow.

"Lake Cayuga is one of five lakes in central New York called the Finger Lakes—"

"Because there are five of them?" Izzy announced. "Oops! I forgot. I'm sorry."

"Yes, they're called the Finger Lakes because they are five side by side like skinny fingers. Anyway. Your aunt Serenity's father owned a great big house beside the lake where he'd dug a secret tunnel from the lakeside all the way to his house."

Anne popped up once again. "Why?"

"Anne! *Shh!*" Izzy ordered.

"But why?" Anne whispered.

In a soft, conspiratorial tone, Becca said, "Because he needed a place to hide runaway slaves that crossed the lake by boat, until your uncle Caleb could smuggle them to the next station on the Underground Railroad."

Helen turned her face toward her aunt. "What's a slave?"

Anne popped up once again. "What's an Underground Railroad? Does a train engine really go underground somewhere?"

"We rode on a train once. You wouldn't remember, Helen. You were a baby." Izzy continued, "Daddy and Mommy took us for a ride one Sunday afternoon. It didn't go underground though. And I'm sure I never saw any slaves."

"What's a slave?" Helen insisted.

"Obviously this isn't going to work." Becca yawned and rubbed her eyes. "I could sing you a song about a railroad. Would you like that?"

"About the train that goes underground?" Izzy asked.

Anne peered over her sister at Becca. "What about the treasure hidden in the cave?"

"What's a slave?" Helen asked a third time.

Becca blew out a stream of air in frustration. "I've been working on the railroad," she began singing. "All the live-long day. I've been working on the railroad just to pass the time away. Don't you hear—"

A knock sounded on the bedroom door. It was Aaron's voice. "Hey, you girls. Don't you think you'd better get some sleep?"

"Yes, Daddy," the three girls answered.

Becca sighed with relief. As her eyes closed, she felt a tap on her arm. It was Izzy. "Tomorrow, you can tell us about the cave and the treasure and the railroad that traveled underground and the slaves."

"What's a slave?" Helen whispered between yawns.

Morning dawned too soon. Sunlight streamed into the spacious farm kitchen through white embroidered café curtains as Rebecca stood at Lilia's new wood-burning cookstove, turning out silver-dollar-sized, heart-shaped flapjacks while the three little girls seated at the dining table raced to see who could eat the most.

Upstairs, Grandma Fay was dressing baby A.J. while his mother succumbed to a renewed bout of morning sickness. Aaron had already left for work at the supply depot when the girls heard a wagon stop in front of the house.

"Daddy's home!" Izzy shouted and dashed through the kitchen door onto the wide porch that encircled the house.

"Daddy!" Anne and Helen followed their sister.

What is he doing home at this hour? Wiping her hands on a dish towel, Rebecca followed the girls outside. She stopped short upon seeing Hobie and Mr. Joe alight from the wagon.

"Where's my daddy?" Helen's lower lip quivered into a pout.

"He's not here, honey," the owner of the mercantile explained. "He's at the supply depot loading goods on a wagon for our return trip to Placerville."

Hobie hung back, allowing his father to precede him up the porch steps.

"Rebecca, good to see you. Where's your mother?" Mr. Joe pounded his wide-brimmed leather hat against his pant leg to shake it free of dust.

Becca looked beyond the merchant, hoping to see her father. "Where's Papa? Did you bring Papa with you?"

Mr. Joe shook his head and slowly climbed the steps. "If your pa had had his way, he would be here. It took all of my jawing, along with threats by Sheriff Tate to let him cool his heels in the county's only jail cell to keep him from coming. I didn't realize how stubborn our parson could be." He shook his head and clicked his tongue. "Now we need to talk with your mama. Got any coffee brewing? Sure could use a cup."

"The coffeepot is on the stove. Help yourselves." Becca pointed toward the kitchen door. The three Cunard girls cowered around the corner of the house while Becca led Mr. Joe into the kitchen. When Hobie smiled at Izzy, the girl screamed and dashed from view. The other two followed her example.

"Please make yourselves comfortable while I get my mother for you." Becca started toward the kitchen stairs, but not before her mother appeared with A.J. in her arms.

Fay knitted her brow. "Is Eli all right? Are you here to take us home?"

"Not exactly, Mrs. Cunard," Mr. Joe said hesitantly.

"What is it? What has happened?" The baby in Grandma Fay's arms sensed the woman's concern and began to fuss.

Mr. Joe pulled out a chair from the table. "Why don't you sit down, Mrs. Cunard while I tell you? You, too, Miss Rebecca." The women did as told. "State Senator Stanley has formed a five-man posse of hired guns to track down the person who tried to kill his only son. He believes the killer is your daughter. The senator also posted a thousand-dollar reward for Rebecca's capture. The man announced to everyone in town that he would find her and string her up in the town square."

"Has young Bart awakened from his coma?" Fay asked, bouncing the baby, more out of nerves than necessity.

"No, Mrs. Cunard. The boy's condition hasn't changed. He awakens only long enough to mouth Rebecca's name and immediately slips into unconsciousness. Doc doesn't hold out much hope for the young man's recovery."

Becca pressed her hand against her forehead. "Now what should we do? Obviously I can't go back to Placerville right away."

"That's why Hobie and I are here. I've discussed a plan with your husband and, while he's not happy, I think he sees the wisdom in it. Rebecca's pursuers won't know whether she's hiding in Sacramento, San Francisco, headed north to Oregon, taken a ship around the Cape, or boarded the eastbound Butterfield Overland Mail stagecoach."

The girl shook her head as if trying to remove giant cobwebs from her brain. "Wait! I don't understand. Will I or won't I be staying alone in San Francisco?"

The delighted baby gurgled and laughed as Grandma Fay's bouncing intensified. "I don't like this! I need to return home to my husband. I don't want to go be holed up somewhere in San Francisco!"

"You're right. You do need to return to Eli, if for no other reason than to keep him from doing something stupid or dangerous." Mr. Joe pursed his lips. "That's why my son Hobie and your daughter Rebecca will take the paddleboat to San Francisco, where they'll board the eastbound Butterfield Overland Mail stagecoach to your other son's place in Missouri. I know this is an extreme plan, but the situation calls for extreme measures!" He waved his hand to silence the women's objections. "As I told your husband, I feel extremely responsible for the situation that occurred in my store. And I know a pastor's salary wouldn't cover the expense, so I will foot all travel expenses." His lips formed a thin determined line.

"But Mr. Joe, that costs a lot of money! We can't allow you to do that," Fay protested.

"Trust me! I'm in a better financial position than Eli and you are. Just consider it my gift to the church this year." He chuckled, and then quickly sobered. "I hate to lose the help of both Rebecca and my son at the mercantile, but this appears to be the only possible escape for Rebecca. If Bart awakens and clears up this mess, they'll come home. If not . . ." He sighed. "Hobie is certainly man enough to protect your daughter from harm should they need to make the two-thousand-mile journey, aren't you, son?"

"Yes, Pa." Hobie reddened and stared down at his boots. "Along with all those angels Pastor Cunard requested."

Missing the angel comment, Fay gasped in horror. "But he's a man! I can't allow him and my unmarried daughter to travel across country unchaperoned!"

"The couple will be well chaperoned, I assure you, Mrs. Cunard. I've arranged for Mrs. Pettigrew, a personal friend of my deceased wife, to accompany them aboard the *Antelope* to San Francisco. She has a son in the Bay Area," Mr. Joe explained. "As to the trip east, the two will be more than well chaperoned by a stage driver, a conductor, and as many as seven additional passengers."

"Mrs. Cunard." Hobie fumbled with the brim of his hat. "I promise I will deliver Rebecca safely to her brother in Independence. I will allow no one, including myself, to harm her in any way."

"I-I-I didn't mean to imply that you might—I just need to protect my daughter's reputation," Fay began.

"Do you mean as a murder suspect or as a lady?" Mr. Joe reminded.

Becca whirled her five-foot-two-inch body about to face the people plotting her future. She planted her hands on her narrow hips and glared. "I don't need Hobie or any other man to protect me! I can take care of myself!"

By the look in her mother's eye, Becca realized that instead of successfully declaring her independence, she'd sealed her fate. She either would become a sitting duck for the senator's henchmen, or she would be making the twenty-four-day trip east with Hobie as her bodyguard. *Twenty-four days, how bad could it be?* she reasoned. *I've had coughs that lasted longer.*

"I'd plan for the worst if I were you, Mrs. Cunard. I am sorry." A tight frown creased Mr. Joe's brow. "The senator is very determined. He won't give up easily."

* * * * *

Tears stained Hobie's ruddy cheeks on Friday morning as Hobie hugged his father goodbye. "Don't worry, Pa. If at all possible, I'll come home on the return stagecoach."

"You stay as long as you need, son." Mr. Joe's eyes watered. "Before I leave town, I'll send a letter to Rebecca's brother by Pony Express, telling him of your pending arrival."

The details were simple. Mr. Joe's plan was put into motion. The Butterfield Overland Mail stagecoach would leave San Francisco at eight forty-five on Monday morning. Hobie and Rebecca would stay with the Pettigrews until boarding the eastbound stagecoach. Knowing the stagecoach passengers were not allowed to carry an abundance of cash or expensive jewelry, and their luggage could weigh no more than forty pounds, Fay and her daughter stayed up most of the night before Rebecca left, sewing the chunks of gold ore into small pockets along the hem of her crinoline. "It's not uncommon for ladies in the east to sew lead into their petticoats to keep the wind from revealing a little too much ankle," Mama explained. "So why not gold?" When finished, the women's fine stitches could hardly be seen.

As Fay helped pack, she advised, "Since they'll weigh your bag but not you, wear as many layers of clothing as you can stand. You can always shed the extra once you're on the road."

"Should I take along my hiking attire?"

"Absolutely." Her mother clicked her tongue. "If the senator's thugs sniff out your trail, they'll be looking for a female, not a young lad. When you need to do so, bind your torso and hide your hair under your father's hat."

Rebecca couldn't pass up the opportunity to tease her mother one last time. "Are you telling me to be dishonest?"

Tears filled the older woman's eyes. "God says to be wise as serpents and harmless as doves. Honey, I never thought I'd be saying this, but do whatever you need to do to stay alive, without breaking God's holy commandments, of course."

* * * * *

The girl stood on the wharf and gazed at the massive paddle wheeler she was about to board. The circus atmosphere on the pier faded. The reality of what she was about to do hit. *This is no game. Anything can happen. I may never see Mama again on this earth.* The girl swallowed hard to keep from losing her breakfast.

"Remember, child, you 'can do all things through Christ' who gives you strength." Fay sniffed into a lacy handkerchief. "That promise guided Papa and me across the plains in our covered wagon. There were times I was so exhausted I just wanted to give up and die, but your father reminded me over and over again that we could do whatever God wanted us to do."

Overwhelmed, the girl leaned forward and kissed her mother's cheek. "Kiss Papa goodbye for me," she whispered. "Tell him I love him; and give Tag-along an extra slab of jerky for me."

Fay crushed her daughter to her breast and held her for several seconds. The woman's breath came in short broken sobs when she finally released her. Taking her daughter's face in her hands, the woman stared deeply into her eyes. "Remember, you are stronger than you may think. You come from hearty pioneer stock. But, as strong as you may be, you can't do this alone. You need to let others help you."

The girl opened her mouth to protest.

"No, my child. Your biggest character flaw is thinking you don't need help from others. But you do, especially from God. And don't forget the sacrifice Hobie and Mr. Masters are making for you. Your survival, and possibly his, will depend more on your cunning and wit than on your six-shooter, as much as you might like to think otherwise."

Fay Cunard took Rebecca's hands in hers and bowed her head. "Please, dear Father, protect my dear daughter from the evils that pursue her and, when necessary, from her own pride. She is a good girl, Lord. Help her to never forget You and Your promises to be with her to the ends of the earth."

Tears blurred Becca's vision as she boarded the paddle wheeler and as she waved goodbye to her mother, her brother and his family, and to Mr. Joe. The girl bit her lower lip to keep from dissolving into a puddle of emotion. She barely noticed the woman with the flashing green eyes and graying strawberry-blond curls that Mr. Joe had earlier introduced as Mrs. Pettigrew. She barely noticed the hulking form of Hobie hovering on her right, as if fearful she might swoon and fall overboard.

Becca clutched the brass railing surrounding the deck and waved until the paddleboat rounded a bend in the river and the city of Sacramento disappeared in the haze.

Once in San Francisco, while Mrs. Pettigrew did her best to entertain, for Becca, the weekend passed in a blur of emptiness. Visits to the Presidio, Nob Hill, and Golden Gate Park did little to coax her out of her sulk. She ignored the worried glances from Hobie as well. For the first time in her life, the future terrified the girl.

Alone that night in the Pettigrews' guestroom, the girl clutched her pillow to her chest and stared into the darkness. The clang of fire wagons, galloping horses, and rumbling service wagons outside her bedroom window kept her awake.

Twenty-four days, she repeated to herself, clenching her teeth as she spoke. *Twenty-four days, and this nightmare will be over.*

Chapter Five

The San Joaquin Valley

A HEAVY FOG ENGULFED San Francisco's skyline as Becca impatiently waited for Hobie to purchase the tickets for their journey east. The words of encouragement that continually poured from his lips did little to comfort her but instead irritated her a lot. " 'We know that all things work together for good to them that love God, to them who are the called according to his purpose,' " he quoted time and again.

As she waited for Hobie to return, the girl carefully reread the list of rules governing the passengers of the Butterfield Overland stagecoach.

1. Abstinence from liquor is requested, but if you must drink share the bottle. To do otherwise makes you appear selfish and unneighborly.
2. If ladies are present, gentlemen are urged to forego smoking cigars and pipes as the odor of same is repugnant to the gentler sex. Chewing tobacco is permitted, but spit with the wind, not against it.
3. Gentlemen must refrain from the use of rough language in the presence of ladies and children.
4. Buffalo robes are provided for your comfort in cold weather. Hogging robes will not be tolerated and the offender will be made to ride with the driver.
5. Don't snore loudly while sleeping or use your fellow passenger's shoulder for a pillow; he or she may not understand and friction may result.
6. Firearms may be kept on your person for use in emergencies. Do

not fire them for pleasure or shoot at wild animals as the sound riles the horses.

7. In the event of runaway horses remain calm. Leaping from the coach in panic will leave you injured, at the mercy of the elements, hostile Indians and hungry coyotes.

8. Forbidden topics of conversation are: stagecoach robberies and Indian uprisings.

9. Gents guilty of unchivalrous behavior toward lady passengers will be put off the stage. It's a long walk back. A word to the wise is sufficient.*

Becca clutched her leather drawstring satchel tightly. *What have I gotten into?*

The ticket agent—a smallish gentleman, his lips pursed into a tight bow, and bottle-thick lens in the spectacles perched on the tip of his pointy nose—stamped the two tickets with the Butterfield Overland stagecoach emblem and handed them to Hobie. As he did, the agent peered around the edge of his iron cage at Becca and sniffed disdainfully. "That little gal will never make it, mister," he mumbled. "Take my word; she's too fragile."

The depot's high-domed ceiling guaranteed that everyone in the room heard his dire prediction. Becca glared and curled the corner of her lip into a snarl. Startled, the man jerked his head back out of her line of sight.

Outside the paned windows of the stone building, the pounding of hooves and the jangle of traces produced a flurry of commotion. A nine-passenger stagecoach, pulled by four matching sorrels, rounded the corner of the building and labored to a stop. A short, wiry man, with a weathered face, hopped off the driver's bench. From beneath his scraggly gray beard came a stream of mild epithets directed toward the station personnel waiting to load the tan canvas mailbags and luggage onto the vehicle.

The man's buff-colored buckskin shirt, black slouch hat, and faded brown duck trousers looked liked they'd seen many miles of wear. He waved a sheaf of official-looking documents over his head.

---

* Elizabeth C. MacPhail, "Wells Fargo in San Diego," *The Journal of San Diego History* 28, no. 4 (Fall 1980).

He yanked both of the station's closed double doors open and planted his bowed legs squarely in the middle of the exit. "Ladies and gents." He nodded toward Becca and a middle-aged woman seated in one corner of the oak-paneled waiting room.

"My name is Sallie, short for Saldana Horatio Medina." In one hand he held a tarnished brass bugle, in the other, a shotgun. He lifted the hem of his buckskin shirt to reveal a big boot pistol in a holster on his belt and a leather sheath that held a long bowie knife. "Before you gents chuckle at my moniker, know that many a smart aleck has come to regret such an action." He paused to eye each of the passengers individually. "I am in charge. I am the conductor of this vehicle. I am the carrier of the United States mail, a task that I take very seriously, more seriously than I take transporting you to your destination, wherever that may be."

The man narrowed his eyes. "Aboard this stagecoach, I am the law! What I say goes! When I say go, we go! If I say jump, you jump; and don't lollygag about it! Do we understand one another?"

He eyed Hobie and the other two male travelers a second time. "The Butterfield Overland stagecoach waits for no man or woman! Nothing and no one must stand in the way of its scheduled delivery of the United States mail." The man warmed to his subject. "We will cover the two thousand eight hundred twelve miles in twenty-four days, traveling round the clock. When the stagecoach stops to change teams of horses, you will have five minutes to visit the outhouse before we hit the road once more. Twice a day you will have thirty minutes to chow down a meal—no more, no less."

The conductor gestured toward a tall, skinny boy, not much older than Hobie, stacking the travelers' carpetbags on the luggage rack. "That's Jehu, our driver. If you remember your Bible, you understand how Jehu earned the name. So keep your hands and arms in the coach at all times. We have a tight schedule—twenty-three days and twenty-three hours to cross two-thirds of this grand country of ours." He gestured toward the third row of seats in the coach. "The rear seat is where the United States mail rides. You folks must cram yourselves onto the two front benches as best you can." He pulled a gold watch from the pocket of his trousers. "Get yourselves on board. We leave in five minutes."

As Becca stepped onto an overturned wooden box to climb aboard the vehicle, Hobie appeared by her side. "Here! Let me help you."

The girl yanked her arm free from his grasp. "I can do it myself!" she snapped. However, lifting herself up into the coach, with the additional weight of the gold nuggets sewn into her petticoat, proved to be more difficult than she had imagined. Frustrated to have to ask for help, she cast Hobie a withering glare.

The young man smiled, placed his massive hands about her tiny waist, and hefted her like a sack of seed into the vehicle, and then assisted the middle-aged woman passenger waiting to board.

"You ladies will be more comfortable sitting opposite one another," Hobie suggested. "The floor space is so narrow, passengers must dovetail their knees with the one seated across the aisle."

Becca blushed at the thought, never realizing the indignities she would endure before she arrived in Missouri. As Hobie climbed into the coach, Becca dropped onto the seat facing the rear. She'd been advised that passengers riding closest to the horses would receive the least amount of road dust in their faces. She also noticed that those seated on the middle row had only a leather strap for back support.

The girl adjusted her brown calico skirt and numerous layers of crinolines around her knees. With only fifteen inches of seat per passenger, comfort would be a luxury. She placed her leather satchel containing her personal items on her lap.

The woman across from her smiled as she tucked her midnight-blue cambric skirt and petticoats about her legs as well. Her blue poke bonnet had slipped from her head and onto her shoulders, revealing a tight bun at the nape of her neck. A myriad of wispy, graying brown curls haloed her face.

"This hat is useless in here, don't ya think?" The woman untied the ribbons, folded the bonnet in half, and stuffed it into a bulging black leather satchel on her lap. "Our bags will make fine pillows tonight when we want to sleep." She drew the leather cord at the top of her bag and wrapped the strings around her gloved hands. "It looks like we'll all be better acquainted than we might like by the time we arrive in Fort Smith." Her dark brown eyes twinkled with laughter. "My name is Agnes, Agnes Sparks. My friends call me Aggie."

Becca nodded and managed a tight little smile in return. "I'm Rebecca Cunard. Uh, my friends call me Becca."

"Good to meet you, Becca. Are you and your husband traveling all the way to St. Louis?"

"Husband?" Becca blinked in surprise. "Oh, no, Mrs. Sparks! This is Hobie Masters. He's not my husband. He's sort of my, uh, bodyguard. My parents insisted—"

"Wise parents, I would say." Aggie nodded. "Goodness, it must be mighty important to them to send you two thousand miles away."

Becca shot a nervous glance toward Hobie, and then recovered enough to force a brittle smile. "Family! I have family in Independence."

"Oh, I see." The woman adjusted her skirts to make room for two additional male passengers who would share her bench. The instant the second man pulled his feet into the vehicle, the conductor closed the coach door, blew a long blast note on his bugle, and climbed into the driver's box. With a shout from Jehu, the horses leaped forward. The stagecoach jounced over the cobblestone streets of the city, jarring Becca's teeth to their roots.

The man seated in the middle, opposite Hobie, looked to be in his late twenties. He wore a black flat-topped hat with a wide brim. His dark, bushy eyebrows almost obscured his piercing dark eyes. The man brushed the collar of his black morning coat as well as the carefully pressed crease of his woolen trousers. As he did, Becca caught sight of a Colt revolver holstered at his waist.

When the last man to board adjusted a large gray snakeskin satchel on his lap, the man beside him clicked his tongue in frustration. "Can you turn that bag sideways? It's poking my arm!" He heaved a dramatic sigh. "I can hardly move in here! Twenty-four days and nights of this?"

"You're welcome to sit over here beside me." Hobie occupied most of the bench on their side of the coach.

"*Hmmph!* I don't see why these two women should have the prime seats!" He continued in a distinctive Southern drawl. "I paid just as much for my ticket!"

The tall gaunt gentleman seated next to the grumbling passenger removed his flat-crowned straw hat from his head and placed it on his lap. His tan duck pants, gray morning coat, and heavy leatherwork boots spoke of rough wear, possibly in the California gold fields. "My name is Jack Hutchinson, and I'm heading home to Washington City. What did you say your name is?" He extended his hand to the complaining passenger.

"Bo Devers, formerly of Memphis, Tennessee," the other man growled.

"Well, Mr. Devers, I don't know how you treat your women in Tennessee, but we men of Washington City treat our ladies like the delicate magnolias they are."

"*Hmmph!* I'll bet this little one here," he pointed toward Becca, "could hold her own against any and all takers from a place like Washington City."

How right you are, she thought. *How right you are!* Becca arched an eyebrow, and at the same moment, slid her hand into the gathered top of the bag on her lap. Her fingers rested on the cool barrel of her Colt six-shooter.

"Mr. Devers, I'm sure we'll take turns occupying the 'comfortable' seats before this journey ends." Becca batted her eyes and shot him a coy grin. Abruptly turning her attention to her fellow female passenger, the girl asked, "And you, Mrs. Aggie, where are you headed?"

For an instant, an almost imperceptible frown flitted across the woman's face. "Oh, I'm going home to see my mother one last time before she dies." Aggie leaned back and closed her eyes as if to silence any further questions. Hobie and Mr. Hutchinson did the same.

As for Mr. Devers, he stared down at his gloved hands folded in his lap. With all trivial formalities shared, the passengers settled into an awkward silence, each lost in his or her thoughts. Only the squeak of wagon wheels and the jangle of traces could be heard. At the edge of the city, the ride smoothed into a gentle rocking motion reminiscent of a baby's cradle.

Hours passed with short stops at relay stations to bring on fresh teams of horses. As the stagecoach ascended Pacheco Pass and then down the other side to the floor of the famous San Joaquin Valley, the cool coastal breezes were replaced by the warmer, dryer air temperature of the Central Valley. Becca realized wearing multiple layers of clothing, as her mama had suggested, would quickly become uncomfortable.

Through half-closed eyes, the girl studied the faces of her fellow travelers. After watching the way Mr. Devers flexed and unflexed his jaw muscles, she decided he was wound up tight like a watch spring, ready to snap at any moment. The set of Mr. Hutchinson's jaw and his lean, muscular face revealed an underlying toughness, a man who lived by his own code of conduct. As for Aggie, Becca figured her to be a sweet, gentle mama, loving and accepting of whomever she met.

The girl glanced at her traveling companion. Hobie's head lolled to one side; spittle dripped from the corner of his lips as he slept. *This is the man my parents chose to protect me all the way to Independence?* She shook her head and stared out of the open window beside her.

She recalled the devastating expressions on her father's and her mother's faces as she had kissed them goodbye. How odd they had become. Papa had always been her rock in any storm, her strength throughout every difficulty, her human face of God. And Mama, in her lace collars and embroidered petticoats, could quiver and burst into tears at the slightest of crises. Yet, when Senator Stanley's henchmen threatened the girl's life, the two switched roles. Her father fell apart while her mother took charge of Becca's escape. She knew both loved God with their entire beings. *But how did this switch of roles happen?* She didn't understand.

Not many miles had passed when Becca's back began to ache from sitting on the wooden seats, and her legs cramped in the tight floor space. It took all her self-control not to shift to new positions every few minutes.

The road narrowed into a cocoa-colored ribbon that wound through a canopy of mighty oak trees and spreading Pacheco Pass sycamores. The hostile forest behind the trees formed a heavy curtain of stinger nettles, wild grapes, and unfriendly stick-tights. Interspersed with the unfriendly landscape were an occasional plowed field and a simple one-room cabin of a hopeful settler who'd come to California for the gold and stayed to homestead the land.

Becca accomplished her wish to shed a crinoline or two when the stagecoach slowed to a stop at Firebaugh's Ferry. The melting snow from the Sierras had flooded the easy, rolling San Joaquin River. The sage-green turbulent waters ran swift and cold. On the western bank of the river, Sallie ordered the passengers to disembark. Grateful for the break, they eagerly tumbled out of the vehicle.

"Due to the danger inherent in the fast-flowing water, the U.S. mail crosses the river first, and then the ferry boat will return for the passengers."

After finding relief in a crude but functional outhouse, Becca rambled along the river's edge among blossoms of purple and yellow, dappled with sunlight. Overhead she heard a lark call to his mate.

What a beautiful place, she thought. Thankful she'd left her bonnet in the stage, the girl laid her leather satchel on the bank and splashed her face and neck with handfuls of the icy water. *Oooh!* Becca tossed her head in pleasure. Her braids swooshed back and forth against her back and shoulders.

In the distance a heavy mountain of clouds threatened the late February day, but she decided she would enjoy every moment of the unexpected stop. To be able to stretch and to walk about felt so good. As uncomfortable as she'd been on this stretch, the girl reflected on how painful making the two-thousand-mile journey across the continent had been the last time.

Spotting Aggie perched on a rock beside the river, Becca stuffed her crinoline into her satchel, looped the bag's handle over her shoulder, and headed toward the cheerful woman.

"Hello, Miss Cunard," a voice called. It was Bo Devers. As Becca glanced over her shoulder to locate the source, the fingers of her right hand automatically gripped the handle of the six-shooter hidden inside her leather bag. Taking long strides, the man quickly caught up with her. "Taking your daily constitutional while you can, I presume?"

Feeling uncomfortable being alone with the man, she glanced about for Hobie. He was nowhere in sight. After Bart, the girl had become suspicious of any male who showed her attention. "Yes," she replied. "As a matter of fact I am."

"May I walk with you?" He fell into step with her shorter gait.

The girl shrugged her shoulders. "It's a free country."

"Yes, it is, isn't it? And a lovely one at that! Did you spot those snow-capped peaks through the trees?"

"Yes, I did, sir. Breathtaking." Snow-capped peaks were hardly anything new to the mountain girl.

"Almost as breathtaking as you, my dear," he drawled, casting her a come-hither grin.

Becca returned the man's flirty glance with a glare. "Do your words cause the hearts of the ladies of Tennessee to go pitter-pat, Mr. Devers? Or does such childish prattle disgust them as much as it does me?"

The man coughed and then touched the brim of his hat. "Sorry,

Miss Cunard, I—"

"Stop!" she shouted, simultaneously removing her six-shooter from her bag and pulling the trigger. The explosion reverberated through the trees in the brisk morning air, sending a terrified Tennessean to his knees.

"Don't shoot! Don't shoot! I meant no harm!" The man's face turned ashen at the sight of the firearm in the girl's hand. He gasped for breath. "Sorry! I meant no ha . . ."

Becca pointed five steps ahead of where the man had been walking. "Over there, by that stump! A rattler!"

The man stared at the headless, six-foot long rattlesnake directly in his path. "What a lucky shot! You saved my life, Miss Cunard."

Blowing a puff of smoke from the end of her gun, she dropped the weapon into her bag and sniffed. "Not luck, Mr. Devers, just hours of practice."

Upon hearing the explosion, Hobie and Mr. Hutchinson came running with guns drawn. As for Aggie, at the sound of the gunshot the woman screamed and instinctively leaped into the fast-flowing river. Seeing the woman flounder about in the current, Hobie plunged into the river and pulled her out of the icy waters. After handing her to Mr. Hutchinson, he climbed up the riverbank to safety.

Mr. Hutchinson removed his jacket and draped it around the woman's shivering form. "Better change into dry clothes on the other side of the river," he suggested. "You don't want to get a chill."

"What happened?" Hobie, soaked to the skin, climbed out of the river.

Mr. Devers pointed at Becca. "This little gal shot the head off a rattlesnake poised to strike my leg! That's what! I've never seen such fancy shooting, and from a mite of a gal at that."

Throughout the ferry ride across the swollen river, the man touted Becca's skills. Sallie waited impatiently as Becca helped Aggie change into dry clothes. Frustrated with the delay, the conductor mumbled under his breath, "Time is money for the Butterfield Overland Mail. We'll have to make up the delay somewhere along the way!"

Within a short time the women climbed into the stagecoach with the help of Hobie, who had also changed into dry clothing. The gentle giant was fast becoming the ladies' personal doorman.

Before blowing the bugle to announce the stagecoach's departure, Sallie became almost loquacious. "Next station of any consequence will be in Visalia, the largest city between San Francisco and El Pueblo de Los Angeles. It's called the jewel of the valley."

This time, instead of being lost in their own thoughts as they had been previously, the passengers were eager to talk.

"That was quite a shot, young lady! Quite a shot!" Mr. Hutchinson clicked his tongue in admiration. "You certainly can move fast."

"Thank you, sir." Becca blushed and then scolded herself for doing so. "Sorry, Aggie, for frightening you so that you fell into the river."

The brown-eyed lady laughed aloud. "No problem, Becca. I needed a bath after riding in this coach for so long! Do it again when we get to the Rio Grande in Texas. They say the water's warmer there."

"I just might do that. They also say the rattlers are bigger and badder in Texas." The girl chuckled at her alliteration. "Perhaps I should have yelled, 'Rattler,' before I pulled the trigger. Papa says I tend to act before I think."

"If you had," Mr. Devers reminded, "I'd be a-sufferin' from a snakebite, possibly dyin'. It really was some mighty fine shootin'; finest I've ever seen by a woman." The first time he qualified her shooting as being unexpected because she was female, it caused the girl to bristle. But by the third or fourth time she wanted to wipe the condescending smirk off the man's face.

Sensing the girl's tension, Hobie spoke before the girl could reply. "Miss Rebecca's pretty good with a knife too. Don't challenge her. She could split a knot in a fencepost at twelve feet with only one toss; at twenty feet with two." He chuckled at his humor.

Determined to keep quiet, the girl took a deep breath and stared at her hands folded in her lap. Across the aisle, Aggie also sensed the girl's discomfort. "Well, our dear little Becca is a woman of many talents, so it seems. What are some of your other talents, dear?"

"She plays a mighty fine mouth organ too," Hobie announced with pride.

Mr. Hutchinson smiled as one would at a precocious child. "Oh? Play something for us, my dear."

"Maybe later," the girl mumbled and glared at Hobie.

"What? What did I do?" He shrugged his shoulders in confusion.

The tension emitted from Rebecca silenced the other passengers. For several hours, they rode without talking. At Elkhorn, while the crew hitched a fresh team of horses to the stagecoach, Sallie gave the passengers a ten-minute break—time to drink a cup of hot tea and eat a bowl of slumgullion. Becca soon learned the definition of slumgullion. It was a watery stew containing a variety of usually unidentifiable ingredients. This one had an abundance of turnips.

The bugle sounded as she slurped her final mouthful.

Night had fallen by the time the passengers climbed into the stagecoach for the next phase of their journey.

"It's as black as tar pitch in a Mississippi swamp," Mr. Devers murmured as he settled into the unenviable middle seat once again. "How Jehu can see the road ahead, I'll never know. Those two carriage lamps can't help much."

At the darkest hour before dawn, the heavy band of clouds that had preceded them through the valley broke, releasing a torrent of rain. The air crackled with lightning. Waves of thunder rumbled across the valley toward the foothills. A strong wind blew the leather shades meant to cover the windows, letting in the rain. The road quickly became a quagmire of mud and fallen debris.

Desperate to stay as dry as possible, the travelers stuffed their coats and leather satchels in and around the edges of the leather curtains. The blankets supplied by the stage company barely covered the shivering passengers. Aggie spread her heavy woolen cape atop the blankets, as did Becca. Grateful for any available warmth, the five passengers huddled in silence.

Becca could hear Hobie murmuring a biblical promise her father often quoted. " 'He shall cover thee with his feathers, and under his wings shalt thou trust. . . . Thou shalt not be afraid for the terror by night; nor for the arrow that flieth by day.' "

A soothing warmth grew inside the girl. Instead of dwelling on her own discomfort, she thought about Jehu, Sallie, and the poor horses exposed to nature's fury. Even Sallie's waterproofed beaverskin jacket had to be damp enough to be uncomfortable.

CHAPTER SIX

THE JEWEL OF THE VALLEY

BECCA HAD BARELY CLOSED her eyes when a deafening crack of thunder and a blinding light rattled her awake. The horses whinnied and reared in terror, jostling the startled passengers.

"Whoa! Whoa!" Jehu shouted above the din. A string of expletives spewed from the conductor's lips. Less than fifteen feet in front of the stagecoach, the bolt of lightning had split a pine from top to bottom. The tree had crashed to the ground, blocking the narrow roadway.

Sallie climbed down off the driver's box and opened the stagecoach door. "Men, I need your help to clear the road." By the look on the man's rain-streaked face, Becca knew that for Sallie to admit he needed anyone's help was distasteful. The girl understood this emotion all too well.

"Is there anything we ladies can do, Mr. Sallie?" Aggie asked.

"Pray we can clear enough of the road to get through to Visalia tonight. Otherwise, we'll be stuck here until the line brings out a fresh team of horses and another coach from the Visalia station."

"I'm good at praying," the woman admitted, reaching for Becca's hands.

Reluctantly, the girl allowed Aggie to take her hands. The woman bowed her head. "Father God, Thou dost understand our predicament. That tree looks mighty big, and those men look mighty miserable out there working in the rain." The women could hear the men shouting and chopping wood between thunderclaps. "A few dozen of Thy burliest angels would be a big help about now," she reminded. "I thank Thee for answering my prayer in whatever way Thou seest fit. Amen."

With nothing else to do, Aggie took a ball of yarn and knitting needles from her satchel. "Figured this would idle away the hours," she explained.

"You can knit in the dark?" Rebecca exclaimed.

"My yes, I can knit my way through any crisis." Two hours later, the men, soaked to the skin, their teeth chattering, and their bodies shaking from the cold, returned to the stagecoach. Immediately following one blast from Sallie's bugle, the wheels of the stagecoach began to roll through the mud once again.

Earlier, before the men returned to the stagecoach, the women each removed one extra petticoat for the men to use as towels.

"I never thought I'd ever use a lady's unmentionables as a towel." Mr. Devers laughed. The man appeared to be in a good mood despite his discomfort. "Sallie says we're less than thirty minutes from Visalia, where we'll get another bowl of slumgullion and a change of clothes—maybe even a dry bed!"

Mr. Hutchinson added, "Fortunately for us but unfortunately for Sallie and the Butterfield Overland stagecoach, Jehu found a crack in the rear axle that will need to be repaired before we head over the mountains at Grapevine Pass—unless the Visalia station has a spare stagecoach, of course. Either way, it looks like we're going to enjoy a longer rest stop than scheduled."

"By the way, Mr. Masters," Mr. Devers nodded toward Hobie. "That was some display of brute strength when you single-handedly shouldered that one massive branch. You are quite a man."

"What I'd like to know, how did you determine which branches needed to be removed in order to clear the road enough for the stagecoach to pass?" Mr. Hutchinson wiped the rain from his hat. "Impressive calculating!"

Hobie grinned and shrugged. "I don't know. Just uncommon common sense, as my dad always calls it. Plus I had a little outside help." He glanced heavenward.

When the men returned the saturated petticoats, Aggie and Becca wrung them out and stuffed them into the cracks around the stagecoach's windows.

The first streaks of dawn rose over the snow-capped Sierra range as the stagecoach lumbered down Visalia's quiet, and almost empty, Main Street. Becca sighed with pleasure seeing the grove of oak trees, several adobe houses, and a few larger red brick buildings. *So this is the "jewel of the valley."*

Hours earlier the patrons from the string of gambling parlors and bars had disappeared to sleep off their night of gaming and drinking. The ladies of ill repute had extinguished the red lanterns in their windows and had called it a night as well. As the stagecoach rolled into town, a mangy yellow dog uttered a perfunctory yip from under the edge of a loose plank in the boardwalk, but he lifted only one ear in greeting.

However, despite the early morning hour, the news of the stagecoach's arrival spread quickly. As Jehu slowed the vehicle to a stop across the muddy street from the exchange house, also known as the Overland Hotel, four station hands burst through the stable doors. They unhitched the exhausted horses and led them into the stables in record time.

Sallie opened the stagecoach door. "Change into dry clothes and get something to eat while you can. I want to hit the trail again as soon as possible." The rain-dampened travelers groaned. As they emerged from the coach, he added, "By the by, there are many unscrupulous varmints and outright skunks inhabiting this town who will be more than happy to relieve you of any money you might be carrying, so beware."

Becca's high-buttoned shoes squished into the mud as she climbed out of the stagecoach and sloshed across the street to the hotel. Soggy strands of her honey-brown hair had escaped her tight braids and were glued to the sides of her face.

A tall, robust, no-nonsense woman in a green homespun dress and a pink gingham Mother Hubbard apron, her braided hair wound around her head like a halo, beckoned the passengers into the hotel. "Come! Come! We have hot chili on the stove and real cow's milk for sale." She ribbed the conductor with her elbow. "Sallie, what were you thinking keeping these poor souls out in a lightning storm like we had last night? For shame! You could have been killed!"

"You know I can't control the weather!" The man looked absolutely sheepish before the woman's scolding. He turned toward his passengers and gestured toward the woman. "This here's Widow Ruthie. She'll keep you in line while I go check on the stagecoach; I promise."

She clicked her tongue. "At least give these poor souls a chance to dry out and rest—or you'll have five sick passengers on your hands."

When the conductor opened his mouth to argue, the woman tossed her head. "You can come, too, Sallie," she called over one shoulder. "My men don't need you to check out your vehicle. By the way," she turned toward the passengers, "I am the proprietor of this establishment, Ruth Elizabeth Daniels, the widow of Jesse Daniels. Jesse died from lead poisoning fifteen years ago next fall." She chortled. "The sheriff's bullet caught the ornery varmint right between the eyes. I say, that'll teach him to help himself to a man's liquor cabinet without invitation."

Widow Ruthie showed Aggie and Rebecca into a tiny office beyond a well-stocked kitchen. "Use the towels on the back of the door. My men will set your bags outside the office door."

The woman spit out her instructions in rapid succession. "Hang your garments on the clothesline out back. And then, when you feel human again, come out for a hot meal of chili beans and corn bread. I also made a batch of potato pudding and freshly churned butter."

The sound of freshly made anything set Becca's taste buds to salivating. Widow Ruthie continued, "By the way, we have sleeping quarters on the second floor if Sallie doesn't herd you out of town like cattle first!"

By the time the two women changed into dry clothing and restyled their hair, Hobie, Mr. Devers, and Mr. Hutchinson had eaten and left the hotel to explore the small town. Becca found Sallie in the kitchen with Widow Ruthie. They were sharing a large bowl of potato pudding.

"What's the news, Mr. Sallie?" Becca asked. "Was the stagecoach damaged as you feared? Will we be leaving soon?"

The man gave a low growl. "Not likely! Found a serious crack in the rear axle. Made of birch, not oak like it's supposed to be! Not safe to drive! One of Widow Ruthie's men left for the Tule River station to retrieve a spare coach. By the looks of things, we won't be out of Visalia much before dawn tomorrow!" The man glowered into his coffee mug.

"Now Sallie, ya can't change circumstances, so why not just enjoy the break while ye have it?" She handed Becca a bowl that contained two squares of hot corn bread. "Tastes extra good soaked in heavy cream. Eat up. And there's more where this came from, little lady." Widow Ruthie eyed the girl critically. "Little girl, when you cross the pass into El Pueblo de Los Angeles County, the Santa Ana winds will blow you into the sea if you're not careful!" She laughed at her own joke.

Aggie, who entered the room behind the girl, brightened at the delicious aromas coming from the stove. "Food! Real food! I am so hungry. Did you say you have rooms to rent upstairs?"

"First, let me get you some food. What did you say your name was darlin'?"

"Aggie."

Widow Ruthie nodded. "As to our sleeping accommodations"—the woman handed Aggie a bowl of corn bread and a spoon—"it's a big empty room with floor space on which to sleep. The rule is bring your own pallets and blankets. But on the bright side, you ladies will be the first to stake your claims."

"One big room?" Becca cleared her throat. "No walls? No beds? No privacy?"

"Afraid not. Just one big room. I'd advise you to place your sleeping pallets on the floor by the rear windows. Less likely you'll be disturbed by snoring customers or by the noise on Main Street after the sun goes down."

"Thank you for the advice, Widow Ruthie." Aggie spooned a chunk of corn bread from her bowl into her mouth. She'd swallowed her last bites when she glanced toward Becca.

"Shall we stake out our claim? Once we're settled, we could do a little sightseeing."

By the time the two women emerged into the sunlight, Main Street bustled with horseback riders, wagons, and housewives doing their daily shopping. "We should purchase a snack or two to sustain us between here and the fort," Aggie suggested. "Being so far behind schedule, Sallie will be reluctant to slow down for much of anything."

Becca reddened. "You go ahead. I will need to find Hobie. He's carrying our travel money." The girl gritted her teeth at having to admit she was penniless. Then she remembered the gold sewn into her petticoat.

"No problem. I understand. I was married to a man who thought women were not mentally equipped to figure advanced mathematical problems like one plus one or seven plus eight." It was the first time Becca had heard sarcasm coming from Aggie. Aware she'd revealed more about herself than she'd intended, the woman stepped into a nearby general store. "Let me purchase a couple of strips of jerky and some peppermint sticks for us."

"I can't let you do that!"

"Sure you can. Besides, I'll let you return the favor on down the road." The woman chuckled. "And we have plenty of road ahead."

Still steaming over the awkward moment, Becca vowed to trade in a chunk or two of gold for cash before they left town. While Aggie lingered over a display of brightly colored yarns, Becca strolled outside, down the boardwalk to Bridge Street, and then took a left on Santa Fe, where she spotted Fort Visalia, a smallish fortification built by the local citizenry. *What a lovely, peaceful town in which to live,* the girl mused. *I see why it's called the "jewel of the valley."*

She'd barely made her observations when the thunder of stampeding hooves, followed by the whoops and hollers of excited cowboys, shattered the silence of the morning. Rebecca whirled in the direction of the commotion.

A riotous spectacle of terror-stricken horses and shouting riders charged past. Cowpunchers, their courage fortified by hard liquor, twirled their wide-brimmed Texas-style hats high above their heads, as wild mustangs sought an escape. Three of the men were riding bareback on the stampeding mustangs. Mud from the horses' hooves flew in every direction, splattering the faces of the gawking crowd gathered on the boardwalk. Whooping and shooting their six-guns in the air, several other cowboys galloped around the panicky creatures and positioned themselves across the west end of Main Street to block the animals' avenue of escape

As they charged by, several housewives screamed and threw their shopping bags into the air. Vegetables, fruit, and loaves of bread rained down on the heads of bystanders. Mothers dragged their wailing toddlers out of the street toward safety.

A middle-aged man ran from the hotel, waving his fists in the air and shouting angry epithets at the riders. Halfway across the street, a young woman, clutching an infant to her chest, caught the toe of her boot on the hem of her garment and fell facedown in the path of a rearing mustang. Stunned spectators watched as Hobie appeared out of nowhere, dashed into the street, scooped the woman into his arms, and ran to the sidewalk.

"Those foolish Hill boys!" A gray-haired woman standing beside Becca snarled. "Just because their pappy owns the largest spread in the valley, they gotta show off their prowess for the painted ladies of Visalia."

The riders and their bucking animals took their circus farther down the street toward the edge of town.

"Hobie!" Rebecca pushed through a crowd of adoring ladies surrounding him.

The rescued woman shouted over the frightened cries of her child, "I can't thank you enough, mister. I thought my son and I were gonners for sure."

"What a brave thing to do!" a second woman, wearing an emerald-green satin gown and a blue silk shawl, cooed. Cascades of auburn curls piled high on her head tumbled down on one shoulder. She stroked the man's shoulder and upper arm. "What bulging muscles! You are a true hero, mister."

"Shucks, ma'am." Hobie's face reddened at the unexpected attention. He tugged his hat down to hide a large portion of his face. "I only did what any man would do in the same situation."

"Look around, big boy," the same painted lady insisted. "You weren't the only male on the street, but you were the only one who dared risk your own life to save this poor mother and her child. Admit it! You are a hero." Gently, she brushed a blotch of mud from Hobie's cheek with her finger. "After such a feat, you must be mighty thirsty. Why don't you come over to my place," she gestured toward a saloon on the opposite side of the street, "and wet your whistle—at my expense, of course."

"Oh, no! No, thank you, miss, I . . ." The man was accustomed to the attentions of ladies of the night at home in Placerville. He'd grown up around them.

"Hobie!" Becca reached through the crowd and grabbed his shirtsleeve. Standing on tiptoes, she peered between the other women's heads. "Are you all right?"

At the sound of Becca's question, Hobie's bevy of devotees shot daggers at the intruder. They knew a fresh mark didn't come along at such an early hour every day of the week.

Relief flooded Hobie's face. He pushed his way toward her. "I'm so glad to see you, Miss Becca." Before he reached her, his look of relief shifted to fear. "But ya gotta git on back to the hotel!"

"Huh?" The girl blinked in surprise.

"Hurry!" he snapped.

"Skedaddle!" A blond woman, her cheeks red with rouge, her lips painted an orange-red, clutched his arm and leaned her head protectively against his leather vest. "Do what the man says, missy!" She hissed. "Besides I saw him first!"

The redhead tugged at Hobie's other arm. "Back off, Beulah! I already invited him to my place for a drink."

Confused and humiliated, Becca didn't wait to learn which invitation Hobie might accept. She whirled about and fled toward the hotel. Tears stung her cheeks as she dashed through the hotel's swinging doors. *Why did Hobie embarrass me like he did? He treated me like a five-year-old being sent to bed without supper!*

Widow Ruthie met the girl at the front door of the hotel. "Whatever is the matter, child? Did those cowpokes scare you?" She gathered the girl in her arms. Not one to appreciate hugs from strangers, Becca's only thought was to hide from everyone. But the hotel operator firmly pressed the girl to her bosom and held her there for several seconds. "I'm so sorry. Those fool wranglers won't be happy until they kill someone with their antics! Why, just last week, the editor of the *Expositor* railed against the practice of breaking wild mustangs on Main Street. But did it help? It might if those yahoos could read! Our sheriff calls their behavior 'good, clean fun, a way the boys can let off steam.' Huh!"

"I'm fine!" Becca pulled free of the woman's grasp. Before she could escape, Mr. Devers burst through the hotel doors.

"Miss Rebecca, quick! Hightail it up those stairs as fast as you can!" Wide-eyed with concern, the man pointed toward the staircase. "And you best stay there until Mr. Hobie says it's safe for you to come back down."

"Mr. Devers! I don't understand—" Becca began.

"Don't argue. Just do it!" His concern was obvious.

Widow Ruthie glanced from one to the other and back again before taking the girl by the shoulders and aiming her toward the stairs. "You do as Mr. Devers says until I figure out what is happening."

Humiliated beyond words, the mortified Rebecca stormed past the staircase, through the kitchen, and on to the outhouse, a habit she'd developed as a child whenever her parents scolded her. There she stayed, with the only streaks of light filtering between the cracks in the walls. The girl felt foolish for her impulsive display but justified in light of Hobie's and Mr. Devers's orders. While she knew she'd have to emerge from her isolation at some point, she dreaded the moment of facing anyone. As she gathered her courage, she quoted, "I 'can do all things,' " conveniently leaving off the words "through Christ which strengtheneth me." The girl had been inside the tiny cubicle for more than fifteen minutes when someone knocked on the door.

"Go away! Just go away!" She shouted.

"Uh, I can't, miss," said the unfamiliar voice of a stranger, sounding desperate. "I got nowhere else to go."

Color flooded her face as she unlocked the outhouse door. "Sorry," she muttered as she skittered past a short, rotund, and balding, middle-aged man waiting to use the facility.

When she entered the kitchen, Hobie and Mr. Devers stood on one side of a butcher-block worktable; Widow Ruthie stood on the other. Mr. Devers was the first to speak. "Miss Rebecca, just before the hullabaloo began, a scruffy-looking man, along with two equally unsavory sidekicks, rode into the Butterfield Overland stagecoach livery, asking if anyone had seen a runaway girl who was wanted for attempted murder. It seems Mr. Masters was coming to warn you when the horses stampeded."

"You poor child!" Widow Ruthie pulled the girl into her arms a second time. "Mr. Masters explained everything. The senator's hirelings threaten to search every building and stop every vehicle leaving town to find you."

"We don't believe for a minute that you did what he says you did. So we're here to help you get out of town safely," Mr. Devers explained. "Fortunately, a few minutes ago the new coach arrived from the Pack-wood station."

Not to be outdone, Widow Ruthie went on to explain. "My men are already hitching up a fresh team of horses. Sallie wants to hit the trail as quickly as possible."

Becca recalled the face of the stranger she encountered at the outhouse. "Was the man I passed . . ."

The innkeeper chuckled aloud. "Oh, no, James Martin is harmless, unless you're a Northern abolitionist or you choose to break wild mustangs on Main Street. Jim's the editor of our local newspaper, the *Expositor*. His print shop occupies the other half of this building."

"Becca, did you bring along your prospecting garb?" Hobie asked.

"Sure did. Mama insisted. Why?"

"The hired gunmen are looking for a woman." Hobie thoughtfully stroked his chin. "Widow Ruthie suggested the best way to get you out of town is for you to dress like a young boy."

Rebecca gazed at the three faces watching her. Hobie's motive to help her she understood, but not Widow Ruthie's and Mr. Devers's. *Am I walking into a trap?* she wondered.

"I know what you're thinking. Why are we doing this? Well, when I walked over to the stables to speak with Sallie," Widow Ruthie began, "one look at that hornswoggler from up north and both Sallie and I knew whose story to believe! Don't worry, honey! We'll get you out of here safely."

Mr. Devers shrugged his shoulders and grinned. "Hey, you saved me from a deadly snakebite. You've won my eternal devotion, little miss." He glanced toward the widow. "You should see this gal shoot. She could shoot a ladybug off a fallen log at fifty feet and not leave a mark on the bark!"

Becca chuckled. "Not hardly, Mr. Devers, but thank you for the compliment."

Widow Ruthie planted her left hand on her hip and pointed toward the stairs with her right. "Then it's settled, Miss Rebecca. Go change your clothing. Mrs. Aggie went upstairs to pack a few minutes ago. You, Mr. Devers, find Mr. Hutchinson. Tell him the stagecoach is leaving in fifteen minutes."

The girl dashed up the stairs two at a time. A niggling voice inside warned her to obey though her naturally petulant nature wanted to rebel. She knew Hobie and the others were only trying to help, but she felt her life had spiraled out of her control. And, more than anything else, Rebecca Cunard hated being out of control. Everything was happening too fast and with other people making her decisions.

Before Aggie and Rebecca left the second-floor hotel room, the girl had been transformed from a petite young lady into a slightly overweight twelve-year-old boy. Aggie had wrapped the strips of fabric, which Becca's mother had insisted on packing, around the girl's middle. The woman helped her into the bulky trousers, heavy boots, and a plaid wool shirt.

"Here!" Ruthie burst into the room carrying a worn leather vest. "This should help camouflage your femininity a little more."

The hotel owner tied a man's red-and-white checkered handkerchief around the girl's neck and stepped back to admire the transformation while Aggie anchored Becca's braids with several whalebone hairpins also donated by the widow.

Plopping Becca's father's floppy suede hat atop the girl's head, Aggie asked, "Well? What do you think?"

The woman shook her head. "I don't know. One stiff wind will send that hat sailing into the next county and the jig will be up. No self-respecting boy would wear his hair that long."

Aggie agreed. "The wisest thing to do would be to cut off those braids!"

"No!" the girl wailed and grabbed the back of her head. Memories of evenings when her father would watch her mother brush the honey-brown locks popped into her mind. "No! No! I can't! I can't!"

"It's only hair! It will grow back," Widow Ruthie soothed. "Besides, you'll find traveling bareheaded in the coach a whole lot more comfortable, especially in the heat of New Mexico and Texas."

"Well, what will it be?" Aggie had retrieved a pair of scissors from her carpetbag. "Remember, 'be ye therefore wise as serpents, and harmless as doves.'"

The girl started in surprise at the pair of scissors going *snip, snip, snip,* in Aggie's hand. The woman's lips moved but Becca heard only her mother's warning, "Be wise as serpents, and harmless as doves." She could almost hear her mother say, "This is the time to be wise."

One of the station handlers knocked on the door and called out, "Ladies, Mr. Sallie asked me to fetch your luggage. He's anxious to get rolling." He'd barely finished his message when Sallie's bugle sounded.

"Just a minute," Aggie called out, scissors in hand. "Well, what will it be?"

Becca swallowed hard. "Go ahead! Quick! Before I change my mind."

CHAPTER SEVEN

FUTILE DISGUISE

THE GIRL WINCED AT the sound of the first snip and then again, at the next and the next. Within seconds, her long, heavy braids lay like garden snakes coiled on the wooden floor behind her. Becca grabbed at her bare neck and yelped. The shaggy cut barely covered her neck.

"Would you like to see it?" the widow asked. "I have a mirror in my office."

The girl shook her head. "No! No!" Becca jammed the hat on her head. "Where are my gun and my knife?"

"You can't carry a sidearm! A twelve-year-old boy wouldn't have a—" The set of Becca's jaw warned Aggie that this was a battle she'd lose.

The girl retrieved her weapons and strapped their sheaths to her waist. "May I carry my satchel, or is it too feminine?" she said cattily.

Widow Ruthie patted the girl's shoulder. "There there, honey. We're only trying to help. I'm sure a boy wouldn't mind carrying such a fine leather bag, would he, Aggie?"

Rebecca snatched up the bag and dashed down the stairs with Widow Ruthie dogging her heels.

As the doors of the hotel slammed against the side of the building, the woman shouted, "Gather 'round folks. I want to offer a little prayer before you leave."

"By the looks of things," Sallie chuckled aloud upon seeing the belligerent pout on Becca's face, "we're gonna need all the prayers we can get."

The girl whirled about and glared at the man. "There is nothing funny about my situation, Mr. Sallie. I'd like to see you prancing about in a—a lady's camisole!"

Unnerved by the vehemence in the girl's tone, the stage conductor took a step backward and touched the brim of his hat. "Sorry, miss, er, I mean, mister. What am I suppose to call you anyway?"

"Nothing! Don't speak to me at all!" Tears brimmed in Becca's eyes as she climbed into the coach and slumped down on the seat. Outside on the boardwalk, Widow Ruthie offered a prayer for the travelers' safety. The girl felt a twinge of guilt for not appreciating all everyone was doing for her. After all, her presence risked her companions' well-being too.

One sweep of her fingers across the back of her neck, and her bad feelings returned. She crossed her arms and set her lips into a determined pout. *Who am I, anyway? I've become a stranger even to myself. If I live through this nightmare, I vow I will never allow anyone to tell me what to do, ever again!*

Once Widow Ruthie's men loaded the last of the luggage onto the roof, the other four passengers climbed aboard. If they'd thought to comment on Becca's garb, they changed their minds when she shot them each a withering glare.

Widow Ruthie waved goodbye. "Go with God," she called. "Go with God."

The stagecoach traveled east on Main Street to Bridge Street, where they crossed Mill Creek. As the wheels rumbled onto the wooden post bridge, Aggie announced, "From here on out, Becca is traveling with me. She's my twelve-year-old son! Do you understand?" She gazed at Mr. Hutchinson who hadn't been in on the transformation. "Is that clear, sir?"

The three men nodded solemnly. "Mr. Hutchinson?" she insisted.

"Yes, ma'am. Sallie informed me of the situation before I boarded the coach." His obliging grin quickly faded upon seeing the warning scowl on Becca's face.

They'd barely cleared the bridge when a man in his midtwenties stepped out of a grove of trees and waved for the stagecoach to stop. He wore the navy-blue jacket and dark pants of a soldier in the United States Army; a kepi hat and a heavy sidearm in a holster completed his uniform. The officer peered through the window at the passengers and then up at Sallie. "I see you have room for one more. I'm with the U.S. Army. My horse stepped into a pothole, so I need transportation to Fort Tejon."

Becca ducked her face into her shirt collar while Sallie dickered over the ticket price with the soldier. Once he paid, the man climbed on board, took off his hat, and placed it on his lap. Hobie folded his arms across his chest, effectively blocking the man's view of Becca.

Out of the corner of her eye, the girl studied the man's unlined, well-shaven face and his parade-ready uniform. "Mornin' folks," he began. "I'm Lieutenant Wyatt Milburn from Rochester, New York."

The passengers nodded their greetings, all except Becca, who stared out the window beside her. If the soldier thought he wasn't warmly welcome, he concealed it. "I've been in the Visalia area dickering with the local ranchers for beef cattle."

"Did you get a good deal?" Mr. Hutchinson asked.

"Better than I thought. I was ahead of schedule when my mare stepped in a hole and wrenched her leg, so I have to leave her in Visalia until she mends. The doc says she should be ready to ride in a few weeks. In the meantime, I'm due back at the fort."

"You just abandoned her?" Aggie's voice raised several tones in surprise.

The soldier chuckled. "I'll be returning for her. She's a good horse. I wouldn't want to lose her."

"Well," the woman huffed. "I am certainly glad to hear that. Welcome Lieutenant Milburn to our cozy little coach. My name is just plain Aggie." She offered her gloved hand.

He nodded and grinned. "It's a pleasure to meet you, just plain Aggie."

Aggie giggled at the flirtatious twinkle in the young man's eyes. "This is Mr. Devers and Mr. Hutchinson and Mr. Masters from Placerville." Fearful she'd revealed too much, the woman shot a wary glance toward Becca.

"And who might you be, young man?" The soldier smiled at Becca.

Without thinking, the girl replied, "I'm Reb—" Suddenly, she froze and inhaled sharply.

"Reb? Like Johnny Reb?" The soldier's eyes narrowed.

Unable to take back her utterance, she shook her head. "No, I'm simply Reb."

Aggie hurried to her aid. "My son's full name is Reuben Sparks. For obvious reasons we didn't like the nickname Reub, so we called him Reb."

"Glad to hear that, Reb. I'd hate to think I was riding in a coach with a Southern sympathizer." The soldier's brown eyes twinkled as he chuckled. The dimple in the cleft of his jaw deepened. Momentarily forgetting her ruse, Becca cast the soldier a coy little smile.

The soldier blinked in surprise, causing Hobie to lean forward, blocking the man's view. Hobie gave Becca a tiny dig in the ribs and whispered, "What do you think you are doing?"

Across the coach, Mr. Devers quickly interjected, his voice dripping with Southern charm. "You could do worse than to be forced to travel with a Southern sympathizer, sir."

"Of course, you're right, sir." The officer grinned again, but his voice lacked even a speck of humor.

"I forgot! I'm sorry," Becca simpered to Hobie.

"You should be!" he hissed. Fortunately, the rattle of wheels rolling over the rocky road and the jangling of the horses' reins drowned out their exchange. Pretending to go to sleep, Becca slouched down in her seat and pulled her hat over her face.

The stagecoach angled toward the mountains to the east when three seedy-looking men rode up on horses and blocked the road in front of the coach. Those in the stagecoach stiffened and reached for their guns. They'd all heard of dangerous highwaymen robbing the stagecoaches along the Butterfield route. The leader of the interlopers shot his rifle into the air. "Stop!" he shouted.

"Whoa!" The driver yanked on the reins, bringing the horses to a stop.

"What's the big idea?" Sallie demanded, his shotgun resting on his lap. "Get out of the road!"

The leader of the group yelled, "We represent State Senator Bartholomew Stanley. We are looking for a young female, a fugitive from justice."

"We ain't got no fugitive from justice on board," Sallie snarled. "And while you may represent a state senator, I represent the United States of America!"

When the two other men peered through the windows into the

coach, Lieutenant Milburn unsheathed his military issued pistol and aimed it at the chin of the nearest hoodlum. "I, too, represent the United States government, and, as you can see, we ain't got no young females on board!" He shot a quick glance toward Aggie's ashen face. "Begging your pardon, madam. You're a fine specimen of a woman, you are, but hardly as young as these hooligans describe."

Aggie blinked and nodded. "No offense taken, Lieutenant."

"Be gone with you!" The officer stuck his head out of the carriage. "Sallie, move on out!" The conductor nodded toward Jehu, who flicked the reins, and the carriage began to roll. The lieutenant holstered his gun and mumbled, "Highwaymen! They are why the army needs to establish a fort down here—to protect the good people in the valley from such riffraff."

Relieved, the other passengers leaned back in their seats. No one spoke for several miles. When the stagecoach rolled into the Tule River station, everyone stayed on board while a team of fresh horses replaced the tired ones. Within five minutes, they were on the road heading toward the town of Porterville.

"See that massive oak tree over there?" The soldier pointed as the stagecoach passed the center of town. "The good people in these parts call it the hanging tree. A while back two men from a local Indian tribe were strung up for killing a couple of white miners. Unfortunately for the two Indians, the people later discovered the white men had shot each other over a poker dispute. In the meantime, the town's vigilantes chased and slaughtered several of the local tribesmen. To avoid the same fate, the women and children hid in the caves in the hills east of town."

"That's terrible!" Aggie gasped.

"It happened all too often during the last ten years." The man heaved a heavy sigh. "Yeah, I've fought the elephant." The other men nodded solemnly.

" 'Fought the elephant'?" Aggie asked.

"That means Lieutenant Milburn has seen battle," Mr. Devers explained.

The lieutenant gave a humorless laugh. "Sometimes I think my eyes have seen more than any human being should . . ." His voice faded. As Becca stared toward the eastern hills, she imagined seeing women and children running for their lives and hiding for weeks in caves. She thought about Aaron's brood, especially Izzy. *What if Izzy got caught in such a slaughter? So much pain for so many tears—why?* she wondered.

Hobie's face remained expressionless. Beyond him, the soldier silently stared out the window. Becca wondered, *Just what have you seen, Lieutenant, since you joined the cavalry? And what more will you see and do before your time on this earth comes to an end?*

Whenever Becca's father discussed with the other men in town the growing threat of a civil war breaking out somewhere in the East, she and her mother found other places to be. Yet refusing to hear about the conflict didn't stop the girl from thinking about the possibility. *Will it begin with an exchange of gunfire between neighboring farmers? From an argument between U.S. senators on opposing sides in Congress? Or during a street brawl in New York City?*

Frightening memories came to her of nights in western New York when she watched her older brother Caleb ride pell-mell into the barn. There he disappeared into his "hidey-hole" in the hayloft until the bounty hunters in pursuit tired of searching for him. She recalled taking a bucket of fresh water to her brother and catching glimpses of the terror-stricken faces of dark-skinned men and women crouched in the hayloft with him. She shivered as she remembered the night Serenity's fine home on the banks of Lake Cayuga burned to the ground. *Surely we left all that violence behind when we came to California,* she reasoned. *At least, in California we can choose not to get involved.*

After a brief stop at the Mountain House station to switch teams and again at Gordon's Ferry, the stagecoach rambled south toward a range of mountains growing out of the floor of the San Joaquin Valley. Watching the mountains loom closer, Becca tried to determine which way the road would go over the hills. Would it veer around the mountains to the left or angle off to the right? Either path would be difficult. Whenever the officer glanced her way, the girl closed her eyes and pretended to be asleep.

Mr. Hutchinson awakened, his voice was groggy, "Where are we?"

The lieutenant blinked awake. As a man who obviously loved to talk, he leaped at the opportunity to share his knowledge of the area with someone. "We're nearing the Tehachapi Mountains. Fort Tejon is just beyond the crest. Originally, the government hired a Mr. Beal to build a road from the El Pueblo de Los Angeles basin across the Tehachapi

Mountains to the San Joaquin Valley. The facility was designed to protect the settlers from marauding Paiutes." The officer heaved a heavy sigh. "The First Dragoons arrived at Fort Tejon in 1854. The fort's complex of adobe buildings house two hundred and twenty-five soldiers. The fort cost a half a million U.S. government dollars to build. Because of the rough terrain of Grapevine Canyon, we are approximately one hundred and fifty miles from the fort. If all goes well, we should arrive there in thirty-two and a half hours, a good record by the way this Jehu drives."

"Thirty-two hours," Becca mumbled to herself.

"Do they call it Grapevine Canyon because of the vineyards growing there?" Mr. Hutchinson asked.

The officer snorted, shifting his weight in the narrow seat. "Hardly! They call it Grapevine Canyon because the road to the pass is twisted like the stalk of a grapevine. The shoulder on the single lane road drops several hundred feet into the canyon below."

Aggie stirred uncomfortably, as did Mr. Devers.

"I've heard you soldiers ride camels imported from the Middle East instead of horses." Mr. Hutchinson twisted his head to remove a crick from his neck, or at least that's what Becca surmised.

The lieutenant's loud guffaw awakened Hobie, who'd been snoring lightly. "That's a rumor started by an East Coast reporter. The camels were not shipped to Fort Tejon but to El Pueblo de Los Angeles County." The disappointment on the faces of his audience encouraged him. "A part of the story is true. Soon after they arrived in the West, a few of the mangy creatures escaped into the mountains. I've been told that if you're lucky, you might see one or two of the ornery beasts grazing in a mountain meadow."

"Really?" Becca peered around Hobie's relaxed face at the soldier. "Do you know anyone who's actually seen a camel?"

"Why, young man! You sound skeptical! I heard tell last summer a Mormon family was camping near French John's Station. The man's first wife sent her two daughters to a nearby spring for water. After filling their buckets, the girls heard horrid, unearthly grunts, wheezes, and squeals coming from the brush. The girls darted behind a clump of thistles and watched three humpbacked creatures with long necks and bobbing heads charge toward the spring. Later, after the little gals told their tale, soldiers from the fort hunted for the beasts but never found them."

Becca leaned back against the seat. *What a fanciful tale,* she thought. *Camels! Humped backs and long necks? No one I've ever known has seen such an animal!*

Capturing the attention of the other passengers, the man continued. "Our stop at Rose station will be brief, just time to switch teams. Later, after the Kern River station, we will pass through the Sink of Tejon or Comanche Point." The lieutenant took a gulp of water from his tin canteen. "If the rain hasn't made the post road through the swamp impassable."

He paused and glanced at Becca. "So, Reb, have you ever felt the earth shake?"

The girl started to tell about an earthquake that struck Sacramento when she and her parents were visiting Aaron and Lilia, but quickly bit her tongue. "Yes, sir, I have, not a very big one but an earthquake nonetheless."

"Well, last year, we had a mighty big one at Fort Tejon. I was in the sick bay with a broken foot when it hit. The force threw me off my cot and slammed me into the wall across the room. And I fared better than some of my buddies, however. What a mess! Most of the buildings at the fort were damaged, and several soldiers were injured." Satisfied he'd gotten the desired reaction from the two Easterners, the officer closed his eyes and leaned his head back against the bench. "But, for all of the destruction, only two people died."

The late winter sun quickly set beyond the ridge to the west, wrapping the passengers in a cozy cocoon of night. The only sounds were the clop of the horses' hooves, the wheels rumbling over the rocky ground, and the carriage's squeaky springs.

While her traveling companions snoozed, sleep evaded Becca. She stared at the dancing halos—the two lanterns guiding the coach. Her thoughts bounced from one memory to another; from one person in her life to another. The ache in her heart grew. She felt so alone. On an impulse she placed her left hand on Hobie's. And as natural as rain, and without opening his eyes, he turned his hand over and wrapped his giant fingers gently around hers. Silently, they rode throughout the night. When the first rays of sunlight glinted through the brush along the road, she reluctantly withdrew her hand from his.

Throughout the next day, it was hard going for the stagecoach and for the passengers. At one point, while Aggie picked her way along the shoulder of the roadway, the male passengers, including Becca, pushed the vehicle through the axle-deep mud.

"I can do all things," she muttered as the sticky clay splashed her face and clothing. "Please, God, don't let me fall on my face in this sticky mess."

At the south end of the swamp, the horses regained their footing; the wheels of the coach took hold of solid ground. The horses leaped forward; Jehu and Sallie cheered. "All right, men." The conductor eyed Becca as he spoke. "Take a few minutes to clean up in the spring over there at the edge of the woods, and then we'll be on our way."

Becca splashed water on her face and rinsed the mud from her hands. How she maintained her cover in front of the military man, the girl didn't know. It didn't hurt having Hobie and Mr. Devers shadow her every move. By late afternoon the fort's rough-hewn wooden post walls could be seen in the distance. After what seemed like hours, the stagecoach stopped in front of the fort's massive wooden gates. With a signal from Sallie to the soldier standing guard on the wall, the gates swung open.

Becca was exhausted. All she wanted to do was sleep. Since this was the longest meal stop they would have before crossing the southern range into the El Pueblo de Los Angeles basin, Aggie insisted the girl eat something. The aroma of bubbling venison stew simmering over an open-hearth fireplace accosted the women's senses as they entered the mess hall, awakening Becca's taste buds. When the cook handed her a bowl of the stew, the girl almost drooled upon seeing real vegetables floating in a thick broth.

Aggie and Becca sat down at a long, narrow wooden table. In the center of the table, several oversized handwoven baskets held hot-from-the-oven soda biscuits. Remembering her mother's Sunday morning breakfast of Southern biscuits and gravy brought tears to the girl's eyes.

Mr. Devers parked his body across from her and handed her a bread basket. "Here, help yourself."

Becca mumbled a Thank you and took two biscuits. All too soon both she and Aggie saw the bottom of their bowls. When the cook came by to replenish the empty bowls, Aggie asked, "Where do you get such delicious vegetables? From El Pueblo de Los Angeles?"

The cook's chest puffed out with pride. "I grow 'em in a small garden out back. It seems everything grows in this rich soil."

Becca had barely emptied her second bowl of stew when Sallie announced that the Butterfield Overland stagecoach would be leaving in fifteen minutes. Full for the first time since she left the Pettigrews' home in San Francisco, the girl reluctantly pushed back from the table.

She'd barely risen to her feet when Lieutenant Milburn appeared, grasped her arm and, without a word, marched her from the building.

"You are no twelve-year-old boy, Miss Rebecca Cunard. I've been watching you. You can't fool me. You walk like a female; you eat like a lady."

Becca whirled around in surprise. "How did you know my name?"

"I happened to be in the livery stable when those henchmen inquired after you."

"If you knew, why didn't you report me to those bounty hunters?"

"I didn't report you for two reasons: one, I didn't trust the unsavory demeanor of the men pursuing you; and two, I needed to return to the fort as quickly as possible. By the way, when you gave me that saucy smile, all lingering doubts I might have had were laid to rest."

"Th-Th-Thank you, Lieutenant Milburn." She stumbled over her words. "For not saying anything. I truly didn't do what they claim I did."

"Of course, you didn't. I knew that. But I wouldn't be surprised if they continue to dog your trail. It's the only way they can collect a reward. And should these guys fail, chances are good that this senator fellow will hire additional ruffians from across the country—just a warning." Gently releasing her arm, he leaned closer to her. "I think I'd like you better as a woman. I wish we could have met under different circumstances." Abruptly he turned and strode into the nearest barracks, leaving Becca speechless.

"What was that all about?" Hobie stepped out of the building's shadow.

"I guess I didn't fool the man with my disguise."

Hobie glowered. "I was afraid of that. I was praying he'd keep quiet."

Becca nervously licked her lower lip. "He also said that the men won't stop until they find me. It's the only way they can collect the reward."

"I know, but remember that God promises to cover you with His feathers. He already sent a blue uniformed angel to watch over you this far." He shifted his weight from one foot to the other. "Besides, you do know I'll always be here for you, Rebecca."

"Don't you worry, Hobie." She patted the sidearm in her holster. "If I see those three bandits again, I know what to do!"

Hobie shook his head slowly. "Sometimes I wish I'd never taught you how to use that thing."

CHAPTER EIGHT

EARTHQUAKE!

WITH THE LIEUTENANT GONE, the interior of the stagecoach felt almost spacious to Becca, still dressed in what she called her prospector's garb. She and Aggie had agreed to take turns riding in the middle seat. Since it was Becca's turn, the girl clutched her leather satchel to her chest and leaned back against the leather straps as best she could.

"Hey, Reb," Mr. Devers took delight in referring to the girl by the Southern moniker. "Do you still have a mouth organ in that bag of yours? I feel like singing."

"Yes." She glanced at the faces of the other passengers.

"Good idea, Mr. Devers. I think some music would be lovely." Aggie nodded toward the young woman. "Maybe we'll all sing along."

Becca found her harmonica at the bottom of the bag and ran her mouth across the instrument's comb.

"Do you know 'Sweet Betsy From Pike'?" Mr. Devers asked.

Becca nodded and played several bars of the popular ditty. The other passengers joined his clear tenor voice, filling the carriage with the familiar words. Hobie's strong, rich baritone voice surprised the girl. She hadn't known her friend could sing so well. Of course, she hadn't been listening.

> "Singing too-ra-li-oo-ra-li-oo-ra-li-ay,
> singing too-ra-il-oo . . ."

As the passengers added creative verses of their own, the song continued for what seemed like forever. Before long, everyone was laughing at the ridiculous rhymes created. Finally, when they'd exhausted every possible variation, Rebecca paused for a much-needed break.

She'd barely had time to swipe her moist lips across the comb once more when Mr. Devers asked, "Reb, how about 'The California Stage Company'?"

The girl shook her head. "I think I may have heard it once at a Saturday-night potluck, but I don't know it." The memory of Bart's invitation to the weekly event, which had triggered her flight from her home and family, caused her to wince.

"I think I can do it a cappella if you give me a low C to get me started." She obliged and then leaned back to listen to the ballad written about the earliest stage line in California that transported eager forty-niners to the gold fields.

> "There's no respect for youth or age
> On board the California stage."

Becca and the others laughed at the song's humorous lyrics. Even the stoic Mr. Hutchinson joined in the fun. "How about 'Yankee Doodle'?" he asked.

"Only if we follow up with 'Dixie,' " Mr. Devers snarled at the man.

Becca was surprised at the level of anger that passed between the two travelers. *I guess civility only runs skin deep.* Hobie didn't wait for further conflict to break out, but began singing. "Yankee Doodle went to town a-ridin' on a pony." When he finished the last chorus, he switched into "Dixie." "I wish I was in the land of cotton . . ."

As upbeat as "Yankee Doodle" had been, singing "Dixie" held a note of nostalgia, especially for Mr. Devers. The last chorus ended with a sigh from the man. "I've been away from home too long." A gentle smile crossed his lips. "God willing, by the beginning of April, I'll be able to plant these boots on Tennessee soil once again."

Even Mr. Hutchinson's face softened. As for Hobie, he heaved a sigh of relief at a conflict averted. Becca remembered being a part of the wagon train west. The biggest dangers for the travelers didn't involve snakes, Indian attacks, or wild animals. More people were injured or died from personal feuds, little skirmishes over spilled coffee, loud snoring, drunkenness, and jealousies over positions in the wagon train lineup.

For several minutes, they rode in silence. Grateful for the break, the girl dropped her mouth organ into her bag once more.

"Mr. Devers, do you know 'Down in the Valley'?" Aggie asked, barely above a whisper. "It was my husband's favorite song."

Husband? Numerous questions came to the girl's mind. At the moment, Becca dared not ask.

Mr. Devers nodded and obliged her by singing the words to the familiar ballad. Hobie and Mr. Hutchinson joined in on the third line. Tears filled Aggie's eyes as the men harmonized. She dabbed her eyes with a handkerchief.

"Roses love sunshine; violets love dew;
Angels in heaven know I love you."

A somber mood settled over the travelers. Instead of enveloping the passengers in an atmosphere of intimacy, the darkness isolated them with troubling thoughts and tender memories. For Becca, the melody transported her back to her childhood in western New York state. She recalled Saturday nights when her family gathered around a roaring fire in the fireplace to sing hymns and ballads, such as "Bonny Barbara Allen," and to play Bible charades.

The girl could almost smell hot popcorn flavored with her mother's freshly churned butter. She could almost hear the crunch. She could almost taste the tangy sweetness of a crisp, McIntosh apple picked off a tree behind the parsonage.

Cold mountain air blew through the coach. By the variety of snores from the male passengers, she knew they were asleep. Bundled in her cape and with her corner of a buffalo robe lying across her legs, Becca spotted a mother bear and two cubs standing beside the rocky mountain road, watching the stagecoach pass by. She glanced across the carriage at Aggie also staring out her window.

"Can't sleep?" Becca asked.

The woman shook her head.

"Missing your husband? How did he die?"

Again the woman shook her head. "He didn't. It would have been much easier if he had."

"Oh." Fearful she'd asked too many questions, the girl bit her lip. "I'm sorry. I didn't mean to pry."

"Don't be. You're not the only person on the run. I left him in a drunken stupor in San Francisco. I'm going home to my parents in Indiana."

"Oh."

"I should have left the man years ago before he lost at the poker table the sizable inheritance I received from my grandmother. I'm just thankful I thought to salt away small amounts of cash over the years, or I could never have saved enough to make this trip!"

"Oh, I'm sorry."

"Don't be. My parents warned me about Harry, but I was madly in love with love and with Harry's roguish, naughty-boy image; I couldn't resist. Foolish me! I thought once we were married, he would change." She paused. "He changed all right. He drank more; gambled away our Nob Hill three-story townhouse, including all our expensive furnishings; and accused me of being a nagging wife. Maybe I was—toward the end." Again she paused before continuing. "When I complained because he pawned my grandmother's diamond brooch to pay off his gambling debt, he slapped me so hard my ears rang for hours afterward."

"Oh!" Becca couldn't picture her gentle father or either of her brothers ever hitting their wives. The only man she could picture being so cruel was Bart Stanley, her nemesis.

"After fourteen years in a childless marriage, I went to the local constable for advice. He shrugged off my complaint with, 'I don't interfere in domestic disputes.'"

"The police officer wouldn't help you?"

Aggie shook her head. "When I asked if he'd interfere when my husband killed me, he grinned and spat a wad of chewing tobacco into a brass spittoon in the corner of his office. 'Ah, lady, don't be ridiculous. A man needs to keep his feisty woman in line somehow.' So here I am."

"Do you think Harry will follow you?"

Aggie snorted. "Only if I'd dumped the bottles from his liquor cabinet before I left."

"What if he does come after you? What will you do?"

"I don't know. By law a man can drag home a runaway spouse whether or not she wishes to go."

Becca thought about the woman's plight for several minutes. "Aggie, you are a very brave woman. I admire you for your courage to leave him."

"Don't. It might take bravery to leave him after so many years, but I was foolish to marry him in the first place. When it comes to choosing a husband, I should have listened to my grandmother's wise counsel. She told me to 'winter 'em and summer 'em before you marry 'em.' She also used to say, 'Marry in haste; repent at leisure.' If only I'd listened." Aggie stared out of the carriage window into the darkness. "I've had many days to repent."

The woman left the girl with much to think about. After several minutes, Becca added, "Frankly, I don't see any advantages marrying at all. I may not be the marrying kind. I like being free to come and go as I please."

The woman smiled. "Oh, Becca, you are so young. Life can be mighty lonely without a caring spouse. Sitting alone in my Nob Hill mansion, surrounded by expensive furniture from the Orient, exquisite carpets from Persia, and carved mahogany sideboards filled with gold-rimmed china and silver goblets from Belgium and Germany, I would have given it all for my husband's affection and companionship."

"I-I-I'm sorry," Becca mumbled, burrowing deeper into the buffalo robe covering her lap and torso.

Suddenly, the silence of the night was shattered by a loud rumble and shake. The horses reared and whinnied.

"Whoa! Whoa!" Jehu shouted. The stagecoach's back wheels skidded sideways and screeched to a stop. Becca and Aggie screamed. Several heavy canvas mailbags shifted forward, tumbling onto the heads of Hutchinson and Devers. The men cried out in pain.

"Hey!" Hobie started awake as Devers's leather satchel landed on his lap. "What's going on?"

From the driver's seat, Sallie shouted, "Earthquake. Everybody out!" As he and Jehu leaped to safety, the stagecoach's doors flew open and all five passengers fled the coach. Becca hit the rocky bank beside the road.

"Get away from the coach!" Sallie's hat flew off his head and disappeared into the night. A second tremor rolled along the roadway.

It wasn't until the third tremor stopped that the girl heard a groan come from Hobie, lying next to her on the bank. "What? What happened, Hobie? Are you hurt?"

His voice was husky with pain. "I guess I wrenched my knee."

"Are you sure? Could it be broken?" she asked.

"Naw, it's not."

"Well, let's check to be sure." He winced from pain as she rolled up his pant leg, uncovering his right knee. She felt around the area, which had already begun to swell. "I can't feel anything out of place. Nothing seems to be broken. Sallie," she called, "can you please bring a lantern over here?"

"Nothing's wrong. I'll be fine." Hobie grunted.

Becca clicked her tongue as she'd seen her mother do when caring for a recalcitrant patient. "If your knee swells inside your pant leg, we'll need to remove your pants entirely."

"What?" The man scooted backward.

"I will if I have to!" Becca snapped. "And I'll get Sallie and Devers to help me! Besides, who is going to see you out here in the wilds of the San Gabriel Mountains?"

"Hey, what's going on over here?" Sallie walked toward Hobie, carrying one of the carriage lanterns.

"Hobie wrenched his knee." She rose to her feet. "I don't think it's broken, but he's acting like a skittish colt having me examine it. Maybe he'll hold still for you."

As Becca walked toward the carriage, she spotted the light from the other lantern bouncing along the narrow roadway. She figured Jehu was checking to see if the road was passable. The girl met Aggie climbing out of the ditch.

"Are you all right?" Becca asked.

"Other than losing my favorite bonnet and my dignity, I'm fine. How about you?"

"Aggie, make sure the men stay away from the stagecoach for a few minutes while I metamorphose back into a female." She unfastened the buttons on her shirt. "Even if he didn't break a bone, Hobie's knee should be wrapped to keep it from swelling too much. Will you help me unwind?"

"Unwind? Oh, yes." Aggie laughed. "I'd forgotten about the cotton strips around your midriff. Hey, I have Epsom salts in my bag in case of snakebite. That should cut down on any swelling."

"Good idea. That's what my mother always used." The girl finished

81

removing the strips of cotton and slipped into a camisole and eyelet blouse. Slipping out of the canvas trousers, Becca found a red cotton skirt in her carpetbag. "Take the fabric strips and the salts to Sallie while I finish dressing."

Following one more minor tremor, the two male passengers helped Hobie and the ladies into the carriage. Even Sallie, who complained when they fell behind by as little as five minutes, seemed grateful the mailbags were safe and the Butterfield Overland stagecoach was ready to roll once again.

Mr. Devers was the first to comment on Becca's change in appearance. "Very nice, Miss Cunard. You make a much prettier girl than you did a boy."

"Thank you, Mr. Devers, for the compliment." Becca frowned as she pushed a lock of her hair behind one ear. Aggie understood her distress.

"It will grow back quickly. You'll see," Aggie encouraged. "Besides, did you know that without the weight of your braids, your hair is curling? It's quite attractive really."

CHAPTER NINE

ON TO THE MOJAVE

A NOTHER DAWN. BECCA ETCHED a mark into the belt of her gun holster. Seven marks. Seven very long days and nights had passed. Since leaving San Francisco, the stagecoach had traversed mountain passes, swamps, and valleys, stopping only long enough to switch to a new team of horses while the passengers took care of their physical necessities and purchased a quick meal in the station house, if the typically tasteless gruel could be called food.

"Hobie, let Mr. Devers and Mr. Hutchinson help you into the station while I purchase a bowl of slumgullion for you." As much as she felt sad over the pain her friend was experiencing, she liked being able to order him around for a change.

"I can get it myself!" A note of petulance edged his characteristically calm voice.

"Now, now, don't be like that. Your knee is doing so much better today. You don't want to put unnecessary strain on it while it heals." The girl skipped into the adobe station house before he could complain further. As it was, the two male passengers had graciously agreed to help him take care of his personal needs at each stop. If they hadn't been willing to help the man, Sallie told Hobie he'd have to stay behind until his leg healed enough to travel.

Determined to get the Butterfield Overland stagecoach back on schedule, Sallie pushed across unbelievable terrain without a full night's sleep for him and without changing drivers. After Becca had enjoyed a hot meal of rice, refried beans, and enchiladas at Campo de Cahuenga on the El Camino Real, she noticed that a strange young man with fiery red hair tied back at the base of his neck, sat atop the driver's bench. She asked Sallie where Jehu had gone.

"He's right up there, ready to roll." The conductor pointed at the new man.

"That's not Jehu," she protested.

"Oh, you mean Wendell Gates. No, this is Oscar, Oscar something or other. He's our new jehu." Up to that moment she hadn't realized jehu was the title for the stagecoach drivers, not their given names.

At each stop Aggie wrapped Hobie's swollen knee in an Epsom salt plaster. Having to hobble around with a makeshift cane at each station grated on the young man's pride. It didn't help that Mr. Devers had been showering Becca with attention both on the stagecoach and off.

At a *Californio*'s family ranch, Becca traded a couple chunks of gold ore for cash with Mr. Velasquez, the station proprietor. A few coins in her satchel gave the girl a renewed sense of security.

Though Mrs. Velasquez, the wife of the station manager and a fabulous cook, said Fort Yuma wasn't much to look at, Becca could barely wait to reach it. It would be their first overnight stop. They'd be able to catch a few hours of uninterrupted sleep. On board the stagecoach, Aggie discovered that by shifting the mailbags around in the third seat, they could spread a buffalo robe on top of the canvas and make a reasonably comfortable bed for one person.

Using a satchel as a pillow, the travelers agreed to take one hour long turns on the new surface. Yet despite the more comfortable sleeping accommodations, nerves began to fray. Long hours in the cramped vehicle brought out the worst in everyone. Rising daytime temperatures added to their discomfort. As a result, spontaneous bouts of scrapping erupted like brush fires following a lightning storm in the desert. Becca burrowed into her own space to avoid the conflicts as much as possible. Keeping her head from lolling onto the shoulder of the individual seated beside her when she slept gave the girl a stiff neck and grumpy attitude.

Mr. Devers accused Mr. Hutchinson of napping fifteen minutes longer than his time allotted on the makeshift bed, while Mr. Devers's snoring irritated Hobie. Whenever Hobie tried to shift his injured leg, the dried Epsom salts filtered out of the bandage and onto Aggie's skirts.

And though the woman held her tongue, Becca could see the irritation in her face.

With every passing mile, even Sallie's level of tolerance waned. Becca stopped counting how often she heard him berate one passenger or another for not reboarding quickly enough. "This is why I prefer transporting the U.S. mail to human beings. I get no back talk out of canvas bags!"

The overnight stop at Fort Yuma will bring much-needed relief for everyone, Becca decided.

"They claim Fort Yuma is the hottest post in the country," Mrs. Velasquez confided. "The story is told about a particularly evil army sergeant stationed at the fort. The night he died, the devil took him to his just reward. After two nights in his new digs, the sergeant asked for permission to go back to his barracks for a few blankets. He said he could no longer stand the devilish chill."

The girl laughed, but before boarding the stagecoach for the next leg of the journey she removed all but one of her remaining petticoats. Miles earlier, both ladies agreed to store their bonnets except when walking in the sunlight.

They crossed the Colorado River in the middle of the night. The toll keeper charged an exorbitant fee. But because his raft was the only option for the travelers, each doled out his or her share of the cost while Sallie paid for the coach and horses.

A cool breeze ruffled Becca's hair about her neck as she watched the swift-flowing water pass under the raft. She started at the sound of Mr. Devers's voice behind her. "What are you thinking?"

She smiled over her shoulder at the young man. "I'm thinking how good it will feel to get a full night's sleep again."

"I agree." He placed a protective hand on her shoulder. "And to think we aren't halfway yet."

"Becca, there you are. I've been looking for you." Hobie limped around the end of the stagecoach.

"My," the girl pointed toward his injured leg. "You are certainly doing much better with that makeshift cane." She gritted her teeth against the petulance in his voice. "Please tell me, Mr. Masters, just where did you think I might be hiding on this rather small raft? Under the mailbags? On the roof? Between the horses?"

Hobie's face reddened. "I was worried about you."

She shook her head in disgust. "Just what do you think might happen to me during our short ride across the Colorado River? Could a bear have devoured me? Could I have fallen into the river and drowned? Been kidnapped by a band of marauding Paiutes? Got lost and wandered across the border into Mexico?"

Hobie glanced from Becca to Mr. Devers and back again. He narrowed his gaze. "What's he doing out here with you?"

"Perhaps he's getting some fresh air like everyone else." Disgusted, she whirled around to face the river. "Sorry, Mr. Devers."

Mr. Devers patted her shoulder tenderly. "Please, call me Bo. And don't be cross with poor Hobie. He's just being protective of you."

"You are very understanding, Bo. However both you and Hobie should realize that I don't need protection. I can take care of myself! In fact, I prefer to do so." Realizing her words sounded harsh, she shrugged and flashed him a coy smile.

"You, my dear, are so unlike any female I've ever met. I admire your spirit. May I call you Rebecca?" he asked.

On the Arizona side of the river, the horses drew the carriage to the nearby stables while the passengers walked the short distance to the fort. Becca felt like a silly little girl sashaying along beside the suddenly loquacious Mr. Devers. While Bo talked about his parents, his three sisters and four brothers, she began to feel bad for snapping at Hobie. Bo was right. The poor man only was trying to take care of her as he had promised to do so many miles earlier.

I'll apologize later, she decided. In the meantime, she would enjoy Bo Devers's attentions. The Tennessee man described the family's sprawling log cabin in the Smoky Mountains. When he talked about his hunting dog, Digger, she thought of Tag-along and wondered how he was doing without her. By the time they strode into the fort's mess hall, everyone else was eating a meal of beef jerky, wormy crackers, and slumgullion stew. The chunks of parsnips, small ears of corn, and an unidentifiable green herb floating on a gray-colored liquid, did little to stimulate Becca's appetite, nor did the swarm of flies attacking the stew from all angles. As the girl spooned the last of her slumgullion from her bowl, Aggie whispered in her ear. "Are you as sleepy as I am?"

The girl nodded. "I'm having trouble keeping my eyes open."

"Me too. Nothing can stop us from catching a short nap, you know," the woman coaxed.

"Let's do it!" Becca placed her spoon in her empty bowl and asked to be excused from the table, as did Aggie. The two women rushed into a small storeroom beside the mess hall, which had been assigned to be their sleeping quarters.

Aggie eyed the sleeping arrangements. Along the back wall of the nine-by-nine-foot cluttered storeroom was a wooden bunk bed especially reserved for female travelers.

Becca brushed past the woman and announced, "I'll take the top bunk. You can have the lower one if you like." She placed her carpetbag on the dirt floor beside the bedstead.

Aggie gave her a relieved smile. "That's very sweet of you, Becca. When I saw the bunk bed, I had dire images of climbing up there and worse yet, tumbling off in the night." She laughed at herself. "Even as lumpy as those mattresses appear to be, I doubt I'll have any trouble falling asleep."

"Me either." The girl yawned, hiked her long skirt up about her hips, and scrambled up the side of the bunk. The open beam ceiling cleared the top of her head by less than six inches. Becca sighed as she stretched out on the mattress. "Who knows how soon Sallie will announce our departure! The man's worse than a Viking slave master!"

Several hours later, Becca awakened with a terrified start. She sat straight up and bumped her head on the ceiling. The bottom bunk was empty.

She recognized Bo's raised voice coming from the other room. "Withdraw your slur against the South, sir, or we'll meet on the field of honor!"

Mr. Hutchinson's low, calmer voice followed. "Are you challenging me to a duel, son? If that is the case, I believe it is customary I choose the weapons."

"That I am, sir. You're an abolitionist, just like your Mr. Lincoln," Bo sneered.

Becca inhaled sharply at Mr. Hutchinson's studied reply. "Lincoln's not an abolitionist, nor am I. I am merely a humble American who fought in the war against Mexico and who cherishes his country—the United States of America!" He emphasized the word *united*. "Tell me, young man, does your family run slaves?"

Bo sniffed and cleared his throat. "I object to having you call them slaves; they're almost members of the family!"

"Oh, really! Do they live in the family home? Are they free to come and go as they please, like you seem to be able to do?"

"You don't understand, do you, Mr. Hutchinson? Our servants are barely off the ship from Africa. They would die in the Tennessee wilderness if we didn't take care of them."

Mr. Hutchinson snorted. "How Christian of you!"

"My daddy's slaves are content and happy. You should hear them singing while they work in the tobacco fields. All you Northerners want to do is stir up trouble!"

"Hmmph!" Mr. Hutchinson grunted. "So content they run away to Canada when given the chance?"

Fury filled Bo's voice. "Never fear. The day will come when the South will deal with abolitionists like you if you force our hand!"

Becca climbed off the bunk and pressed her ear against the closed door. Mr. Hutchinson continued, "That would be an unwise move. Remember, the Bible says, 'Every city or house divided against itself shall not stand.'"

"Quoting scripture won't change the outcome. You'll sing a different tune, sir, when the streets of your cities run ten feet deep with the blood of the Northern dead!"

Becca gasped. Childhood nightmares of raids and violence swirled through her brain. Dressing as quickly as possible, the girl ran her hairbrush through her curls and opened the door between the bedroom and the mess hall.

Several soldiers, eating their evening meal, froze with forks in hand, transfixed by the unfolding drama. Mr. Hutchinson sat in a straight-backed chair beside the glowing fireplace on the far side of the room. Bo stood at the end of the nearest long dinner table.

Becca inhaled sharply as he slid his hunting knife from the sheath on his belt. Simultaneously, Mr. Hutchinson rose to his feet, thumbed back the hammer on a big boot pistol, and aimed it at Bo's belly.

Bo jerked his hand away from the knife handle like it was hotter than Mrs. Velasquez's chili.

Standing near the outside door, Aggie hissed, "You better apologize,

Mr. Devers, or he'll blow a hole in your brisket."

"Apologize? For what?" Bo blustered defiantly. "He needs to apologize!"

Mr. Hutchinson leveled his fiery gaze at his adversary. "Mr. Devers, I will not withdraw a word I've said—not today, not ever!"

Everyone gasped when the door to the mess hall flew open and banged against the wall. Sallie strode into the room with his shotgun loaded and ready to fire. A strand of straw hung from his lips.

"Well, someone had better back down," Sallie began. "If either of you ever hope to see the sights of your homes anytime soon. The war between the North and the South isn't going to start on my run!" He shifted the straw to the other side of his mouth and announced, "If you don't both agree to contain your political views for the duration of this trip, your journey aboard my stagecoach has come to an end." With his free hand, he tipped his wide-brimmed felt hat back from his face. "Keep in mind, sirs, you are more than fifteen hundred miles from Fort Smith, several more from Fort Tejon, and about the same to the border of Texas. You are less than fifty miles of hard wallkin' from Mexico; and at this moment, six feet from perdition!"

Sallie leveled his shotgun at Bo. "Mr. Devers, if you plan to continue your journey on my stagecoach, hand me your weapons—all of them. Your revolver, the derringer in your right boot, your bowie knife—everything!"

Sallie stuffed them into his thick leather belt. "Did I miss anything?"

Bo shook his head.

"Good! And now it's your turn, Mr. Hutchinson." Sallie held out his free hand. "I will return your arsenal when you reach the end of the line."

"But, sir," Bo protested, "you can't leave us defenseless out here in this wild country. We're about to travel through some mighty dangerous territory filled with warring Indian tribes, unscrupulous highwaymen, and fearsome varmints of all kinds."

Sallie's eyes twinkled. The corners of his lips lifted a hair. "Well, Mr. Devers, you should have thought of that before you shot off your mouth and challenged a fellow passenger to a duel."

"Sir!" Mr. Hutchinson growled, "You can't do this. Isn't this the fort commander's jurisdiction? You are not the local law enforcement here."

"Try me, Mr. Hutchinson. I can and I will decide who I let ride on my stagecoach and who I don't!" He shouldered his shotgun and tipped his hat toward his stunned audience. "Drink up, boys, we're heading out in fifteen minutes."

"Fifteen minutes?" Aggie exclaimed. "I thought we were leaving in the morning."

Sallie shook his head. "Just got a report that a band of Apache renegades held up the westbound stagecoach three hours ago. We gotta get as far away as possible while the warriors are celebrating their victory."

"Sir?" A soft-spoken army corporal spoke like his mouth was filled with corn bread and molasses. "Last night I spotted fresh moccasin prints along the river. I told the commander about them."

"Hmm." A young captain, barely out of military academy, scowled as he rose to his feet. "Did any of you hear the inordinate ruckus the coyotes were making last night?"

Several of the military men nodded and exchanged nervous glances. "I'm thinking, maybe it wasn't coyotes howling. I'll talk to the commander about doubling up our guard for the next few nights. To be forewarned is to be forearmed."

"This doesn't make sense." A grizzled sergeant with deep-set brown eyes lumbered to his feet. "But didn't the Butterfield Overland Stage Company work out a deal with the tribes along the route that if they wouldn't shoot the braves for stealing a mule or two every now and then, the tribes would allow the stagecoach to safely pass through their territory?"

Sallie nodded. "So I understand. Probably some inebriated yahoo from one side or the other incited his people to riot. Whatever the reason, I don't have time to dilly-dally while a bunch of stodgy diplomats work out the particulars. A mule team is hitched to our stagecoach, leaving in ten minutes. Has anyone seen Mr. Masters?"

Mr. Devers gestured toward the barracks behind the mess hall. "Hobie's asleep back there."

"Well!" Sallie clicked his tongue. "Go waken him! Come on, folks. We've got to outrun a bunch of warriors who may or may not be eager to repeat their earlier victory."

As Becca stuffed her clothes into her carpetbag, she thought of Hobie. *If he'd been in the mess hall, what would he have done? Would he have sided with Mr. Hutchinson against Bo just because of his dislike for Bo? Does he even have an opinion on the issue of slavery?* In all the time she'd known him, the girl realized Hobie was the only male in Placerville whom she had never heard voicing a political preference regarding the possible conflict.

As the stagecoach left Fort Yuma, the passengers rode in a tense silence once more. Becca licked her cracked lips. She could barely breathe from the dust kicked up by the mules pulling the stagecoach. Hobie's eyes were closed and his hands folded across his stomach as if all was right with the world. But it wasn't.

The sullen faces of Mr. Hutchinson and of Bo sitting opposite one another warned Becca that, while their differences might be temporarily tabled, the issue between them was far from settled.

CHAPTER TEN

A NEW PASSENGER

THE VILLAGE OF MARICOPA Wells, nestled against the base of the Sierra Estrella, could be seen for miles before the stage pulled into the station. Torrential rains in the mountains had swelled the arroyos to a dangerous flood level, forcing the newest jehu to veer farther south from the customary route. This delay put Sallie in a sour mood.

When Bo spotted a rattler coiled beside the carriage, he asked Sallie to return his gun. The conductor shook his head. "Nope! Ain't gonna do it."

"But I have no way to protect myself," the man argued.

Sallie lifted one eyebrow and shot him a sardonic grin. "Better stay close to Hobie or to Miss Rebecca then. They're both sure shots."

It was late afternoon when the exhausted travelers disembarked from the coach at Maricopa Wells. The ride over the mountain range had been bone shattering. Becca ached in places she never before knew existed.

Looking around the area, she made her way to the little outhouse behind the station. Thousands of giant black flies nipped at her exposed flesh, leaving small red welts on her face, neck, and hands. A swarm followed her from the outhouse to the adobe station. The ones diving at her nose bothered her the most.

By the door of the station Bo was beating off a battalion of the irritating creatures when she returned.

"Ah, the flies are Montezuma's curse to the Wells," the man standing nearby spoke with a Spanish accent.

"Is there nothing that can be done?" Becca asked.

The man shrugged.

Bo opened the door for Becca. A long table filled the dark, cavelike room. A white linen cloth covered the far end of the table. A silver candelabrum with four candles lit that end of the table. Seated there, a man, a woman, and their two teenage daughters ate roast chicken, greens, and small potatoes off of gold-rimmed china with polished silverware.

"Just make yourselves comfortable anywhere along here." A dark-skinned man wearing a buff-colored cotton shirt and matching pants, gestured toward the empty benches on either side of the closer end of the table, covered with a worn and soiled oilcloth.

Aggie, who'd been watching the strange proceedings since before Becca entered the building, asked, "And how does one qualify to dine at the far end of the table?"

The man shrugged and smiled through a picket fence of teeth. "Sorry, madam. Only the station manager and his family sit down there."

"Well, I never!" the woman snapped. "Fine! Here's money for my food. It had better have no dead flies floating in it!"

Becca shuddered and followed Aggie to two empty spaces next to Sallie.

"This place makes my skin crawl," Becca hissed.

"Mine too," Sallie admitted. "Don't worry. I plan to report these people to Mr. Butterfield the first chance I get."

When a young boy placed a bowl of slumgullion in front of her, Becca stared at the greenish-gray mixture with several unidentifiable objects floating in a sea of greasy water. Her stomach turned. She gulped down the sudden urge to lose what food remained in her stomach. After sniffing the concoction, the girl gagged a second time. "A lot of good Mr. Butterfield's knowing will do me after I die a painful death from some disgusting intestinal distress!"

Reluctantly, she sipped a spoonful of the watery liquid and then ate a chunk of what she hoped was meat floating in the bowl. As she chewed on the tough, gristly flesh, the girl grimaced. *This tastes worse than it looks!*

A hired worker seated across from her whispered, "Haskell, the family mutt, took one sniff of this stuff and hid beneath the porch!" He snickered and ate another spoonful. "Smart dog! Maybe we could cut down on the coyote population by feeding 'em this stuff."

"Horace!" a shrill female voice from the far end of the table screeched. "If you don't like my cookin', you can do your own!"

"Yes, miss." The man bowed his head and hurriedly scooped the remainder of his stew into his mouth.

Becca found the woman's behavior abominable. The girl could only imagine what her mother would say, considering that the woman believed hospitality and good manners to be one of a Christian woman's most valuable virtues. Becca eyed the station manager's wife at the far end of the table and whispered to Aggie. "That woman is certainly a pleasant sort, isn't she?"

At the far end of the table, the woman's head popped up. She cast a piercing glare at Becca. "Do you have any complaints, Miss Fancy Skirts?"

With one gulp, a giant chunk of potato unintentionally slid down Becca's throat. She choked. "Uh, no ma'am. Not me!"

Satisfied she'd silenced the girl's complaints, the station manager's wife picked a breast of chicken from her plate with her fingers, took a bite, returned the remaining chicken to her plate, and then licked the grease from each finger.

Becca stole a furtive glance at the others seated about the table. All eyes were focused on their bowls. When she turned toward Hobie for support, she realized that sometime during the exchange he had left the room.

Unable to bear the strained atmosphere around the table, she hissed at Aggie. "Excuse me, please. I think I'm going to lose my supper or whatever meal this is."

Without glancing in Becca's direction, Aggie nodded. The girl bolted for the door. Once outside, she inhaled the fresh, clean desert air, swarming flies and all. "Sir," she asked the worker still standing near the horses' stall. "Did you see which direction that tall man went?"

He pointed down the muddy street past two hastily built one-room adobe homes. "To the chapel," he said. A long tan fringe dangled from the sleeve of his homespun cotton shirt. "The señor go to the chapel," he said in broken English.

The chapel? Why the chapel? she wondered as she hiked her skirts above the ankle of her black leather high-top shoes and began walking in the direction the young man had pointed. At the second of the two adobes, three little girls, the age of her niece Izzy, played tea party. Seated on the ground around a wood scrap for a makeshift table that was covered with a dishrag, three flour sack rag dolls waited to be served.

Seated barefoot in mud drying in the sun, dirt splashed on their faces and on their hand-sewn flour-sacking dresses, the girls squinted up at Becca and grinned.

"Hello, pretty lady," the tallest of the girls spoke, revealing a space where a front tooth had recently come out. In broken English, she asked, "Would you like to join our tea party?"

"A tea party? What fun!" Becca bent down beside the girls' make-shift table. The self-proclaimed hostess handed her a tiny porcelain cup. She pretended to take a sip. "How very nice. Thank you. Have you girls ever attended a real tea party?"

"No." The hostess shook her head sadly. "But my mama did before she married Papa in Mexico. Mama says that my grandma held tea parties for her friends every week."

"Really?" Becca set the cup on the wrinkled dishcloth.

The girl gave a condescending nod as if Becca didn't believe her. "Really! And someday, when my papa finds his silver mine in those mountains, we're going back to Mexico, and I will be attend my grandma's tea parties."

"How exciting! You are a very lucky little girl."

"I know. Mama says I am much blessed." The child preened before her awed friends. "And I will wear a dress of red taffeta and slippers of pink satin."

"Oh, how utterly elegant you will look." Becca glanced down the empty road and then back at the girls. "Please, can you help me?" she asked. "Did you see my friend, a very tall man, walk by here a few minutes ago?"

"S'," the girls chimed.

"A very big man." The hostess measured Hobie's height with her hand.

Becca straightened. "Did you see where he went?"

"To the mission at the end of the road. Can you see the bell tower beyond the clump of eucalyptus trees? Would you like us to take you there?" the smallest girl asked.

"Do you think I might get lost?" Becca's eyes grew big with feigned fear.

The girls giggled into their muddy hands. "Oh, no, you won't get lost," her hostess assured her. "But we will walk you there if you'd like."

"That's very sweet of you, but if you don't think I will get lost, I think I can find it alone." She rose to her feet. "*Mmm*, good tea. Thank you so much."

Becca's steps lightened as she thought about the girls and their tea party. Since spending a short time with her nieces in Sacramento, the girl was surprised how much she missed them. She wondered if they missed their auntie Becca as well.

A sun-baked brick wall surrounded the adobe chapel. In the middle of the wall, an iron bell hung suspended over a narrow archway. She stepped through the opening onto the mission grounds. In front of her, two carved black oak doors stood ajar as if coaxing her into the cool darkness of the building. Feeling uncomfortable in the candle-lit chapel, she paused to allow her eyes to adjust to the dimness of the light. *What's the daughter of a Baptist preacher doing in a . . .* She immediately sensed she was not alone. Hobie stepped out of the shadows. "Becca! What are you doing here?" he whispered. His whisper echoed off the room's high ceilings and open beams.

"Looking for you. I hope I'm not intruding."

"Of course not. Is something wrong?" he asked.

"No, I was just curious where you'd gone." The flustered girl was grateful that the dimly lit room hid the sudden blush of her cheeks. "So what are you doing here?"

"Worshiping."

"Worshiping? But, Hobie, you're not a papist." She touched his lower arm. "Hobie, you're Baptist."

The man grinned and patted her hand. "I know that."

"So why would you—"

"What I miss most—besides my family, of course—is worshiping each week at your father's church. So whenever we stop long enough for me to scout out a place of worship, whether it be a building or a large rock in an isolated spot, I spend a few minutes talking with God."

"You do?" She blinked in surprise. "I never noticed." As soon as her words came out of her mouth she realized how it must have sounded to him. "Sorry, I didn't mean . . ."

He heaved a heavy sigh. "I understand. Bo Devers can be quite distracting."

"No, it's not that." She licked her suddenly parched lips. "It's good that you want to spend time with God, Hobie. My father would be pleased. I admit that one thing I miss, besides my folks, of course, is my time alone on the mountain each morning with Tag-along. Jammed in a stagecoach with four strangers doesn't leave much room for meditation."

"I'm not a stranger, am I?"

"Of course not. I didn't mean you, Hobie. But honestly, don't you ever feel the need for more elbow room?"

"It can be difficult. Sometimes when I get too uncomfortable, I pretend to be asleep. That's when God and I visit. He's a good listener." Hobie gently took her arm in his. "We'd better head back to the station. No one knows when Sallie will get a bee in his bonnet about leaving."

"Or, in this case, a fly!" Becca laughed as she gathered her skirts with her free hand. "Speaking of which, how did you like tonight's dinner?"

"Hmmph!"

"Aw, come on," she teased. "You must have some opinion."

"Just food. Tomorrow's another day."

Becca giggled and fell into step beside him. "For some reason, you just reminded me of my dad, of all people. That's the same response he would have to a less-than-tasty casserole he'd had to endure at a church dinner."

Hobie threw his head back and laughed. "At times, the fewer the words spoken, the better."

"You're so cute." She cast him a teasing smile. "And sometimes you can be quite profound, my friend."

He stopped, turned, and gazed into her eyes. A wave of conflicting emotions swept across his face. "I am your friend, aren't I?"

"Of course you are, Hobie. How could you ask such a thing? Actually, you're more than a friend. I think of you as my—my brother."

The man's face fell; he heaved a deep sigh, shrugged his shoulders, and silently strolled toward the station. Confused by his reaction, she watched as he entered the building. *Whatever did I say wrong? I thought he'd be pleased.*

A new team of horses pulling the stagecoach driven by a new jehu rounded the far end of the building. Sallie burst out of the station, record book in hand. And in a voice that would terrify the wildest of critters, he shouted, "The eastbound Butterfield Overland Mail stagecoach is pulling out in fifteen minutes!"

By the number of station hands pouring out of the building, she assumed the conductor had made the same announcement inside the dining room. He strode over to the coach and threw open the passenger door, and then, pointing to the row of tin water containers dangling from the boot of the coach, he called to the new jehu. "Did you fill all the water jugs? We'll be needing them for the next leg of our journey."

"Yes, sir!" The smooth-faced driver, not much older than Becca, touched the brim of his brown straw hat in respect. "We're ready to hit the road, sir."

"Indeed!" Sallie blew his bugle and glanced over his shoulder at Becca. "We have an additional passenger, a Mrs. Cora Day. I've been warned she's a lot to handle." He snorted, tipping his hat back on his head. "By the sound of it, I'm sure glad I'm sittin' out here in the elements."

Becca blinked in surprise. Beyond his threat to throw Devers and Hutchinson off the stagecoach for threatening to fight a duel, the man had seldom uttered an opinion on anything or anybody except keeping to his precious schedule.

By four o'clock, Becca and the others had climbed onto the stagecoach. The driver cracked the whip, and the stagecoach rolled eastward, over the rutted, dusty road. As the stagecoach passed the site of the tea party, she waved to the three little girls standing in front of their home. Becca could only wonder if the little hostess would ever wear that red taffeta dress and a pair of pink satin shoes. She'd seen more than one prospector return to his family broken and empty handed during her years in Placerville.

Inside the coach, Aggie was introducing Mrs. Day to the other travelers. With each introduction, the newest passenger, wearing a black crepe dress and cape, nodded and barely made eye contact. "By the way, you may call me Aggie. May I call you Cora?"

The woman bristled and dabbed at her eyes again. She spoke with an irritatingly high, whiny tone. "Absolutely not! I am Mrs. Horatio Day!"

"Welcome to our little traveling family, Mrs. Horatio Day. So what takes you east, er, Mrs. Horatio Day?" Aggie asked, her voice friendly and open.

The woman reached under the waist-length cape and into the bodice of her dress to withdraw a lacy hankie and dab at her eyes. "I am going home to bury poor Horatio." She opened her cape and revealed on her lap a rectangular bronze box with carvings of cherubs on the cover.

"Oh." Aggie gulped in surprise. "I am so sorry. When did he die?"

"A year ago, come May." The woman eyed each of the passengers as if challenging someone to object to the additional passenger on board. "The conductor offered to allow me to place poor Horatio in the boot, but I insisted on keeping him close to my heart."

Once Mrs. Day began talking about poor Horatio, she didn't stop. Even Mr. Devers couldn't get more than five words in edgewise.

"Yes, poor Mr. H—that's what I called him. Mr. H died in a house fire from burning green wood in the fireplace, don't you know? Fortunately, I was off visiting an invalid neighbor. By the time I returned home, there was so little left of Mr. H that Jess Harper, our family doctor and the town undertaker, suggested he finish the job. Ashes to ashes, don't you know?"

"It must have been a very difficult time for you, deary," Aggie comforted. Becca stared at the brass container with cherubs on top. A tiny silver lock bolted shut the cover.

"Oh, it was. It was. You have no idea . . ." Mrs. Day blew her nose. "After the legal affairs were said and done, all I had left to my name was my dead spouse's ashes and a will that ordered me to return him to his parents' graveyard in Texas if I intended to inherit his family's piddlin' fortune! Hardly pays for my stagecoach ticket! Talk about spending good money after bad!" the woman continued. "But then what could I expect? The man couldn't manage to keep two gold pieces in his pocket at one time. If I'd known he would up and die, I would have insisted he not spend his money quite so freely. I tried to tell him, but would he listen? If I didn't know better, I'd think he died to spite me!"

Becca shot a startled glance toward Hobie. His eyes were shut. A tiny smile hovered at the edges of his lips. *Stop it, Hobie. It's not funny! I know what you're doing. And just what is God telling you?* To hide an irrepressible urge to giggle, she quickly looked out the window at the reds, oranges, and purples glowing in the sky.

"And just how did you come to board the stagecoach at the Wells?" Aggie feigned a convincing interest in the woman and her stories. "Is that where you lived before Horatio, er, died?"

"Of course not! The Wells is hardly fit for humans or beasts. I lived in Gilroy, California. But thanks to a belligerent conductor who dumped me in the middle of nowhere, I found it necessary to await the arrival of the next eastbound stagecoach. Can you believe it? He said I was annoying the other passengers. I never heard a one of them complain—not one!" she huffed. "I admit that I have an opinion or two, and I'm not afraid to voice them, but to call me annoying? You can be sure, when I reach Texas, I will be writing a letter of complaint to the Butterfield Overland stagecoach headquarters! I'm keeping an accurate record of my entire trip and of every discomfort I suffer."

CHAPTER ELEVEN

DEVIL WIND

A CCOMPANIED BY MRS. DAY's incessant whine, the night seemed endless. First, she was too chilly; then, she was too hot; then, Mr. Hutchinson's elbow dug into her side; then, she complained about too much dust coming through the windows, despite the drawn shades. "Why anyone would choose to live in this desolate land I do not know!" The woman's shrill voice invaded Becca's dreams as well.

Doesn't that woman ever sleep? the girl wondered.

During the night, the roadway grew more difficult to detect in the darkness, forcing the driver to drive more slowly. The dim moonlight, not the carriage lights, lit the roadway. How the driver found his way through the wilderness, Becca couldn't imagine. She uttered a sigh of relief when Sallie blew his bugle, announcing the next relay station break.

While three local tribe members, dressed in buckskin breeches and no shirts, hitched fresh horses to the stagecoach, the station manager, disheveled from sleep and smelling of cheap spirits, sold the passengers goat jerky that had been dried over buffalo chips, grilled onion rings, and wormy crackers. In less time than it took to chew and swallow the tough jerky strips, the stagecoach was off again.

Revived by the food, Mrs. Day resumed her litany of complaints. "This country is totally uncivilized! I am growing to hate cacti. They're everywhere. And those natives with their lack of proper clothing would strike terror to the core of any well-brought-up female! And I can only imagine the filth on the hands of the individual who prepared that jerky!

If we survive this journey, it will have little to do with luck and everything to do with divine intervention!"

"You can say that again!" Bo muttered from his perch on the mailbags.

"Amen!" Hobie mumbled. Becca faked a yawn to conceal her grin.

Uncertain she'd heard Bo's remark correctly, Mrs. Day shot him an angry glare and continued. "And the heathen legends these people believe! Did you know that the local people see the profile of a sleeping Montezuma at the southern tip of the Sierra Estrella? Imagine! They believe the god will one day awaken to rescue his downtrodden people and restore his kingdom." Mrs. Day clicked her tongue in judgment. "Actually, if you look closely at the sides of the mountain, you will see campfires the locals keep burning in anticipation of his return."

Becca lifted the canvas shade hoping to see the glow of a campfire. In the moonlight, she did detect, along the ridge of the mountain, the profile of a man snoozing. *How frustrating it must be for the people awaiting the man's awakening. Despite the tribe's belief, their cry for justice never quite reaches the warrior's deaf ears.*

The stagecoach slowed to a stop at the next station. Grateful for the break, Becca and the others tumbled out of the vehicle and raced for the outhouse. It had been a long run with very short middle-of-the-night stops to take care of personal necessities. Needing to stretch her legs, Becca hitched her gunbelt tighter around her hips and strode toward a nearby boulder to watch the breaking sunrise. Intent on her destination, she failed to notice a huge brown cloud sweeping across the desert from the west. The sudden gale whipped her skirts about her legs, almost toppling her facedown on the desert floor.

"Watch out!" she heard someone call. Two hands grabbed her about the waist, flung her to the ground behind the nearest boulder, and then someone landed on top of her. Trying to rise to her feet, Becca sputtered, "Sallie! What in the world?"

The conductor rolled off of her and leaned the back of his head against the boulder. "Sit still, woman! It's a sandstorm! These winds can sheer the skin off the side of a mule and the paint off the door of a stagecoach."

By now, a whirlwind of sand and pebbles whipped around and over the top of the boulder. Rebecca licked the grit from her parched lips. "How long will it last?"

"It's a devil wind. Only he knows how long it will last."

Hunkering as close to Sallie as possible, there was nothing she could do but wait it out. "So how far are we from Texas?" she asked in her most nonchalant voice.

The man chuckled. "So Mrs. Day is getting to you too. I was warned she might, but I'd hoped she could distract Hutchinson and Devers from firing the first shot of an ideological war."

"It's working. Everyone pretends to be napping. So, how far is it to Texas, or wherever the dear lady's destination may be?"

"Too many miles to contemplate. I should tell you that I'm leaving you folks at the Soldier's Farewell station in New Mexico." He removed his neckerchief and handed it to the girl. "Here. Rub that grit out of your eyes."

"Leaving? You can't. We depend on you, Sallie."

He shrugged. "I already took three divisions more than I was suppose to, without a break."

The girl knew each division equaled two hundred and fifty miles in length. "Why?"

"Well, there've been several stagecoach breakdowns and one conductor quit after four highwaymen tried to rob his stagecoach. The line was shorthanded. And well, I feel sort of responsible for you, young lady. I wanted to make sure you get to wherever you're going."

Becca brushed a stray curl from her face. "So why are you leaving us at Soldier's Farewell? What attracts you there?"

"Not much. Soldier's Farewell is one of the most remote and primitive outposts along the route. The cook's tea tastes like sandy water with a dishrag and old bacon scraps added." The man chuckled. "And there's nary a speck of sugar or milk to make it palatable."

Becca snorted, "Sounds delightful. I can hardly wait." She paused for several seconds. "Obviously, you aren't planning to stay at Soldier's Farewell. Where will you go from there?"

"I'll make another trip west to San Francisco. Hawk, the conductor on the incoming westbound stagecoach, will need spelling off. If not, I'll wait for the next one. I got no one to answer to, and I go where I pretty well please."

Becca's lips curved into a soft, dreamy smile. "I do so admire you. It must be nice to be so free, to go wherever your spirit leads, to stop whenever you like."

"Don't. It was fun at first. But in time, aimlessly wandering gets old with no one traveling beside you on the trail and no one waiting for you at the end. All of my family's gone. My mama died last winter; my family's homestead in Arkansas had to be sold to creditors. All I can call my own are the clothes on my back, the boots on my feet." He tapped his right boot with the barrel of his gun. "And old Caroline, my shotgun."

The girl fell silent for a time. She closed her eyes and listened to the roar of the wind and the swoosh of sand pelting against their stone fortress.

"You're the one to be envied, little lady. But you're not smart enough to know it." Sallie drew his left knee up to his chest. "You act tough like you don't need anyone, but you do. You have a family who loves you, who've sacrificed everything to keep you safe. And you have Hobie, a good man to protect you."

"Oh, Hobie. He's just a friend—"

Sallie shook his head and wagged a finger in her face. "No, he's more than a friend, little girl. And mark my words: he's twice the man that Bo fella is. Hang onto him. And let him know you appreciate him before it's too late and another filly comes sniffing around."

"My, are you ever full of advice today." Becca resented the fact that Sallie wasn't the strong and free adventurer she'd thought him to be. "Maybe you should take your own advice, Mr. Sallie. Anyone can tell Widow Ruthie in Visalia has a hankering for you."

"Really? You're joshin' me!" Stunned, the man turned his face toward the girl.

Becca giggled. "Even though I was dressed as a young boy, I'm still very much a woman. I see things. Trust me, one female can sniff out the affections of another a mile away. And, believe me, Widow Ruthie has a yen for you."

A slow smile crossed Sallie's face as he slowly shook his head. "I'm going to miss you, gal. I sure am going to miss you." The conductor stood up and brushed dust off his pants and shirt. "Looks like our sand storm has move toward the northeast. Good for us since we're angling to the southeast." He reached down and helped Becca to her feet.

Stumbling over dirt clods, she trailed after him toward the stagecoach where the other travelers were emerging from their hiding places. Each step hurt due to the sand in her boots. They hadn't gone far when

Hobie came running toward them. "Becca! Becca! Are you all right? I was worried when I didn't see you anywhere. No one knew where you'd gone."

Her initial reaction was to snap at the man, but then she remembered Sallie's advice. "I'm fine, Hobie. I just need to dump the sand out of my boots." She pointed toward the muddy brown clouds in the eastern sky. "Where did you find cover?"

"I piled inside the coach with Aggie, Devers, and Mrs. Day. We burrowed under the mailbags. Hutchinson and the jehu climbed into the boot. At one point I thought the entire coach would overturn, horses and all."

"Where is Aggie?"

"The woman is sweeping out the vehicle with a whiskbroom she carries in her travel bag." Hobie scratched his head. "Is there anything she doesn't carry in that poke?"

Soon they were on the road again. Mrs. Day continued to complain about being jostled. "My poor body is covered with bruises. I've never been so uncomfortable in my entire life."

Becca felt the same way but bit her tongue. The woman was doing enough complaining for both of them. During the heat of the day, the rocking of the coach lulled the passengers into a comfortless sleep. As the sun disappeared behind the stagecoach, they began to stir once more.

Mr. Hutchinson leaned forward and gagged. "I think I'm going to be sick." His face turned pea green.

"Hang out the window," Bo shouted, giving the man a push toward the closest door.

In advance, Mrs. Day covered her nose with her handkerchief. "That'll teach you to eat a second helping of that cook's revolting slumgullion! Anyone could see the stew had been exposed to all kinds of vermin before being served!"

Everyone held their collective breath when Mr. Hutchinson relieved the discomfort in his stomach through the open window.

"I, myself, wouldn't touch such repulsive food under any circumstance." The woman made it sound like Mr. Hutchinson became sick on purpose.

"Mrs. Day, please be quiet for a few minutes. You're not helping here!" Hobie patted the weakened Mr. Hutchinson on the back and handed him a tin canteen of water. Becca couldn't believe that her friend had the courage to say what everyone else in the coach wanted to say but didn't dare. Hobie continued, "Are you feeling better now, Mr. Hutchinson?"

Piqued by Hobie's direct request, Mrs. Day wrapped her arms about Horatio's brass box, pressed her lips tightly together, and stared straight ahead. Aggie, who had been stretched out on the mailbags, sat up as best she could. "Here, Mr. Hutchinson, you lie down a while."

"Oh, no, Aggie, I couldn't," he protested.

"Nonsense!" She scrambled over the leather straps and into the second seat. "Trust me, I'm being a tad selfish. We will all feel better when you feel better."

Aggie's words proved true. The food in Becca's stomach had begun rolling and tumbling about. Grateful to be sitting on the opposite side of the vehicle from Mr. Hutchinson, the girl turned her face toward the moonlit desert rushing by outside the vehicle.

Shortly after midnight, the stagecoach slowed to a crawl as the horses pulled the massive coach up a steep incline. Sallie stuck his head around the edge of the stagecoach and shouted, "Straighten up!" In Sallie talk, this warning meant "Hold on to your possessions. We're in for a rough ride."

The higher in altitude the stagecoach climbed, the lower the temperatures dropped. For warmth the passengers huddled together under every available blanket, cape, and overcoat on board. The advantage of being squeezed together so tightly was less jostling, thus the bruising was kept to a minimum. When they rolled over a large rock in the road, the stagecoach's left rear wheel lifted off the ground. The passengers gasped in unison when the stage tipped, threatening to overturn. Terrified, Becca held her breath and prayed, "Oh, Lord, help us!"

She glanced toward Hobie. His eyes were tightly closed. Without a word, he placed his massive hand on hers. Rebecca relaxed, for she knew he was praying too.

After an hour of teeth-jarring crunches and rugged bone-bruising potholes, the driver halted the horses in front of the Dragoon Spring station. At the "swing" station there was only time to use the facilities and change teams before Sallie hustled the passengers back onto the stagecoach for the Apache Pass station.

Built of stones indigenous to the area, the partially constructed

Apache Pass station sat next to a running stream, a rarity in the vast southwestern desert. Relieved to escape the close quarters, Becca allowed Hobie to help her out of the coach.

"I could use a hand, too, young man." Mrs. Day's screechy voice sent shivers up and down Becca's spine. Hobie, being a gentleman, extended his hand toward the irritating woman.

"That's better!" she huffed and stepped down onto the dusty soil. "So this is the Apache Pass station."

Bo Devers crawled out next and stretched. "What a beautiful spot. Look at that mountain range. I've heard a lot about this place, not all good." Recalling the Butterfield Overland stagecoach rules about sharing tales about bands of marauding Indians, he clamped his lips shut as Sallie sauntered toward him.

"Whatever you heard is probably true—which is why we won't stay here any longer than necessary." The conductor squatted down to check the rim of the wheel that had hit the rock. "This is Apache country. Up there in the Dragoon Mountains is Chief Cochise's stronghold."

"Do you think he's in the area this early in the season?" Mr. Hutchinson sidled up to the conductor.

"Oh, I knew it! I knew it! We're all gonna die, be massacred in our sleep. And it's all Horatio's fault!" Mrs. Day wailed, throwing herself into Hobie's arms. As gently as possible, he disentangled himself from the sobbing woman's grasp.

"Probably not." Sallie rose to his feet and pointed toward the stone corral behind the main station house. "We won't be here long enough to find out, though this wheel won't make it over the rough terrain ahead."

Becca blinked in surprise. *This wasn't rough enough terrain for you?* she thought.

The conductor shook his head and pursed his lips. "Folks, as soon as the station hands bring a new coach and team from the stable, they'll reload the mailbags and we'll be on our way."

Becca groaned, as did Aggie. Mrs. Day wailed and touched the back of one hand to her forehead as if she were about to faint.

"Aw, come on, ladies," Sallie snorted. "No one said this trip would be a piece of blueberry pie at a July picnic. Go on into the station and buy yourselves a meal."

"Beef jerky and slumgullion?" Mrs. Day whined. "Hardly a meal!"

"No time to eat stew at this station. Goat jerky and stale crackers will have to do." Sallie pointed to a wooden pen of goats.

Mrs. Day gave a weak groan. Becca noted that the conductor enjoyed baiting the poor woman.

"Pulling out in fifteen minutes in a new coach." He strode toward the station. "Fill your water containers and check for all of your belongings. Anything left at Apache Pass station becomes the property of either the station manager or Chief Cochise."

While the other travelers purchased food or headed toward the outhouse behind the station, Hobie helped Becca transfer their belongings to the other stagecoach.

The station hands wore pantaloons made of a coarse canvas fabric, which were stuffed into leather boots. Their silver spurs jangled with every step. Beneath their well-worn, dusty wide-brimmed hats were faded navy-blue woolen shirts. Long military-issued revolvers hung from leather sheaths on each man's wide leather belt. They performed their tasks without as much as a glance at the travelers.

When Sallie blew the bugle and ordered the new driver to head out, all were on board. With the addition of a new mailbag headed for El Paso, sleeping atop the mail was no longer possible.

As the day grew warmer and boredom set in once again, Bo suggested, "Hey Rebecca, how about a round of 'Sweet Betsy From Pike'?"

The girl maneuvered her harmonica out of her satchel. But when she tried to lift the instrument to her lips, she was sandwiched in so tightly between Hobie and Mr. Hutchinson that she couldn't move enough to play it.

"Did I ever tell you about the unlucky miner with a peg leg who was bitten by a rattler?" Bo adjusted his trousers. "Why, they say his fellow miners got seven cords of firewood off his fake leg before they could get the swelling down."

Everyone laughed; even Mrs. Day. Becca flashed him a teasing smile.

"I heard tell," Hobie began, "that a settler scattered pumpkin seeds on the spring side of a mountain. When a grazing goat wandered into the pumpkin patch, he got tangled in the vines. He didn't show up until fall. By then the pumpkins had grown to such gigantic proportions that one fell by its sheer weight off the vine, rolled down the hill, and busted against a big boulder. Out popped the missing goat. He'd been grazing inside the pumpkin and got caught in the process."

Becca clicked her tongue and grinned at her friend. "Hobie Masters! That's as tall a tale as I've ever heard."

"That was pretty tall, Mr. Hobie. However, we ladies can give you a run for your money. Have you ever heard of Molly Pitcher, a real, live Revolutionary War heroine who carried water from the spring to the exhausted soldiers fighting in one-hundred-degree temperature?" Aggie leaned forward. "During the Battle of Monmouth, she came upon a soldier who'd fainted beside his cannon. Despite the barrage of cannon balls bombarding the ridge, Molly loaded the cannon and fired until she ran out of ammunition. At one point an English cannon ball shot right between her legs, ripping her cotton petticoats to shreds. She was said to have looked down and shrugged, 'Oh well, that could have been worse.' "

"Aw, come on, I don't believe that one any more than I did the previous two," Mr. Hutchinson chortled.

"It's a true story," Aggie insisted. "The story has been part of our family legend for years. My great-great-great-grandpa Benjamin Allen fought beside her on that ridge. In fact, later, when General Washington became our first president, he made her an honorary sergeant in the army."

"A female sergeant? That will be the day!" Bo snorted. "What woman do you know could load a cannon, let alone fire it?"

Hobie chortled. "I know a gal who could hold her own against any enemy fire."

Bo shot a worried glance at Hobie and then at Becca. "No offense, Miss Rebecca. Shooting the head off a rattler with your, uh, trusty sidearm is a mite different from firing a heavy cannon."

The girl drew her gun from her holster and examined it first one way and then another; then she cast the Southerner a teasing grin. "You say that after I saved your life with this little old six-shooter. And just where is your rifle?"

Hobie chuckled, as did Aggie, since both Bo and Mr. Hutchinson were weaponless.

Aggie had been watching the exchange between Bo and Rebecca. "Son, as any successful gambler knows, you need to know when to place your bet and know when to fold. I advise you to fold. I'm a good judge of horseflesh. This little gal looks like she could be a direct descendant of the famous Molly Pitcher."

The girl laughed. "Hardly. I come from a long line of pacifists, but I do know how to take care of myself."

The woman leaned across the carriage and patted the girl's knee. "I'm sure you can do whatever you put a mind to, sweetie."

CHAPTER TWELVE

HELLOS AND GOODBYES

FATIGUE FROM BEING CROWDED in the most uncomfortable positions, along with the uninterrupted day and night travel, took its toll. Becca wondered if she might go insane before she reached Independence. At times it was only Hobie's calming presence that kept the girl from screaming and clawing her way out of the swaying vehicle.

"Hold on, girl. You're tough. You'll make it," Hobie would whisper in her ear. "Some day we'll look back on this and laugh."

Whenever he'd make such a prediction, she had the wildest urge to scratch out the man's eyes. When her sanity returned, she'd descend into a profound sulk that would last for hours. The other travelers didn't help because their moods had grown equally dark.

Becca awakened when she heard the driver yell, "Whoa." It had been a long, tiring run for man and beast. The heat of the morning sun had already risen to uncomfortable temperatures. A dry wind pelted her face with sand—New Mexican sand. The girl barely glanced about the conclave of buildings, typical of the stations in the Southwest: an adobe station house with an outhouse out back, a corral of eight to ten donkeys, and a stone-walled stable.

So this is Soldier's Farewell—a hundred and eighty-four miles from Tucson and one hundred and fifty miles from El Paso. Rebecca groaned. "I'm gonna die before we reach Missouri; I just know it. They'll leave my body in the desert to be eaten by wolves and coyotes."

She glanced toward Sallie as the man strode toward a tough-looking hombre of undetermined age and questionable character. The man looked as if he could hold his own against rattlers, highwaymen, and anything else the devil or God could throw his way.

The station manager stood beside a wooden hitching post and a watering trough encrusted by dried mud. "Sallie, my friend." The man extended his hand to the conductor. "I was wondering when you'd be pullin' in. A little behind schedule, don't you think?"

Knowing how sensitive keeping on schedule was to Sallie, Becca hurried past the two men and into the building. After gulping down a noxious tasting tea and a handful of stale crackers, she made a stop at the outhouse. While there, a second stagecoach arrived from the east. The weary passengers tumbled out of the conveyance, looking as exhausted as she felt.

Six mules had replaced the tired horses on the eastbound stagecoach. A short, wiry man, with long gray hair held behind his ears in a brightly beaded braid, chatted with Sallie. Station hands tied mailbags to the top of the coach, along with several additional pieces of luggage. Inside, the stack of mailbags had multiplied into a perpendicular wall behind the middle seat.

As Becca peered inside the coach, she asked, "Where did all this mail come from? Who'd be mailing letters back east from way out here in this desolate place? There can't be more than fifteen souls counting the staff at the station."

Sallie turned toward the girl. "That's true. But there is a small settlement of miners in those hills. The last coach heading east broke down. So you folks will be hauling all of their mail as well. Fortunately, that coach contained only two passengers who need a ride." He gestured toward the man at his side. "Rebecca, meet Buck, your new conductor. He and Ed, your new jehu, will be with you for the next two hundred and fifty miles or so, right Buck?"

The jehu peered at her from around the head of the lead mule while the conductor shyly nodded and tipped his hat. "Good to meet you, ma'am."

Sallie strode to the other side of the coach to examine the rear wheel. He didn't look her way.

"Hey, did you think I'd leave without saying goodbye?" she asked.

The man reddened and tugged at his collar.

"You don't like goodbyes, do you?" Becca placed a gloved hand on his callused, chapped one.

"No, ma'am, I sure don't. I've seen more than my share in fifty years of living." He stared down at her hand resting on his. "You, young lady, have a way of worming your way into a man's heart—Hobie's, Bo's, mine." A gentle smile crossed his face; his eyes glistened with tears. "I'm proud to have made your acquaintance."

She made eye contact with the man. "Sallie, mark what I said. The jewel of the valley has a lot to offer you."

His face flushed a second time. "So you say. Well, I might just head that way."

"Give Widow Ruthie a big smacker for me." Becca rose on her tiptoes and planted a kiss on his grizzled cheek.

Before Sallie could respond, Buck gave one blast on his bugle. The travelers, including the two from the other stagecoach, poured out of the station. Bo and Mr. Hutchinson were each examining their recently returned weaponry. Mrs. Day was harping at Aggie about the two new passengers: a slight, disheveled man, dressed in a wrinkled, pinstripe linen suit and a bolo hat; and a six- or seven-year-old boy in short pants, a striped shirt, and suspenders.

"Where are we expected to . . ."

Becca climbed into the coach once more. If it had been crowded before, nothing could have prepared her for the crush of bodies squeezed inside the coach. Buck could barely secure the latch on the stagecoach door.

"Don't worry," the stranger began immediately after the vehicle pulled out of the station. "My son, James Junior, and I will be leaving the stagecoach at Fort Smith. Mr. Butterfield hired me to run a station near there."

"And your missus?" Mrs. Day leaned forward, checking out the man from head to toe.

The man tugged at his collar before speaking. "My wife died in childbirth last winter. We buried her at Fort Tejon."

"I see Sallie returned your weaponry, gentlemen," Aggie interrupted. A grin teased the corners of her mouth. "Do you think you can play together nicely for the rest of our journey?"

Mr. Hutchinson sniffed. "I can if Devers can."

Aggie nudged Bo in the ribs. "How about you, Mr. Devers?"

The Southern gentleman gave the woman a playful grin. "I think I can manage, Miss Aggie, with your help, of course."

Mr. Hutchinson leaned back against the leather straps supporting the middle seat. "I sure won't miss old Sallie. He was an ornery cuss! Just because he was our conductor, he thought he's was a great mogul, king of the trail. Even the jehus jumped when old Sallie spoke." The man rolled the brim of his hat in his hands. "I hope Buck has a heart under that shoe-leather skin of his."

"I doubt there will be much change. The stagecoach still has a schedule to keep," Hobie reminded.

"I'll miss him," Becca replied softly. "I found him to be a man of intelligence, insight, and courage. Can you imagine how exhausting it is for the driver and the conductor to sit atop the stagecoach through rain, sandstorms, and swarms of insects hour after hour?"

Conversations dwindled as the sun burned hot throughout the day. Seeking relief from the heat, the ladies waved silk fans before their faces; the men waved their hats. Short stops at Cow Spring station and Murphy's Station afforded short breaks for the travelers. When the stagecoach rumbled over teeth-shattering rocks outside Fort Cummings, a Mormon military settlement, two mailbags tumbled onto the heads of Mrs. Day and Hobie.

"Ouch!" The woman bolted awake. The tiny black straw hat perched on the front of her head slid down over the woman's nose.

As humorous as the woman looked, the other passengers sighed and quickly returned to his or her "cave of misery," as Becca called the mental retreat each person established to survive the long hours of boredom. Hobie rubbed his head and hefted the canvas bags off his neck with the help of Mr. Hutchinson.

Finally, the constant shaking and rattling of the coach stopped. "Everybody out," Buck called. "Got a broken spring. We'll be changing coaches. We leave in an hour," he warned.

Bo helped Becca from the stagecoach. "I don't like this. This is Apache country; I can feel it."

She ignored the man's paranoia and hurried toward a row of outhouses behind the fort's main building, as did Mr. Hutchinson, Aggie, and James Junior. By the time she emerged from the facility, the others had exited to the dining hall. She spied a stone-faced, dark-skinned man wearing Apache garb, leaning against the wall behind the station. His waist-length ebony ponytail was woven with brightly colored feathers and beads. When their eyes met, a sudden chill skittered up her spine.

She glanced first one way and then the other, looking for a means of escape. The area between her and the fort's administration building was empty. Her hand slid to her holster. Unnerved by the man's intent gaze, she stumbled over a pothole but caught herself before falling to her knees. As she straightened, she prayed, "Oh, dear God, protect me, please."

Her father's policy to befriend strangers popped into her mind. Flashing her sweetest smile at the man, she greeted him politely. "Good evening, sir. Mighty hot today, isn't it?"

That was a stupid thing to say. It's always hot out here in the New Mexico desert! Besides, he probably doesn't speak English. A quick glance over her shoulder revealed that the warrior had straightened as if poised to follow her. *Don't run! Whatever you do, don't run! You can't show fear.* Becca maintained an even pace along the side of the building. Once inside, she flattened her body against a wall to steady her nerves. Then she slid onto an empty spot beside Hobie.

On the wall over the exit hung a sheet of yellowing parchment that read, "Indian country. The safety of your person cannot be vouchsafed by anyone but God."

Hobie eyed her curiously. "Where have you been? I was getting worried." He lifted a spoon of potatoes and meat to his lips. "I don't know what's in this slumgullion, but it's the best we've had yet." He slurped the stew from his spoon and smacked his lips. "Here! Try some."

While sharing a spoon and a bowl with her friend or with anyone else wouldn't usually appeal to her, the girl was hungry, hungrier than she'd been in days. And the mixture of meat and fresh vegetables tasted good. She'd eaten more than half of Hobie's bowl of slumgullion before hers arrived. The fluffy Southern-style biscuits did not disappoint her appetite either. Hobie laughed at her enthusiasm and ordered a second basketful.

Before the passengers left the dining hall, an army captain clanged his spoon against his tin cup. "Attention! Attention, everyone! All passengers, ready your weapons at the slightest sign of Indians, especially as you cross into the Mescalero Apache region of west Texas. The military calls this territory the Badlands of New Mexico. By all accounts there are more than one hundred and fifty pioneers buried along the next three-mile stretch of road. Let a word to the wise be sufficient."

The girl had barely digested the officer's warning when the bugle announced the stagecoach's departure. Her steps toward the coach were slow and deliberate as an icy fear prickled the hair on her neck. Reluctantly, she climbed into the conveyance, dreading the next leg of the journey. Aggie followed, as did the two Jameses, Bo, and Hobie.

"Daddy, I'm afraid," the boy whispered to his father.

The man tousled his son's strawberry-blond hair. "So am I, son, but we've come too far to turn back now."

Hobie patted the man's shoulder. "We all feel a bit jumpy right now. Maybe we should ask for God to send His armed guard to travel with us."

"Armed guard? He can do that?" The boy looked up at Hobie's face.

"Yeah, don't you know about God's armed guard? He promises to send ten thousand of them whenever we ask."

"Ten thousand?" The boy's eyes widened.

"Hey, I'd settle for a half dozen, myself." Bo gave a nervous chuckle. "Sure glad Sallie returned my weapons."

"If it's all right with you, sir," Hobie directed his question to the boy's father, "we can make that request right now before we climb into the coach."

The man gave an enthusiastic nod, as did the boy. Gathering everyone into a circle, Hobie bowed his head. "Dear heavenly Father, Thou hast offered to deploy a regiment of Thy strongest angels whenever we ask. Alone, we are weak, but Thou promised a thousand shall fall on our right side, and ten thousand on our left. We're not greedy, Lord. The number of heavenly troops Thou chooses to send is up to Thee, however many Thou thinks it takes to do the job. Amen."

A wave of amens passed through the small assembly that included Buck and Ed the driver. The girl noticed a heavy mantle of perspiration on Ed's knitted brow and upper lip. The man appeared paler than normal for a man accustomed to sitting in the sun all day.

As Becca climbed into the coach, she was surprised to discover that several of the mailbags had been removed from the third seat to the roof. This would allow the travelers to take turns stretching out once again.

The two Jameses climbed aboard as Becca adjusted her skirt about her ankles. Due to the extreme heat, she'd long since shed all of her crinolines, including the one concealing the gold nuggets. She sighed at the jangle of the jehu's spurs as he climbed into the driver's box. After such a good meal, she was ready to nap.

"Ladies and gentlemen, make yourselves comfortable." Buck poked his head around the stagecoach's open door. "We'll be traveling light on this leg of the journey. Mr. Hutchinson and Mrs. Day have decided to wait at the fort for the next eastbound stagecoach." His mouth widened into a picket fence grin. "Guess the meal was too irresistible." He slammed shut the door and climbed on board. And before the six passengers could digest his announcement, the jehu shouted and the stagecoach lurched forward.

With Mr. Hutchinson's and Mrs. Day's absence, the interior of the coach felt almost spacious. Aggie flashed Becca a knowing smile.

"The poor man," the woman murmured under her breath.

"Huh?" Hobie looked confused.

"The poor man is doomed. He may never reach Washington City— single, that is."

Hobie shook his head in wonder. "I'm confused."

"Don't tell me you didn't notice the admiring glances Mrs. Day sent the man. Poor Mr. Hutchinson. She'll have him hog-tied and to the altar within the month, mark my words."

Hobie turned his puzzled expression toward Becca. "Did you see anything developing between the two?"

"Maybe a little." What could the girl say? Hadn't she told Sallie that a woman always senses another woman's yearnings of the heart? Thinking of Sallie, she wondered if he were on his way west to Visalia, or would he be forced to spend a few days at Soldier's Farewell.

They'd barely ridden for an hour when the mules stopped. Becca started awake. She'd been dreaming she was twirling in a field of clover, her skirts billowing in the wind, and her once-long brown hair loose and swirling freely about her shoulders.

"Men!" Buck swung open the coach's left door. "I need your help out here. Ed's mighty sick. I need help lowering him to the ground." As the men scrambled out the opposite door, Buck added, "If you ladies know somethin' about medicine, the lad could use your help."

"I know a little. Tell me what's wrong." Aggie hopped out of the stagecoach. Within a few seconds, the woman had spread a blanket on the ground, and the men had laid the jehu onto it. Becca stood by helplessly watching as the boy writhed in pain. "My side! My side!" he moaned.

"Get me some water. He's burning up!" Aggie ordered.

Instantly, the conductor removed a tin flask from his hip and handed it to her. While Hobie cradled the boy's head in his hands, the woman gave Ed small sips of water. "Is this all you have? We must soak a blanket and wrap him in it to bring down the fever." She touched the back of her hand to his forehead as she spoke.

Becca helped James and Bo douse a woolen blanket with water while Hobie and Buck helped Aggie remove Ed's outer clothing. After covering the man's quaking body with the soaked blanket, Aggie waved a hand in the air. "Shoo! Shoo! Give the poor man some privacy."

Buck stood and gazed toward the nearby foothills. "There is a spring of fresh water in that cave on the side of that hill. It's one the Apaches use to water their horses. Miss Rebecca, would you mind refilling our water containers? Maybe the boy will go with you to help carry 'em."

"Be glad to." She smiled at the young boy. "Can you carry a couple of those tin buckets for me? I'll carry the rest." The girl picked up four of the tin water containers and slung them over her shoulder.

Behaving like a skittish colt, the boy hefted one empty container into each of his hands and followed her in the direction of the mountains.

"If you need help, fire once," Hobie called.

She waved and turned toward her goal. "So, this your first time east?"

"Yessum."

Late-afternoon shadows mottled the valley floor by the time they arrived at the foothills of the mountains. "It shouldn't take us more than a half hour to climb to that cave, fill these containers, and head back to the stagecoach."

When he failed to reply, she turned to see the boy's terrified eyes dart first one direction and then the other. "What's wrong? Are you all right?"

"Yessum. Jest skeered of Injuns, I guess." He hung his head and dropped back a step.

"James, do they call you James, Jim, or Jimmy?"

"My ma called me Jimmy."

Becca grinned. "Then Jimmy it is. You don't talk much, do you, Jimmy?"

"Pa says, 'Unless you have something worth sayin', don't say anything at all.' "

"Yes, I notice he doesn't talk much either. So how do you like the New Mexico wasteland?"

He shrugged. "It's all right I guess. Wouldn't want to live out here though."

Becca chuckled. Her laugh echoed off the sandstone cliffs. "Me either! If I never see another cactus, it will be too soon!"

They walked in silence for several minutes. The distance had been greater than the girl had estimated. By then, the afternoon sun hung lower in the sky than she imagined. She bent down and examined a narrow trail leading up the side of the first hill. "Unshod horses. Unless I miss my guess, I'd say the tracks will lead us straight to the cave and the spring." She eyed the massive ball of fire hovering in the western sky. "We need to move fast. That sun won't stay above the horizon for long."

They'd climbed less than fifty feet when they discovered a large opening in the side of the mountain. The ground outside the cave had been cleared of all cacti and rocks. A large circle of stones surrounded a pit of ashes. Cooled chards of burned wood and cinders assured her that the blaze had been extinguished hours earlier.

Becca went to the cave opening and took a deep breath. "Ah, smell that—the aroma of fresh water. See the horses' tracks? The source can't be too far inside the mountain." She gestured toward a large rock beside the entrance. "Sit down a spell while I locate the spring. If you spot any trouble, give me a holler."

"Yessum." The fear on his face had intensified.

She placed her hand on his shoulder. "Jimmy, are you sure you'll be all right? I won't go far, I promise."

"Yessum." He handed his water containers to her and plopped down on the rock, as he'd been told to do.

Struggling to carry six empty water buckets, Becca wondered how she'd get them out of the cave once she had filled them with water. Small holes in the cave's ceiling let in just enough light so she could identify a stash of weapons, food, and trophies from battle. *Apache,* she assumed. Cold chills darted up and down her spine at the sight of a pioneer woman's calico dress, several iron cooking pots, a boy's toy rifle, and a little girl's rag doll along one wall.

Stop wasting time, she scolded herself. *Just fill the buckets with water and get out of here.*

CHAPTER THIRTEEN

BAT CAVE AND APACHES

BECCA FILLED THE SIX tin containers with water and dragged them toward the entrance of the cave. Suddenly, something swooped in front of her face. Dropping the pails, she swatted at the air. A second creature grazed her shoulder. Again she batted the air, flailing her arms in defense. She looked up to see hundreds of bats hanging from the ceiling, having been awakened from their sleep by her invasion. The girl screamed, drew her sidearm, and shot wildly at the cave ceiling. The explosions prevented her from hearing Jimmy's terrified cries.

Her bullets ricochet off the ceiling and surrounding walls, scattering shards of rock. When a piece of shrapnel sliced the sleeve of her dress, she stopped shooting. The echo of the shots reverberated deep inside the cave. Having fired her six bullets, she stuffed the gun back in its holster and dragged the six containers of water toward the mouth of the cave as quickly as she could.

Several bats dived at her head and shoulders as she fled the cave. At the entrance, Becca stopped abruptly. In the gathering dusk, fifty raven-black eyes stared at her and knives were leveled at her chest—Apache knives. She dropped the water containers and raised her hands to indicate her surrender.

"Where is Jimmy?" she called to the man who appeared to be the leader. She took two steps forward. "Does anyone speak English? Where is the boy?"

The Apache leader held up his hand, ordering her to stop. He glanced over his shoulder at a stocky warrior holding Jimmy by the arm. "The boy is safe."

"Are you all right, Jimmy?"

The quivering boy nodded. Undaunted, the girl strode forward and stopped inches from the leader's face. As she studied the contours of his face, a wave of surprise swept through her. "You're the man I saw back at the fort."

The corners of the leader's lips twitched ever so slightly.

As if accusing the leader of wrongdoing, she charged, "You understand me! You speak English!"

The man gazed at the girl, from her boots to her honey-brown hair. His eyes narrowed. "What are you doing here? Are you stealing from our camp?"

She pointed back toward the six water buckets on the ground. "I took water from your spring, nothing else. I did not touch your belongings." The word *belongings* held a tinge of sarcasm.

"You are a brave woman. Back at the fort, instead of screaming and running from me or fainting at the sight of me, you smiled and greeted me in a civilized manner. I don't think I've ever had a white woman respond to me in such a manner. Don't worry; I won't hurt you." The leader sheathed his knife. His men did the same.

The word *civilized* sounded strange coming from the mouth of a man her fellow Americans considered to be a savage. "Your English is amazing. Where did you learn to speak so well?" she asked.

His lip curled into a sneer. "The United States government sent me to a mission school in Texas. A Methodist couple, the Marshes, ran it. At thirteen, I ran away to rejoin my people." The man lifted his chin as if expecting her to disapprove.

"Do your men understand English too?"

He shook his head.

"I'm curious," Becca continued. "Why were you standing by the wall at the fort?"

He didn't speak for several seconds. "It would have been a coup to kidnap a white woman on the grounds of the fort. But your smile and your kind words reminded me of Mrs. Marsh, and I couldn't do it." He swallowed his last phrase, fearful his men might hear and understand what he said. "I had one of my men stationed on the other side of the wall. I would have passed you to him."

"Why? Why would you do such a thing?"

"Besides the right to brag to other Apaches? The army at Fort Cummings pays very well to ransom white women as not too many live around these parts. The men in charge of the fort are Mormon, you know." Suddenly he stopped speaking and whirled about to face his men. A flurry of what sounded like gibberish sent the braves scrambling behind nearby rocks and boulders. The leader tossed her over his shoulder like a sack of grain and dashed into the cave.

Becca pounded on his back. "Stop it! Put me down!" Before her feet touched the ground, he whipped her about and clamped his hand across her mouth. She wriggled and squirmed, trying to escape, but was as effective as a kitten caught in the jaws of a coyote.

"Be quiet!" the man ordered, tightening his grasp on her waist. "Your people are coming for you. They probably heard the shots. I will remove my hand from your mouth if you promise not to shout. Do you promise?"

She nodded. When he lifted his hand, she inhaled sharply as if to scream. But before she could, his rough fingers clamped over her mouth.

"I mean it. Your screams would only lead your men into an ambush. Do you want that?"

Rebecca shook her head.

"Good! Then we understand one another." He slid his hand down to the heavy gunbelt at her waist and removed the six-shooter from its holster. "*Hmm,* good weapon; nice balance. What were you shooting at in the cave? You could have killed yourself."

Still trying to break free, the girl chomped down and ground her teeth into the tender flesh between the man's thumb and forefinger. The man yelped and let go long enough for her to scream, "Apaches! Watch out!"

"You little wild cat!" The leader clamped his hand over her mouth again. She could taste the blood oozing from the bite she'd inflicted on the man. He dragged Becca to the open space in front of the cave entrance.

"We know you're out there. We have the girl and the young boy. Both will die at the sound of one gunshot." His words reverberated off the sandstone cliffs. "As much as I might enjoy keeping this young lass as my squaw, it's been a tiring day. My men and I don't want a bloodbath.

Besides, we outnumber you three to one. Send one of your men as insurance, and we will release the hostages to you unharmed."

Becca froze, expecting the reply to come in a barrage of gunfire. Instead, a long pause followed. Her heart skipped a beat when Hobie stepped out from behind a boulder on the desert floor, his hands lifted over his head. "Take me. Let the boy and the woman go. Take me." Carefully he placed his handgun on the ground by his feet and then straightened to his full height. To the quaking Becca, her friend appeared ten feet tall.

"Walk toward me," the Apache leader demanded.

Hobie did as told.

"Order your men to return to the stagecoach!"

"Do as he says," Hobie shouted over his shoulder.

The stagecoach conductor signaled to Bo and James. Becca's heart sank as she watched the men head toward the stagecoach.

"You promised to release the woman and the boy." The set of Hobie's jaw remained firm and determined, as if he were in charge of the situation.

The Apache nodded. "And I always keep my word." With a slight gesture he ordered his man to release Jimmy.

"Go back to the stagecoach," Hobie shouted as the boy stumbled past. "And my woman?"

"She is your woman?" The leader eyed Becca and then Hobie.

"Yes, she is my woman." The set of Hobie's jaw hardened more. "Take me, but release her as you promised."

The Apache stepped closer. "Haven't you heard how cruel and bloodthirsty we Apaches can be? You would risk possible torture and death for a simple woman?"

"Becca is no simple woman, I assure you." Hobie gazed into her tear-filled eyes. "I would travel to the ends of the earth for this woman. Indeed, I already have! And I would protect this woman with my very lifeblood, if that's what it takes."

"Hobie!" Becca whispered. "I don't know what to say."

"Don't say anything, Becca. Pray. Pray for us both." It wasn't an urgent cry to pray for divine intervention, but a simple directive.

"You're not afraid of what we may do to you, are you?" The Apache frowned as he sucked the blood from his wounded hand.

Hobie shook his head and grinned. " 'Thou shalt not be afraid for the terror by night; nor for the arrow that flieth by day; nor for the pestilence that walketh in darkness . . .' "

Almost without thinking Becca mouthed the words with him, " 'For he shall give his angels charge over thee, to keep thee in all thy ways.' "

The Apache leader blanched. Beads of sweat coated his forehead. Suddenly, as if she were a burning firebrand, he released Becca. "Go! Go back to your people," he ordered. "You too." He gestured toward Hobie. "Get out of here. I don't want any of your hocus-pocus religious tricks played on me and my men."

Becca stumbled into Hobie's waiting arms. Instead of hurrying away from their captors, her rescuer held his ground. "You recognized those words from Psalm 91, didn't you?" The gentle giant smiled at the agitated Apache.

"Yes," the Apache mumbled, casting furtive glances toward his baffled men. "Mrs. Marsh used to repeat those verses each night as she tucked us boys into bed. She said that the words gave her a mighty courage—and they would give us courage as well. Now, go, get out of here before I do something I'll regret." The Indian picked up Becca's gun and handed it to her. "Don't forget you sidearm, little girl. You'll need it. The state of Texas houses some pretty ornery hombres."

With Becca securely protected under his giant arm, Hobie turned to leave, "May God bless you, sir. May His angels guard you from all evil."

"How could you say that?" the girl whispered as Hobie led her across the darkened desert floor. "Surely God wouldn't protect evil men like that."

"They are only defending their homes and way of life, Becca. We're the invaders. Remember?"

"*Hmmph!* Let's hurry before they change their minds," the girl urged. "You may trust them, but I don't. Oh no, I forgot to take our water containers! Should we go back?"

Hobie tightened his hold on Becca's waist and stepped up their pace. "No, we'll have to make do until we reach the next station."

Remembering the reason she'd gone for the water, the girl asked, "By the way, how is Ed?"

"His fever broke, but he's too weak to drive."

"What will we do?"

"I've been driving supply wagons for my dad since I was a lad. I imagine I can manage four mules and a little old stagecoach—at least until we reach the Fort Fillmore Pass."

"You are incredible, Hobie Masters. You truly are."

An easy grin filled his face. "Why, thank ye, ma'am."

The reunion at the stagecoach was short lived. Nervous about the encounter, Buck and the passengers wanted to put as much distance between them and the band of Apaches as possible. With Ed lying on the mailbags in the third seat, Hobie helped Becca into the vehicle and climbed on the driver's seat beside the conductor.

Except for the exhausted patient, sleep eluded the passengers inside the coach. Rebecca fielded their barrage of questions, especially the ones about the Bible text that unnerved the Apache leader.

"I always knew God's promises were powerful, but to affect the heart of a savage like that?" Aggie shook her head with wonder.

"The man is not a savage. Actually, he was polite and articulate. Under different circumstances, I would have asked him a boatload of questions."

"Savages, all of them!" Bo snarled.

"No more than the white soldiers at Fort Tejon that Lieutenant Milburn told us about."

"You'd be singing a different tune if that scalawag had kept you as his squaw, milady!" Aggie huffed and turned her face toward the window.

The tight lips of the other passengers told the girl they agreed with Aggie. Even Jimmy, resting in the crook of his father's arm, looked unconvinced.

Sitting next to Becca, Bo tried to change the mood by telling another tall tale. His efforts failed. No one was in the mood for laughter. He switched to describing his home in Tennessee, especially the acres of pine trees and cool green forests. Rebecca leaned her head back and closed her eyes. She could almost see and feel a drop in temperatures.

"My mama would love you." Bo drew gentle circles on the back of her gloved hand. This sent delightful little chills up and down her spine. From across the aisle, Aggie glared.

In the dark of night, they covered the distance between stations in record time. At each stop when they switched to a fresh team, Buck inquired of the station manager about a spare driver but returned each time shaking his head. If they hoped to keep to the schedule, Hobie would need to continue driving. As for Ed, Buck decided the sick boy would leave the stagecoach either at the first station where they found a driver or the first place where he could get proper medical attention. Except for occasional spikes in his fever, the boy slept much of the time.

Days later, the stagecoach, pulled into the sleepy little community of El Paso. The station consisted of several small adobe huts and a corral that held fifteen horses. The station keeper waved them into a low-slung hut with a doorway barely wide enough for an average man to slip through. Hobie had to duck and worm his way into the building.

The floor inside was hard-packed clay. There were no shelves or cupboards for storage. Between the sacks of flour were a collection of blackened kettles, a tin coffeepot, a bag of salt, and a side of raw beef along the walls of the room. A fire roared in a six-foot-wide stone fireplace on the side wall. While Buck took Ed to the town's physician, the station keeper sliced off a slab of beef of a questionable age and fried it in an iron skillet wiped clean with his shirttail. A chunk of stale bread and a measure of moldy cheese rounded out the meal.

When Buck returned, the station manager introduced the passengers to their new conductor, Pete, and to a driver named Fenn. Becca studied the two men. Except for the conductor's pronounced limp, it was difficult to tell them apart. Both men had greasy blond hair and chins that looked as if they had been trimmed with bowie knives. Several layers of grime and sweat coated their brown canvas pants and once buff-colored muslin shirts. Aggie wrinkled her nose and whispered to Becca, "I'm glad they're sitting outside the coach and not inside with us."

On the trail, no one could practice good personal hygiene, but Becca was certain these men's lack of cleanliness left a horde of dead flies in their wake. Whenever possible, she and Aggie took what the ladies called "spit baths"—soap and water in porcelain basins. After their baths, they'd wash their "linens" or unmentionables. Drying their wet clothes involved modestly covering their "linens" with outer garments and pinning them to a cord stretched across the top edge of the coach. In the Texas heat, the garments dried in record time.

Grateful for a two-hour break, Aggie and Becca took their spit baths, washed their undergarments, and then wandered through the dusty streets of El Paso.

"Nine hundred miles—that's how far the station manager says it is to Colbert's Ferry at the edge of the Choctaw and Chickasaw reservation." Aggie groaned. "I'd forgotten how big Texas is."

Once they had explored the small border town from one end to the other, they returned to the station house for a bite of food. Becca enjoyed her platter of freshly made tortillas between layers of refried beans, rice, ground meat, and goat cheese.

"Imagine!" The girl mopped up the remaining green chili salsa from her plate with her last morsel of tortilla and tossed it into her mouth. She licked her fingers, savoring the lingering flavor of the green salsa. "*Hmm,* Texas, Oklahoma, Arkansas, and finally Missouri! We're almost there!"

Aggie cast her a lopsided grin. "Yeah, almost there!"

With Hobie riding inside the coach once more, Bo kept an appropriate distance between himself and Becca, though he continued to charm her with his tales of life in Tennessee.

The Texas heat soon lulled Becca into a dreamless sleep. She awakened hours later and gazed out the window at the endless landscape with nary a building in sight. By the third day when Becca napped and awoke to the same blistering sun and the same arid landscape, she groaned. "Nothing's changed! Is our jehu driving in circles?"

Bo laughed. "That's Texas for ya darlin'."

They changed horses every ten to twenty miles throughout the day and night. The horses fairly flew over the hard, level road. Each time the coach stopped, the passengers tumbled out to stretch their legs, and before anyone could wander far, the bugle sounded, and they once again hit the road.

At Fort Chadbourne, a tall, angular black man avoided Becca's gaze as he helped her down from the carriage. A swarm of flies descended toward her face in beeline formation. *Ah, memories of Mariposa Wells,* she thought. It wasn't until she studied the faces of the workers at the fort and those working in the surrounding fields that she realized these people were slaves.

At the sound of the dinner bell, the flies followed her into the dark dining room. As with many of the eating areas she'd visited, a fire roared in a huge stone fireplace at the back of the room. One look at the table and Becca gasped in horror.

The wooden tables were black with flies. The clustering pests were dining on the crumbs from earlier meals. Gingerly, she followed Bo's example and brushed the dead flies off the table. Bo slid into the seat beside her. When a slave younger than Jimmy placed a cup of sun-flower tea in front of her, the girl inhaled sharply. "Look!" She poked Bo on the arm with her teaspoon.

He leaned forward and chuckled. "Mighty good swimmers, I'd say."

"That's not funny! Imagine what terrible diseases they carry!"

Bo shrugged. "If you don't like them, spoon them out."

"A lot of help you are," she mumbled, examining the contents of her teacup.

His eyes narrowed. "Would you like me to call Hobie to rescue you from the devil's own horde of bugs?"

She glared at him. "That's not nice. Hobie is my friend."

Bo rolled his eyes toward the fly-covered ceiling. "So I've noticed. I can't get a moment alone with you without his ambling over at his slow, aggravating pace."

"You want to be alone with me?" She batted her eyes at him in sur-prised.

Bo grinned. "You know I do."

A warm glow filled the girl's heart as she anticipated spending time with Bo without an audience present.

* * * * *

Because the conductors and the drivers changed every two hundred to two hundred and fifty miles, the passengers no longer attempted to become acquainted with them. No one mentioned Sallie, but Becca compared each new conductor to her friend. They always fell short. In time, the girl ceased trying to remember the names of the men on each new shift.

The girl wondered if Sallie had found his way back to Visalia. In her imagination, she created a touching reunion between Sallie and Widow Ruthie. Following her romantic interludes, the girl would study the face of her dependable friend Hobie, and then the rakishly handsome face of

Bo Devers. She imagined what life would be like being wed to each of the men. Once, when the women were alone, she shared her pleasant little imaginings with Aggie.

The older woman shook her head. "Becca, my dear, always remember brass ain't gold. The shine of brass tarnishes quickly, while genuine gold warms with wearing."

Becca mulled over the woman's advice across the miles of Texas wasteland. But to say Bo's dazzle didn't tickle her fancy would be a lie.

However, as the hours dragged into days, and the days dissolved into nights, exhaustion and sore, aching muscles replaced the attraction she had for either Bo or Hobie. Confined in a tight space for days on end robbed any human being of his or her natural wit and charm.

CHAPTER FOURTEEN

INTO THE UNKNOWN

THE ANTICIPATION OF LEAVING the state of Texas for the Chickasaw Nation at Colbert's Ferry kept Becca awake long after the sun set in the west. Like the girl, the other passengers, even Bo, had long since tired of idle banter. Their periodic sighs and groans reminded her she was not alone in her misery.

With the leather curtains fastened down, the stagecoach became as dark as the interior of a closed coffin. The girl had lost all sense of time passing. It was Jimmy's hour to stretch out on the mailbags.

"I'm skeered," the boy confessed as he swung his legs over the back of the seat onto the mailbags.

"Why are you afraid?" Aggie asked, more out of politeness than curiosity.

"Goin' into Indian country. Maybe they'll scalp us or torture us for our money," he continued.

Bo chuckled. "Money? Considerin' what we've shelled out for food along the way, no one has any money left."

"That's for sure," James interjected. "I thought the price of our tickets would be our biggest expenditure, but I was wrong."

Becca heaved a giant sigh. The sound of the other passengers' voices had begun to grate on her nerves.

"Trust me, boy," Aggie began, "no torture any human could inflict on me could equal the black-and-blue marks on my poor body. If such a place as purgatory exists," Aggie shifted her weight from one side to the other, "this is it!"

The jouncing of the conveyance intensified as the stagecoach headed north. Small rivulets threaded the bumpy terrain. Without warning, Becca gave a startled yelp as her body flew forward, unexpectedly, onto Bo's lap. Aggie landed on James's lap.

"Hey! Hey!" Hobie snorted as Jimmy, who'd been asleep on the mailbags, slammed against the man's neck, sending both of them onto the heap of dazed passengers. Dust from the mailbags billowed about them. Seconds later, the team of horses flew across a stream and up the opposite bank, flinging the passengers toward the rear of the stagecoach like toys being cast aside by a child throwing a tantrum. Becca found herself pinned between Jimmy and Bo.

"Why, Miss Rebecca," Bo chuckled as he sprawled across her body, "fancy meeting you here."

How the man could find humor at such a time, she did not know. "Your elbow is—*aachoo!*" She showered Bo's face with a gigantic sneeze. Aggie and Hobie sneezed as well.

"Jimmy! Take your knee out of my back," Becca snarled.

"Sorry." Jimmy scrambled to oblige.

Hobie, between several ear-shattering sneezes, hefted the boy back onto the mailbags. "It's all right, Jimmy-boy. You couldn't help it. You're doing fine."

"Is it morning yet?" the boy's father mumbled.

Aggie lifted the curtain and peered out. A pale gray light poured into the coach. "Morning can't be far away."

Becca yawned and stretched. A smile teased the corners of her lips. While she was still a long way from Missouri, this was the day she'd eagerly anticipated—leaving the state of Texas.

Less than ten minutes later, the horses stopped running. Smiles flashed across the disheveled passengers' faces. Hobie stuck his head out of the window.

At the Boggy Depot, the last stop before crossing onto the Choctaw reservation, a sizable town had grown up around the station. The conductor had suggested to his passengers that since the town had a U.S. post office, they might write a few letters home. "Tell your family in the west that you got this far safely," he suggested. "We'll be here for thirty minutes."

Becca wrote a short note to her parents in Placerville. Bo and Hobie also sent letters.

"The half hour must be almost up by now. Any minute we'll be hearing a blast of that old bugle! I'm growing to hate that thing." Becca laughed and sashayed toward the door, her skirt swishing behind her.

The girl's prediction proved to be accurate. They'd barely returned to the station in time to watch the jehu adjusting the reins on the fresh teams' backs. As they piled into the stagecoach, the conductor, whose name she'd long since forgotten, announced, "It's a short run to the next station. I don't intend to be there for long."

Twenty miles later, the stagecoach pulled into Geary's Station. Bounding out of a small log cabin, the station keeper invited the travelers inside his home. He introduced them to a short, round gray-haired woman with flashing black eyes, rosy cheeks, and an easy smile. "This is my wife, Mabel." Rebecca noted the pride in the man's voice. "She's the greatest cook this side of Pecos."

"Oh, bash!" The woman dusted her flour-coated hands on her calico apron and playfully swatted her spouse's arm. "Come in! Come in! Make yourselves at home. I've got a batch of chili simmerin' on the stove and corn pone bakin' in the oven. But wait! Where are your manners, Mr. Colbert? These folk must be dry as coyotes in August. Bring in the jug of lemonade from the icehouse. Would you all like a glass of cold lemonade?"

"If it's not too much trouble." Aggie spoke for the others.

"No trouble at all. Go darlin'. Go."

When the station keeper hurried to do his wife's bidding, Mabel smiled at Becca. "You are such a pretty little thing, as cute as a bug's ear, you are."

"Isn't she though?" Bo sidled up to the girl and slipped a possessive arm around her waist.

From across the room, Hobie glared. "Excuse me, Mrs. Colbert, I need to get some air." Their hostess blinked in surprise as the man stormed from the building. She cast a questioning glance toward Becca.

The girl blushed. "It's a long story, Mrs. Colbert. Hobie's a good man. He'll be fine."

A knowing look passed between Aggie and Mrs. Colbert, causing Becca's color to deepen as she wriggled free from Bo's possessive gesture. Having two men vying for her attention was new and exciting to the girl, and a little uncomfortable.

Instead of continuing to play for her favor, Hobie withdrew from the contest. Everyone noted the change. Inside the coach and at each station stop, the man ceased to anticipate Becca's needs. He treated her as respectfully as he did Aggie, but the warmth and the caring for her comfort ceased to exist. With wit and charm, Bo happily filled the void.

At the next station, the conductor, a heavy, lumbering man who wore a constant grimace on his face, announced, "We're having a bit of a problem. I need to inspect the hand brake and possibly repair it before we mount the hills of western Arkansas."

James, Jimmy, and Aggie cheered the welcomed news. As she climbed down from the coach, Becca glanced about for Hobie, but he'd disappeared. The man was nowhere to be seen. In the past, he'd never stayed irritated at her for so long.

Lucy Barton, a slight, birdlike woman of Choctaw heritage, smiled shyly at her guests. She urged Becca and Bo to make themselves comfortable around a rickety wooden table. The red-and-white checked tablecloth added a splash of color to the cabin's great room.

"*Halito!* Come! I will bring you a bowl of hominy. Hominy is part of the Choctaw tradition. My recipe was handed down for many generations. I like to add bits of chicken to the mixture." The woman's soft blue cotton skirt swirled about her ankles as she bustled across the room to the massive stone fireplace. At the sight of the woman's long black braid dangling down her back, Becca instinctively ran her fingers through her shortened bob.

"This is nice." Aggie gestured for Becca to sit in the empty space beside her. "And where is Hobie?" the woman asked.

Rebecca shrugged. "I have no idea. I'm not his keeper."

Lucy returned with a large iron pot and spooned the steaming hot mixture onto the plates. "I also made *banaha* for you."

"*Banaha?* What is *banaha?*" Jimmy asked as he dug into his serving of hominy.

The woman smiled at the boy. "*Banaha* is mixed field peas, cooked cornmeal, and a little meat blended into a mush. Then I shape it into a patty, wrap it in cornhusks, and boil it." She crossed the room to the fireplace and returned bearing a platter of the described food. "My parents and grandparents lived on *banaha* for over a year after surviving the Trail of Tears. That's what my people call the United States government's relocation program to remove us from our homes and places of birth." The woman's smile faded; her eyes grew sad. "My grandfather was a Methodist minister. He believed our family survived because of divine intervention." The woman gave a slight shrug and quickly replaced the pain in her face with a brilliant smile. "Ah, but enough sadness! We survived by the grace of God. What's past is past."

Lucy flitted across the room to the fireplace and returned with a platter of small round balls. She placed one of the sugarcoated balls of dough on Jimmy's plate. "For dessert, you will try my *walakshi*. Usually, this treat is served at Choctaw weddings and other special occasions, but I like to make it especially for my guests."

The boy's face brightened as he bit into the dumpling. "Yum! There's fruit inside."

"You like?" Lucy asked.

"Oh, yes, thank you." He nodded enthusiastically. "May I have another, please?"

"Jimmy!" the boy's father hissed. "Mind your manners."

"Oh, no!" Their hostess giggled with delight. "I have made plenty. Please help yourselves." It had been a very long time since any of them had enjoyed a dessert of any kind.

Becca had finished her third *walakshi* when Mr. Barton, Hobie, the conductor, and the jehu entered the cabin. "Save us a bite, my girl?" The station manager strode to his wife and planted a big kiss on her cheek. The woman blushed and batted at her husband's arm.

"Not with you behaving as shamefully as that!" She filled a plate with food for Hobie. As the others were getting settled, Hobie bowed his head and then started eating.

"Tell me, Lucy," Aggie collected the soiled plates and dinnerware from the table and carried them to the dry sink beside the fireplace. "How do you make these tasty little treats?"

"They're simply dumplings with fruit inside. Fresh fruit is ideal, but out of season any canned fruit will do."

Bored with listening to females sharing recipes, Becca glanced at Bo and smiled. He lifted an eyebrow and gestured toward the door. She nodded.

Always the Southern gentleman, Bo called, "Mrs. Barton, you are a magnificent cook. Your grits put most Southern cooks to shame, and those little puffs melted in my mouth. Thank you so much. And, folks if you will excuse me, I need to stretch my legs."

Becca waited five minutes before she asked to be excused as well. The girl grabbed her bonnet from the peg by the door and exited the cabin. A crescent moon hung low in the star-lit sky. As she stepped outside, a soft breeze riffled her curls. "Bo? Bo?" she whispered. From the branch of a nearby tree, a killdeer answered her.

"Bo? Bo?" She looked inside the empty stagecoach. Her leather sack lay on the seat where she'd left it.

The girl peered around the edge of the cabin. No Bo! *Perhaps he's by the stables,* she thought.

"I'm not in the mood for hide-and-seek, Bo." The horses whinnied when she stuck her head inside the barn. Frustrated, she planted her hands on her hips. Without a sound, someone stepped out of the shadows. Wrapping his hands about her waist, Bo whirled her about and pressed her against his chest.

"Bo!" She squirmed, trying to escape. "This isn't funny! Let me go."

Shadows hid the man's face. "I didn't mean to be funny," he breathed as he undid the ribbons of her bonnet and tossed it to the ground.

"Bo!" She glanced over her shoulder at the main house and then back at him.

With one hand holding her close, he ran his fingers through her curls and dipped his head until his lips lingered within an inch of hers. "Oh, Becca! Do you know how long I've wanted to do this?"

"Bo . . ." Her breath came in short gasps; her pulse raced; her heart beat wildly in her chest. *Strange and dangerous emotions for the daughter of a Baptist preacher,* she thought. *You should push him away.* When she tried, her arms refused to obey. "Bo . . ."

His lips brushed against hers. The kiss became more intense. The girl wished he would stop kissing her, yet prayed he would never stop. He took her face in his hands. "You are so beautiful." He kissed her several times. "I can't get enough of you."

For Becca, the world had stopped turning. She'd never wanted anything so much as to stay in his arms, yet in the recesses of her mind, she heard her mother's voice. "Wait, darling! Something's not right."

Bo made a trail of kisses down her face and neck. When he fumbled with the top button on her bodice, the girl grabbed his hands in hers.

"No, Bo, no!" She took a step backward.

"Oh, darling, please don't make me stop," he gasped, wrapping his arms about her. He tried to capture her lips again, but she swung her head away.

"No, I'm not that kind of girl, Bo."

Behind them, the cabin door swung open and light from inside filled the courtyard. Hobie stepped out of the cabin. An owl hooted in the distance.

"*Shh!*" Bo froze. Without glancing in the couple's direction, Hobie ambled toward the bridge over Little Boggy Creek. In the middle of the bridge, he stopped and leaned on the railing. "When I can read my title clear to mansions in the skies . . ." His clear baritone voice floated over the water.

Any thrill Becca felt when Bo kissed her fled upon hearing her father's favorite hymn being sung. If her father had his way, the congregation would sing it every week. "No, Bo. Let me go," she whispered.

The man's hands slowly slid down the length of her arms to her fingertips. Turning to go back to the cabin, Becca saw Hobie lean his elbows on the railing, fold his hands, and touch them to his forehead. Her eyes misted. He'd come outside to pray, just as he did at almost every stop along the trail.

"I need to get away," she mumbled, fleeing to the outhouse and barricading the door. Once inside the tiny building, she couldn't stop shaking. When the conductor blew the bugle, a knock sounded on the door.

"Becca, are you in there? It's me, Aggie. Please hurry! I need to use the facility before we leave the station."

Crimson with embarrassment, the girl unlocked the door and hurried to the waiting coach. Grateful for the cloak of darkness, she climbed into the vehicle, avoiding eye contact with both Bo and Hobie. A minute or two later, Aggie climbed on board, and the conductor gave a whistle, and the jehu shook the reins. The stage manager and his wife, Lucy, waved from the doorway of their log cabin as the stagecoach leaped away from the station.

They rode throughout the night and the next day, stopping only to change teams at each station. The conductor was determined to get back on schedule before he relinquished the stagecoach and its bags of mail to his successor. But like horses smelling water in the desert, the passengers complained less. Their dark moods lifted; they talked more, sharing their expectations with one another.

Bo continued to court Becca's favor. And slowly, despite the presence of the stone-faced Hobie, an occasional smile brightened her face. Bo's thoughtful little attentions convinced her that his affections were real. Whenever possible the two slipped away from the others to share a tender kiss or two. Becca could tell the older woman did not approve.

After a quick meal of hominy in milk at Riddle's Station, the two women agreed to slip away for much-needed baths. Outside the recently constructed station building and corral, two goats, a doe and a kid, pranced around Becca, begging for food scraps.

"That's Dora and her kid, Rascal," the young station worker harnessing the new team shouted. "They're friendly. You can pet them if you like. But beware of Satan. He's a bad one."

The ram in question eyed them from behind a corner of the stable.

The women walked until they found a shady spot along the stream that flowed into the Fourche Maline River. Becca scrubbed her skin until it tingled. She dipped beneath the cool, clear water, rinsing the lye soap out of her tousled curls.

"How can anything feel so good," she cooed. "Aggie, it's your turn. I'll watch while you bathe."

Aggie stepped into the stream and dipped beneath the water. When she surfaced, the woman sighed, "This is what heaven must feel like."

"I know what you mean. I think I washed ten pounds of sweat and dust from my body!" She dried her hair on one of her crinolines. "There's one big advantage to short hair. It dries so quickly here in the open."

Concerned that the conductor would soon blow his bugle, Aggie undid her braid to wash her hair. And then as quickly as she rinsed the suds out of her hair she scrambled up the bank of the stream and dried her body on a linen towel she'd brought with her from San Francisco. "The station hands must be almost done hitching the fresh team of horses by now."

Fearing the woman might be right, Becca took a deep breath and broached the subject of her growing romance with Bo Devers. The girl didn't know why she needed Aggie's approval, but, for some reason, it had become of utmost importance to the young woman. "I know you don't like Bo," she began. "Why?"

Aggie slipped on her fresh camisole and bloomers. "It's not that I don't like Bo. It's that I care more about you. You are fragile, innocent. You're going to get hurt."

"Hurt? Bo would never hurt me!"

The woman dried her hair with her towel before replying. "Maybe it's because you remind me of myself at your age—I was headstrong, foolhardy, and certain I was wildly in love."

A knot of anger grew inside the girl. "It's not the same. We're not the same. Just because you chose to marry the wrong man doesn't mean I will too," she snapped. "Anyway, who asked you?"

Aggie lifted an eyebrow and grinned. "You did, darling. And you're right; we are two different individuals. I chose unwisely even though I had an abundance of wise counsel from family and friends. While you, you have no one other than Hobie to advise you." She wrapped her wet, freshly washed clothing in the wet towel and rose to her feet. "Remember, you are a long time married, so go slowly. And never forget that no matter how brilliantly new brass shines, it ain't gold and it never will be."

A rush of color flooded Becca's face. "You sound like you think Bo is ready to propose marriage to me or something."

The older woman chuckled. "Oh, he won't do that, honey. Bo Devers is not the marrying kind."

"How can you say such a thing? You hardly know him."

"I know his type." Aggie gathered her clothing in her arms and started toward the waiting stage. Reluctantly, Becca followed. Aggie continued, "Bo is like a fox loose in a vineyard of ripe grapes. He nibbles a little here and nibbles a little there, and then moves on, leaving damaged fruit in his wake."

Chapter Fifteen

Reluctant Groom

ITHOUT ANOTHER WORD, Becca clutched her bundle of clean, wet wash and stormed away. The girl ignored the station hands and the hostler in the corral that were wrestling the fresh team of horses into their harnesses. The hostler called, "Watch out for Satan. He's partial to wet laundry."

At the waiting stagecoach, the girl climbed on the carriage step and strung the rope Aggie had brought to use as a clothesline along the luggage railing from the front to the back.

Removing a couple of willow clothespins from her bag, Becca clamped the teeth down on the ends and strung her wet laundry on the line, carefully concealing her underclothing from view. Her wash would be dry before they pulled into the next station. Seeing Aggie approaching, the girl hopped off the iron carriage step, intent on avoiding her by dashing inside the station house.

Hearing a loud bleat coming from the barn, Becca whirled about to see Satan charging her. Two station hands shouted and ran after the animal while the girl fled toward the station house. Before Becca had reached safety, Satan veered toward her freshly hung laundry. With one leap, the ram grabbed a pair of lacy underwear. The animal shook the undergarment free of the heavier skirt and dashed toward the barn.

"No! No!" Becca screamed and set to chase, her arms flailing. "Not my favorite drawers!"

As she flew past the station hands, one of them warned, "Careful, he bites!"

"So do I!" she shouted over her shoulder.

Aggie stared as the girl ran past. The commotion brought the other passengers and several of the work hands out of the station house. The air was filled with laughter.

Intent on rescuing her unmentionables, Becca charged after the ram. When the goat paused at the open barn door to see if the woman was still in pursuit, Becca snatched at one leg of the garment. "Let go of that!" she ordered.

Instead, the goat clamped his teeth tighter onto the delicate fabric. A tug-of-war ensued—the goat holding on to his prize, and Becca determined to reclaim her clothing. Neither gave in.

"Let go, Satan!" she shouted, wrapping her portion of the garment around her hands and digging her heels into the hardened earth. "If I had my gun, I'd plug you right between the eyes, you worthless creature!"

Fearful that the young woman might get hurt, the station manager waved a stick over the animal's head and danced about the perimeter shouting, "Lady, let him have 'em. Satan will never let go!"

"Neither will I!" she snarled, her boots skidding in the dust.

While neither the goat nor the girl would give in, the garment did. *Riiip!* The startled beast and the angry girl landed on their bottoms. Each was left clutching one wet and very muddy, ruffled leg. Laughter echoed off the barn and off the station house. Becca rose to her feet and held up the torn garment for inspection. Realizing her undergarment was beyond repair, the mortified girl burst into tears and ran into the nearby outhouse. The goat recognized his good fortune, picked up the second leg of his prize, and trotted into the barn, with the station manager in hot pursuit.

At the sound of the bugle, Becca reluctantly emerged from the outhouse. No one spoke as she boarded the stagecoach. At a shout from the new driver, the horses lurched into motion. As they passed the stable, Becca caught sight of a satisfied goat named Satan chewing on her drawers.

Later, while everyone around her slept, she wrestled with her embarrassment and with Aggie's advice. The next morning when the stagecoach stopped to change teams, the girl slipped away from everyone. Fortunately, no one followed to try to comfort her.

By the time they arrived at Watson's Station at Scullyville, Becca's discomfort had faded, and Bo had soothed her with his Southern charm. Still angry at Aggie, Becca needed very little persuasion to talk her into slipping away from the group. Secluded in a grove of blossoming dogwood, Bo took her in his arms and kissed her willing lips. With one kiss, all of her concerns vanished.

What did disturb her was the young man's determination to stray to areas where she feared going. It usually ended in a gentle tug-of-war. But that her best friend treated her with marked distain disturbed her much more deeply. All that kept her going was the knowledge that, if all went well, she would arrive at her destination in less than a week.

The girl welcomed the call of the bugle at Watson's Station in Scullyville. Knowing this was the last stop before their overnight reprieve at Fort Smith, the girl rushed to board, as did the others. The Mexican station hands switched a team of six fine horses for six mules. The men wrestled the semiwild creatures into place and slipped on their harnesses. One man held each mule fast while the conductor and the driver climbed into the driver's box. Unfortunately, the driver lay down the reins to pull on his leather gloves.

Immediately sensing their freedom, the mules kicked, twisted, and whirled, straining the harnesses in six different directions. The two lead mules broke free and disappeared down the road. The four remaining creatures, their harnesses tangled and torn, began dragging the coach in circles.

Frantic, the station hands grabbed for the beasts, shouting, *"Alto! Alto!"*

"We're gonna die! We're gonna die!" Bo wailed, bracing his legs against the seat opposite him.

On the coach's second revolution, the driver and the conductor leaped to safety, leaving the terror-stricken passengers to survive as best they could. The mailbags on the roof crashed to the ground, frightening the terrified mules more. The mailbags inside the coach tumbled onto the passengers, tossing the people on top of one another. Arms, legs, and feet scrambled to get untangled.

"Help! Help!" Aggie waved hysterically out a window as the stagecoach passed the gaping station hands a third time.

Both stagecoach doors flew open. If the coach overturned, they would be trampled to death by the mules. To keep from tumbling out, Becca grabbed Hobie's arm with both hands and squeezed with all her strength. "Those ornery beasts! Somebody ought to shoot 'em!"

Hobie hauled her into his arms. The beating of his heart and the rumble of a prayer reverberating through his chest eased her panic. The girl closed her eyes and prayed too.

Whether halted by exhaustion or by the tangle of harnesses hampering their movement, the four braying mules stopped long enough for the station hands to catch them. While the stable hands led the animals back to their stalls, the passengers staggered from the stagecoach to the station, where the cook offered them cups of chamomile tea.

When it came time to reboard the coach, the passengers found six new mules in harnesses. Becca and the other passengers stared as a sober-faced Bo handed the station manager the front page of a book he carried in his carpetbag. "Here, should I not survive, this is my last will and testament," he said.

Before climbing on board, the girl strode over to the lead mule and ordered, "You behave, you mangy beast!"

The animal brayed and bared its teeth as if accepting her challenge. "Step back, miss," the stationmaster warned. "Old Jedediah doesn't take kindly to females."

"We're even!" she snapped. "I don't take kindly to obstinate mules either!"

Whether or not the beast was defying her or just behaving according to its natural temperament, she did not know. But when the driver grasped the reins and gave a shout, the mule team shot from the station as if a horde of demons were twisting their tails. Becca gasped as the unexpected start sent her flying into Aggie's lap.

Twelve miles later, the animals abruptly halted in front of the Butterfield Overland stagecoach livery. A crowd had gathered to welcome the mail coach—perchance it contained a letter or two from family members and friends who'd gone west.

As James disembarked, the shaken man quipped, "I did say I could barely wait to get to Fort Smith, but I would it had taken an hour or two longer."

The stationmaster, a middle-aged man with a neatly shaped gray beard, sideburns, and mustache, strode out of the stable behind two of his employees. "Take the coach around to the livery before you unhitch the team."

He grinned at the disheveled passengers staggering toward him. "Looks like old Jedediah took you for quite a ride!" Before anyone could respond, he pointed across the street toward a large sign atop a red brick building. "If you're hungry, that's Miss Connie's place. She makes the best fried chicken and dumplings between Fort Smith and Atlanta."

Becca glanced about for Bo. They had much to talk about. Fort Smith was where he would board another stage and travel east to Memphis, while she would go north toward St. Louis. She couldn't find him in the bustle of people.

"Come on." Aggie took the girl's arm. "Let's try Miss Connie's famous dumplings. I bet they're not as fluffy as mine."

"I was just looking—"

"I know. Bo will show up when he's ready." The determined woman led Becca across the dusty street to the boardwalk. "And so will Hobie."

At the top of the steps, a cheery-faced woman with an upturned nose and bright red curls piled on her head greeted them. She stood with her hands folded across a white apron that protected a light green calico skirt and numerous layers of crinolines.

"Come in. Come in. I'm Miss Connie—not Miss Constance, but Miss Connie." From the woman's tone of voice, Becca sensed it would be unwise to confuse the two. The woman continued, "I know you are sweaty and tired from your journey, so feel free to use my little bath chamber to freshen up while I mix up a fresh batch of my famous dumplings." Miss Connie patted the two women on the shoulders and pointed them toward the kitchen. "I make the crispiest melt-in-your-mouth fried chicken. Why, generals stationed in Charlotte say they'd cross the country for my chicken."

The two women had barely entered the tiny cubicle that housed a filled porcelain water pitcher and matching basin atop a small mahogany commode when Miss Connie knocked on the door, "Would you ladies prefer sweet tea or a glass of ice-cold strawberry lemonade with your meal?"

"The lemonade would be nice," Aggie volunteered, and then turned to Becca, who was busy washing the grit off her face. "You don't mind drinking a strawberry lemonade, do you?"

The girl shook her head and emptied the soiled water into a tin pail beside the stand.

After the first bite of chicken, Aggie and Becca agreed Miss Connie's fried chicken and dumplings deserved the accolades given. The two women had barely finished their first serving when Bo sauntered into the restaurant and sat down at their table without invitation. "Hi, y'all."

A slight frown swept across Aggie's face. Before Bo could summon Miss Connie, the woman arrived at the table with a platter of chicken and several dumplings topped with white gravy.

He bit into a chicken leg. "*Mmm!* This is good cookin'! You can't imagine how much this Southern boy missed eating good hometown cookin'. No one, but no one, can fry chicken like a sweet Dixie mama."

Basking in the man's flattery, Miss Connie regaled her visitors with stories of life in town, especially ones about the recently formed Butterfield Overland Express Division Center. "Mr. Butterfield—he loves my fried chicken—said Fort Smith was the perfect junction for the two routes. Why, before Mr. Butterfield came to town, we weren't much more than a sleepy little military outpost. Now we have more than two thousand citizens. Imagine!"

She shook her head in mock amazement. "On mail days, when the coaches arrive from both directions, the town grows by at least a thousand souls. It's good for business too. Everybody needs to eat." The tousle of curls atop her head bounced about when she laughed. "Now, you folks eat up. I have sweet potato pie topped with freshly whipped cream for dessert."

As Miss Connie predicted, several people quickly filled the available tables. James and Jimmy entered the dark wood-paneled dining room and stopped by their table.

"So when are you two heading East?" Aggie asked.

"Not until we've both enjoyed a good night's sleep!" James stated. "How about you folks?"

Becca glanced down at her plate and looked at Bo out of the corner of her eye. Grease dripped from Bo's chin as he bit a chunk from the side of a breast of chicken.

Seeing the silent interchange between the couple, Aggie touched the napkin to her lips. "I agree," she said. "After that bruising journey, I need a short reprieve as well. I'm thinking of staying in town until the end of the week."

When Aggie's, James's, and Jimmy's eyes settled on Becca, the girl mumbled, "The stagecoach north to Missouri leaves Fort Smith later tonight. I imagine I'll be on it. I know Hobie will." Becca placed the chicken bone on her plate and leaned against the ladder-backed chair. "James, you and Jimmy have to try Miss Connie's dumplings. They melt in your mouth."

"So I hear!" The young father turned toward an empty table on the far side of the room. "Come on, Jimmy. I'm starved." As they walked away, James turned and called, "Rebecca, tell Hobie goodbye for me if I don't see him before your stagecoach pulls out."

The girl dabbed at her lips with her cotton napkin. "Whew! When was the last time we ate so well?"

"Well," Aggie touched one finger to her chin, "let me see. Lucy's food was certainly delicious."

The girl raised an eyebrow. "That was a rhetorical question!"

"Was it now?" The older woman pushed back her chair, fished several coins from her bag and set them on the table. "I imagine you two have much to talk about, so if you'll excuse me, I need to secure a room for the night." She stood and slipped her hands into a pair of white lace gloves. "Please don't leave without saying goodbye, my dear. You'll find me upstairs."

"I won't." Tears glistened in Becca's eyes. She'd looked forward to this day for so long, and now that it was here, her heart had begun to ache. Seeing her distress, Bo placed a hand over hers.

She lifted her gaze to meet his. "I am so tired of goodbyes."

"I know! I know!" He gently patted her hand.

"Tomorrow, you'll be gone. Will I ever see you again?"

"Little darlin', of course you will. I'll write regularly. After I spend a few months at home with family and friends, I'll come for you, I promise."

She ached to throw herself into his arms. "Oh, Bo, I will miss you every day until I see you again."

"And I, you."

Becca started as the door to the restaurant flew open and banged against the wall. The jehu from the previous run burst into the eating establishment. "Bo! There's some man out yonder asking for you! I

146

didn't say nothin', but he looks mighty mean. And he has a tough-lookin' posse with him."

Bo shoved back from the table. His hand rested on the gun in his holster.

"Wait!" Becca fumbled in her bag for enough change to cover her meal. "I'm coming with you."

"No, I don't want you to get hurt."

"Hurt? You know I'm a better shot than any four men put together." She was already on her feet and her gun in her hand. "Who do you think it might be?"

"It's not good." He shook his head and strode to the door. Becca hurried to stay by his side when two beefy men with dark handlebar mustaches pushed past the couple.

"We're looking for Bo Devers! Anyone see him?" the scruffier of the two men shouted.

"This is a private establishment, gentlemen!" Miss Connie stormed to the front of the room with a soiled platter in hand as if she might start swinging it at any moment.

Bo straightened his shoulders and jutted his chin. "Who's asking?"

The second man answered. "I am in the employ of Major Jonathan Crabtree."

Bo's shoulders fell as he heaved a giant sigh. Without looking toward Becca, he admitted, "I am Bo Devers." The men grabbed his arms and led him from the building.

"Bo? What's happening? Who are these men? Who is this Crabtree fellow?" the girl cried and burst out of the building onto the board-walk.

A pristine, white four-passenger closed phaeton with a team of matching gray horses was parked in front of the livery stable. Standing beside the coach's open door, a black man garbed in a carefully pressed red jacket and black knee pants helped an impressively rotund man, who was dressed in white from the top of his head to the tips of his shiny white leather boots, exit the carriage. A gold chain divided the broad expanse of his white satin jacket. He also sported a white mustache, a white triangular goatee, and a white felt top hat.

"Well, well." Major Jonathan Crabtree swaggered across the street to the base of the board sidewalk.

"Major! Sir!" Awe filled Bo's customarily boastful voice. "What are you doing in these parts?"

The stranger grinned and tipped his hat back from his face with his gold-tipped walking cane. "Lookin' for you, to make you do right by my daughter Melissa and your two-year-old son, Rupert."

Bo gulped. "I beg your pardon, sir?"

"She and your boy are waiting for you in the phaeton. You're a daddy, son."

"Huh? How did you know . . ." Bo stuttered.

Becca gasped, "You have a child?" By now, a crowd had gathered outside Miss Connie's restaurant. From every window of the two-story hotel, people gaped at the unfolding drama.

"Right nice of you to send a letter telling us you was comin' home. Your pappy became mighty chatty about your return when I paid off the mortgage on his place. Said he always wanted a grandson."

The driver opened the door on the opposite side of the carriage and helped a comely woman swathed in layers of beige lace and silk step from the vehicle. Tears glistened in her eyes. In her arms, a small boy dressed in a linen tunic and silk pantaloons squirmed to break free. "Daddy! Daddy!" the child called.

A terrified Bo shot a quick glance first one way and then the other as if ready to bolt. Holding him fast, both men drew their weapons and aimed them at Bo's chest.

"Don't think about running, son. I spoke with the local clergy this morning. He agreed to do the honors of performing the wedding ceremony. Today!" Major Crabtree's voice hardened. "Gentlemen, please take our reluctant bridegroom to the chapel at the end of this street. We mustn't keep the preacher waiting."

The men half dragged and half carried the humiliated Bo down the steps of the sidewalk. The major called, "Be gentle with him, boys, unless he decides to bolt. I can't have my new son-in-law-to-be injured before the nuptials. Abigail, my baby girl, wouldn't like that, would you sweet plum?" Seeing his weeping daughter, he commanded, "Abigail, get back into that carriage with the child! Abe's gonna drive you and your son to the church."

Chapter Sixteen

REUNION

Stunned by what she had just witnessed, Becca watched until a cloud of dust hid Bo and his captors from her view. *"Bo."* His name stuck in her throat. She fought against the tears welling in her eyes. Many of the travelers followed the magnificent carriage down the street. The faces filling the second floor hotel windows had disappeared behind lacy curtains. Snickering soldiers attached to the military fort ambled up the street toward headquarters.

I've got to get out of here! Becca didn't want to go back inside the restaurant, nor to the livery, nor down the road toward the church where Bo would soon marry the mother of his child. With but one direction left to run, she gathered her skirts in her hands and fled west, which she quickly learned was the direction of the military headquarters and commissary.

The girl rushed past two uniformed soldiers. One called out to her, "Hey, where are you going in such a hurry, pretty lady?"

"Mind your own business!" she shouted over her shoulder. *Men! You're all the same!* "And don't call me 'lady'!"

She didn't slow to hear the man's reply. Spotting a cemetery to her right, she veered off the road and through a pair of iron gates. The girl glanced over her shoulder to be certain the soldiers hadn't followed her.

Finding a secluded tombstone beside a lazy creek, she collapsed onto the ground. "Oh, God, where are You? How could You let this happen to me? I don't understand," she wailed. "You said You wish to give me the desire of my heart. Well, Bo was that desire! How could You let me fall in love with him, knowing this would happen?" A nearby grove of pine trees absorbed the sound of her sobs.

Overhead a wild turkey objected to having his midday nap disturbed. *All I want to do is get as far away from this place as possible!* Fearful she might miss the stagecoach heading toward Missouri, she rinsed her tear-streaked face in the cool stream's water and straightened her bodice. She forced her feet to retrace their steps to the livery stable. Relief flooded through her to find the stagecoach and its six matching horses standing in front of the stable. People she'd never before seen piled into the waiting vehicle. A new conductor blew the familiar off-tune notes on his bugle.

When she asked the conductor how soon the stagecoach would be leaving for Springfield, the man shook his head. "Sorry, lady. This coach is heading to California." He pointed toward a sturdy little vehicle hitched to a team of four wiry mules waiting farther down the street. "That's the one you're looking for."

Breathless from her run, Becca doubled over, gasping. *Mules? I think I'm going to be sick! How much more can I take?*

"Rebecca! Rebecca Cunard!" The girl looked up when she heard her name being called. Aggie dashed through the hotel's swinging doors. Darting in front of a nag pulling a supply wagon and a high-stepping brown-and-white filly hitched to a two-passenger surrey, she bounded across the main thoroughfare, shouting, "Rebecca! Wait! You can't leave without saying goodbye!"

Shame-faced, the girl turned toward the woman who'd been her friend and confidante throughout the journey. "I'm sorry. I just wanted to get out of town as quickly as possible."

Aggie took Becca into her arms and cradled her. "I know, I know! I am so sorry."

"Me too," the girl mumbled. "Where is Hobie? Have you seen Hobie? If he thinks I'm missing this stagecoach because of him, he's sorely mistaken!"

"Becca, I'd like to pray with you before you go." The woman took the girl's hands in her own and bowed her head. "Father, my precious friend is hurting badly right now. Help her to know that Thou art with her and that all things do work together for good to those who love

Thee, Lord. Travel with her as she completes her journey. Fill her soul with peace and her heart with love. Amen."

Becca stared straight ahead, her jaw hard, her eyes filled with fury. Aggie rubbed the girl's upper arms. "Honey, be patient. I know you can't see how right now, but someday you will be thankful that everything happened as it did. I promise you." Tears filled the woman's eyes as she placed a tender kiss on the girl's cheek. "Go with God, dear heart. Go with God."

As Becca lifted herself into the coach, Hobie ambled across the street. He paused to speak with the new conductor, a thirty-year-old clean-shaven man with a deep scar across his left cheek. The jehu, sporting a scraggly beard and unkempt hair appeared to be closer to her age. After a brief conversation with the two men, Hobie hopped aboard.

The girl studied the small coach with a jaundiced eye. Mailbags occupied the floor space. More bags filled the boot. This coach had no place on top for luggage. Her and Hobie's carpetbags had been placed on the seats. *No other passenger? Oh, no, I'll be spending two to three days alone with Hobie. If he tries to comfort me, I'll—*

Slinging Hobie's bag to the seat opposite hers, she pressed the mailbags down with her feet to make a comfortable resting place for her legs. The best she could do was to arch her legs across the bags and onto the opposite seat.

The instant Hobie climbed on board, the conductor blew the bugle. With a crack of the whip the mules galloped down the street as if fleeing the local sheriff and his posse. Becca barely had time to wave at Aggie before they'd left the outskirts of town and were surrounded by overgrown forests.

"What kind of coach is this?" she asked as Hobie adjusted the luggage and mailbags on his side of the vehicle.

"It's called a celerity wagon. The smaller wagon maneuvers through the mountains better than the Concord wagon. And instead of metal springs, it has leather straps supporting the coach."

Long before Hobie had spoken the words *metal springs,* Becca had turned her face toward the open window. Without any signs of slowing, the stage climbed out of the valley and into the steep, rugged Boston Mountains. To keep from being lifted from the seat by the bumps and ruts in the narrow trail, she clutched the door handle until her knuckles turned white. To keep from banging his head against the vehicle's low ceiling, Hobie braced his hands against the sides of the carriage.

Fearing she'd be shaken limb from limb, Becca tried to recall happier times, but none would come to mind. She shot a look of terror at Hobie. His ashen face did little to reassure her.

When the coached pulled to a halt in front of the Butterfield Overland stagecoach offices in Fayetteville, Arkansas, Becca fumbled to unlatch the door. Her feet hit the dusty roadway, and her hands shook; her knees quivered as she hobbled into the stone station house. She and Hobie ate a light breakfast of biscuits and gravy in silence while the station hands changed mule teams and the driver checked the wagon wheels for damage that might have occurred during their wild ride across the mountains.

The station manager entered the dining room. "Is there a Miss Rebecca Cunard here?" He waved an envelope in the air. Being the only female in the room besides the station manager's wife brought a smile to her face, the first since the Fort Smith fiasco.

"I'm Rebecca Cunard."

With the aplomb of the king of England's personal news courier, the man, dressed in bib overalls, a green plaid wool shirt, and muddy work boots, bowed as he handed the white parchment envelope to her. He straightened. "This came in yesterday's mail pouch from Independence."

"Thank you."

Hobie watched the girl break the seal and read the letter.

>Dearest Becca,
>
>We received a note from your parents, announcing the date of your expected arrival in Missouri. Imagine our surprise and delight to learn that we would see you soon. Your brother will meet you in Springfield. I and the children would love to come as well, but, unfortunately, I can't abandon our guests at the inn. Caleb will wait at General Nicholas Smith's Tavern in Springfield for you to arrive. I am so eager to see you once again, little sister. The children can't wait to meet their auntie Rebecca.
>
>Much love, your devoted sister,
>Serenity

"Is it from your brother?"

Becca nodded, her eyes misted with tears.

"What does he say? Do we need to take the stage all the way to Tipton?"

She handed him the letter. "Two more days, Hobie, just two more days!" Her face broke into a broad smile. "At times I've felt trapped in a horrid nightmare from which I couldn't escape."

Suddenly, the usually dreaded sound of the conductor's bugle electrified the girl into action. Her eyes sparkled as she leaped to her feet and grabbed her leather bag. "Hurry, Hobie! We don't want to miss this stagecoach!"

The station manager helped her into the carriage and called to the conductor riding shotgun. "Watch out for highwaymen," he warned. "There've been several holdups between here and the Missouri border. Justice is swift in these parts. When Judge Parker gets his hands on 'em, he'll hang 'em high!"

Becca chortled and patted her holster. "I dare anyone to try to rob this stagecoach. I'll plug 'em right between the eyes."

Hobie looked bemused. "You're certainly feeling a lot better."

The girl squinted out the window at the conductor. "Come on, let's get this stagecoach rolling! We've got a schedule to keep!"

Hobie rolled his eyes and chuckled. "You sound like Sallie."

The pain evident behind his smile saddened her. She knew she'd been punishing him for Bo's duplicity. Yet as much as she wanted to ask his forgiveness, the girl couldn't form the words.

One after another the relay stations came and went—Fitzgerald's, Callahan's, Harbin's, Crouch's, and Ashmore's. At the border between Arkansas and Missouri, a gang of bushwhackers tried to block the narrow road in an attempt to ambush the stagecoach. But with one blast of his shotgun, the conductor sent them flying into the brush.

The night before arriving in Springfield, Becca couldn't sleep. Neither could Hobie. Dark, ominous clouds hung low in the sky. Fearful the stagecoach would lose time if the creeks rose and the rivers flooded, she could see the same anxiety on Hobie's face. *Will we be forced to wait out a gully washer?* she wondered.

Harboring the same concerns, Hobie prayed aloud, "Father, God of the wind and the rain, if it is a part of Thy plan, hold back the waters for us as You did for the children of Israel at the Red Sea. If not, give us the grace to endure without complaining. Not my will, but Thine be done. Amen."

His prayer was simple, trusting; it touched her heart. Staring into the growing darkness of the coach, she asked, "Where were you when Bo was—"

"At the church. I saw them drag Bo into the building," Hobie confessed. "While his bride changed into her fancy wedding dress, Bo asked me to tell you he was sorry, and that he did care for you. He also admitted that the father and brothers of another young woman chased him out of San Francisco."

"I was such a fool!" Becca punched her fist against the wall of the carriage. "How could I have swallowed his lies? It's going to be a very long time before I trust another man, I can tell you that!"

For several miles, a ponderous silence hung between them. Becca assumed that Hobie had fallen asleep. As for the girl, sleep eluded her.

"Hobie? Hobie?" she whispered as the morning light peeked around the leather shades on the window.

"Yes?"

"Promise you won't tell Caleb or Serenity about Bo."

"I promise."

She heaved a ragged sigh. "How soon after we arrive at Serenity Inn do you plan to return to California?"

"I don't know." He paused. She heard his slow, steady breathing. "Probably not before next spring. How about you? Will you stay at the inn?"

"I don't know. I don't plan to head west anytime soon, not after this crossing!" She adjusted her skirts around her ankles, leaned back against her seat, and yawned. "It's going to take months for all of my bruises to heal!" They both laughed.

"What if things haven't changed in Placerville?" Hobie's voice grew solemn. "What if the state senator has issued a warrant for your arrest or something? By now, he must have figured out where you went."

She didn't have an answer.

* * * * *

Becca's breath caught in her throat when she spotted the edge of the small town of Springfield. Her hands jiggled in anticipation as the stagecoach rumbled down the sleepy street. The coach stopped in front of a building with large letters identifying it as General Nicholas Smith's Tavern. As quickly as the wheels ceased turning, the doors of the inn flew open, and out of the establishment poured a welcoming committee of more than fifty cheering people.

Becca scanned the crowd for her brother's face. "There! Over there!" She pointed to her left. "Serenity's with him!" Her body quivered with anticipation. She swiped at the tears streaming down her face.

When her brother rushed toward the stagecoach, the girl flung open the stagecoach door and leaped into his waiting arms. Her feet dangled more than a foot above the ground as he hugged her with all his strength. She buried her face in his shoulder.

"Baby sister! Baby sister!" the man repeated several times as he twirled about in circles. Tears glistened in his eyes. "I never imagined this day would ever come." His voice broke.

Becca's feet had barely touched the ground when Serenity swept her into her arms as well. After a long hug, the older woman held the girl at arm's length. "Look at you! You're no longer my little sis. You've grown into a beautiful woman."

Becca modestly mumbled, "You are being too kind. I haven't had a real bath in, well let's just say, it's been a while."

Serenity laughed. "We'll take care of that. I ordered the hostelry to prepare a hot bath for you in your room. Which would you prefer first, breakfast or a bath?"

There was little doubt in the girl's mind. "A bath!"

The older woman chuckled. "I thought that would be the case."

Behind them, Hobie and Caleb were getting acquainted. "You must be Hobie, Becca's faithful friend and bodyguard." Serenity sized him up from head to toe. "Caleb's mother couldn't write enough good things about you, sir."

She linked her arm in Becca's. "Come, let's head up to your room. I figured that you must be sick of wearing the same dresses over and over again, so I had a dear friend—well, you'll see."

Serenity called to her husband. "Honey, would you please carry your sister's bag to her room; and oh, yes, please show Hobie to his room as well." As an afterthought, the woman added, "A hot bath is waiting for you to enjoy as well."

Caleb chuckled at the surprised look on Hobie's face. "That's my wife, always thinking three steps ahead of the rest of the world."

Massive paintings of early American history lined the walls as the women climbed the broad staircase to the second floor of the tavern. "Your letter said you couldn't come with Caleb," Becca reminded. "I'm so glad you did, but what happened? And where are the children? I can't wait to meet them."

The older woman swung open the door to a small sunny bedroom. Hot steam surrounded a copper tub in the middle of the room. Becca inhaled her favorite aroma. "Lemon verbena, you remembered."

"Go! Get undressed and hop into the water before it cools." A ring of joy wreathed Serenity's face as Becca slipped into the hot, foaming bathwater. "I can't believe you're really here!"

"*Ooh!* That feels divine." Becca picked up a face cloth and a bar of facial soap from the edge of the tub. "So tell me about the children. Where are they?"

Serenity sat on the edge of the room's massive brass bed. "First, let me back up a bit. As you know, I operate the Serenity Inn while your brother runs the accompanying livery stable. When your letter arrived, so did two new guests, a Mrs. Willa Mae Landry and her daughter, Cristabelle. When Josephine, my stepmom, heard I couldn't go with Caleb to meet you, she volunteered to care for our guests and for the children."

"What a dear!" Becca slid under the water and resurfaced, her hair covered with soap bubbles. "I can't wait to meet them." The girl paused. "Josephine—is this the Josephine I met back in Union Springs?"

"One and the same. And she's proven to be a good wife for my father. So tell me about this Hobie fellow?"

Becca sudsed her hair and disappeared beneath the water a second time. When she resurfaced, the girl demurred. "He's a good friend, that's all. I'm sure my folks told you about Bart, the state senator's son, getting shot and me being blamed. And they probably told you how Hobie and his father, Mr. Masters, made it possible for us to flee the senator's henchmen."

Serenity gestured with her hand. "Mama told us all about it in a letter. How frightened you must have been. By the way, I had my father—

he's a lawyer you know, check at the sheriff's office. Rest assured, there are no outstanding arrest warrants against you in the state of Missouri. So you can relax." She paused and then asked, "But, what about this Hobie fellow? He seems nice. Twenty-four days together in a stagecoach? Is there any thing, uh, you know, a spark?"

Water splashed on the oak plank floors as Becca stood and wrapped a thick Turkish towel about her head and a second about her body. "Oh, no. He's just a very good friend."

"Uh-huh." Serenity grinned. "Does he know that?"

"Of course, he does."

"Are you sure? You could do a lot worse," Rebecca's sister-in-law reminded.

"Yes, I certainly could." A vision of Bo flitted through her mind as the girl stepped out of the tub and onto a fluffy cotton bath mat. "I am starving. Now where's that lovely dress you had made for me?"

"Oh!" Serenity dashed across the room and flung open the wardrobe doors. "Right here!" She held a lavender-and-white gown up for Becca to see. "I hope you like it. Annie, you remember Annie, don't you? She operates a dress shop in Independence. She embroidered tiny pink rosebuds across the front of the bodice." The older woman withdrew two crispy white crinolines, a matching camisole, and a pair of lacy drawers from the wardrobe and laid them across the bed. "And what is a new dress without the proper undergarments?"

Becca laughed and removed the towel from her head. "Wait until you see the clothes I brought from home! They're grimy!"

"Oh, and I almost forgot!" Serenity rummaged through a purse she removed from the wardrobe shelf. "Here are some lavender ribbons to tie back your hair." She viewed Becca's head from several angles. "What happened to your hair?"

Suddenly feeling self-conscious, Becca ran her fingers through her shorn locks. "It's a long story. But it's already growing back."

A loud rumble from the girl's stomach reminded both women that breakfast was waiting for them downstairs.

CHAPTER SEVENTEEN

REST AT SERENITY INN

CALEB CUNARD'S FOUR-PASSENGER ENCLOSED carriage, pulled by a matching team of two dapple-gray horses, halted in front of a sprawling white clapboard building. The blue lettering on the sign in front read "Serenity Inn." A myriad of spring blossoms—red, yellow, blue, and orange—blanketed the prairie up to the edge of a waist-high, white picket fence. A blaze of yellow daffodils skirted the circumference of the yard. Behind the house, Becca caught sight of an unpainted barn and livery.

"You've made a lot of improvements since I was last here," the girl commented as Caleb helped her from the carriage. "I remember only the original sod building."

"Yes, God has blessed both the inn and my blacksmithing business. We've had a steady stream of guests heading westward, even after all these years." Caleb's face beamed with pride. "We, mainly my dear wife Serenity, have been able to share God's love with travelers from all over the world. You'd be surprised how many folks do not know how much they need God in their lives."

Becca averted her eyes. Following her heartbreak, she'd wondered if she really needed the God of her parents and of Hobie. She felt a growing satisfaction with how well she'd managed the journey on her own. Suddenly, a giant black blur, the size of an adult bear, barked full voice as he rounded the corner of the inn. The dog bounded toward the guests as if he intended to topple them if given the opportunity.

"Onyx!" Caleb shouted in a commanding tone.

Becca gasped in surprise. "Onyx! Is that you?" She knelt down and extended her arms toward the animal. The dog surveyed the young woman. "It's me, Onyx. You remember me." The girl tossed her bonnet onto the grass. Seeing the girl's face and hearing her voice, the dog's confusion lifted. With his long, red tongue lolling, he charged into Becca's arms, knocking her onto her back. Laughing, she hugged the dog as he slathered her face with big sloppy kisses. Struggling to her feet, she glanced toward Hobie. His hand rested on his sidearm, ready to leap to her defense.

Certain Becca was safe, Hobie assisted Serenity from the carriage. Suddenly, the kitchen door flew open and slammed against the house. A towheaded boy of six bounded from the inn, dashed across the yard, and flung open the gate at the edge of a small vegetable garden.

"Mama! Daddy! You're home! I missed you." The child threw himself into his mother's waiting arms.

"I missed you too." Serenity kissed the top of his head. "Sammy, say hello to your aunt Rebecca and to her friend Hobie."

An unexpected wave of shyness flitted across the boy's face. He extended his hand toward his aunt. "Please to meet you, Auntie Rebecca. And you, too, Mr. Hobie."

Hobie smiled. "Nice to meet you, too, Sammy. And just call me Hobie."

Caleb took the reins and gestured toward Hobie. "Mr. Masters, I'd love to show you my blacksmithing shop, if you're not too tired."

An eager smile crossed Hobie's face. "I'd like that. Please call me Hobie as well. And if you don't mind, I would rather walk to the shop. I've done enough sitting for one lifetime." He rubbed his flanks.

"You gals head on into the house," Caleb called. "Ring the chow bell when it's time to eat."

Serenity headed toward the kitchen door. "Where's your sister?" Becca asked the boy. "Where's Baby Seri?"

"Taking a nap." Sammy shyly took his aunt's gloved hand. "Grandma Jo is in the kitchen baking bread."

"And our guests, the Landrys?" Serenity called over her shoulder.

"Mr. Tavis drove Mrs. Landry and Miss Cristabelle into town." Sammy gazed adoringly into Becca's face. "Mr. Tavis knows everything there is to know about horses. He works for my dad." The boy took a short breath but resumed talking before Becca could speak. "You are just as pretty, Auntie Rebecca, as my mama said you were. Except"—he peered at the back of her sunbonnet—"Mama said you had long brown hair and you wore it in braids. Where are your braids?"

Becca tweaked the boy's rosy cheeks. "You are full of questions, aren't you?"

"Yes, I am. I love asking questions. Mama says I'll become a lawyer like Grandpa Pownell when I grow up, or maybe a preacher like Uncle Ned. Both like to talk. I sure do enjoy jawing a lot. So where are your braids?"

"Well, probably in a town called Visalia, California. At least, that's where I left them."

"Why did you leave them there?"

A baby's cry sent Serenity scurrying into the inn. "Make yourself at home, Becca. Sammy, pour your aunt a glass of Grandma Jo's lemonade."

The boy hurried to carry out his mother's instruction while Becca studied the cozy kitchen. Though no fire burned in the massive river-rock fireplace, the room glowed with warmth. She inhaled the sweet aroma of freshly baked bread. As her eyes adjusted to the room's light, she spotted the red-and-gold crazy quilt her mother had made and given to Caleb and Serenity as a wedding gift. The girl knew her mother would do the same if she ever married, which at the moment she doubted would ever happen.

A small red rag rug covered the dark wooden floor in front of the hearth. A myriad of shiny copper pots hanging over the long, dark wood trestle table reflected the light coming in through the ruffled muslin Priscilla curtains at the room's windows.

Becca eased her tired body into the mahogany Windsor rocker beside the fireplace and set it in motion. The copper kettles hanging over the table reminded her of the copper coffee pots languishing on the mercantile's shelves. *So long ago; so far away,* she mused.

Sammy quickly returned with a tall glass of lemonade. "I put in two chunks of ice to make it extra cold. It's a mighty warm spring day out there."

She lifted the glass to her lips. "Where did you find ice?"

"From the icehouse out back. It's in the soddy part of the inn." With a small glass of lemonade in hand, the boy dropped to the rug at her feet. "I helped my dad cut and haul ice from the river last January. That way we have ice almost all summer long."

"Grandma Jo." The boy leaped to his feet. "This is my auntie Rebecca."

Becca stood to greet an older woman, with blond hair graying at the temples. Grandma Jo's burgundy polished cotton skirt rustled as she glided into the room. "Rebecca, it's so nice to see you again." The older woman stretched out her arms toward the girl. "My, how you've grown. I'm so glad to see the dress Serenity had her friend Annie make for you fits so well."

"Annie?" The girl asked. She hadn't before caught her benefactor's name.

"Yes, you remember Annie, don't you?"

Becca laughed. "Of course, I do. Serenity's best friend. I used to be jealous of their friendship. So how do you and Mr. Pownell enjoy living at the edge of the American frontier?"

"We love it here." Grandma Jo kissed the boy on the top of his head. "Having Caleb, Serenity, and the grandchildren so close by increases our joy. Oh, please forgive Serenity. She's rocking Seri back to sleep. The poor baby is teething again." The woman sighed as she removed six loaves of bread from the oven. "How I hate to see my little bunny hurting so badly. I am so grateful Serenity and Caleb have welcomed me into their family as if I were a blood relative."

Outside the kitchen door, Onyx barked as a rider on horseback rode toward the barn. Sammy hopped up and ran to the window that faced the stables.

"Who is it?" Grandma Jo asked.

"Looks like it's Preacher Ned. The man's in a terrible hurry." The boy dashed through the door. Rebecca pulled back an edge of a curtain to see Sammy run full steam toward the barn and Onyx lope ten feet ahead of him.

"Preacher Ned?" Rebecca asked.

"That's Annie's husband. They have two daughters who are my almost-grandchildren." The woman smiled. "Once I thought the most enjoyable thing to do was to attend fancy balls or listen to chamber music played at afternoon matinees. These days, an afternoon of hide-and-seek with Sammy or taking Seri for a stroll in the sun brings me more joy than I ever could have imagined."

Minutes later, the rider, Hobie, and Caleb rode toward town in the carriage that had brought them from Springfield. And just as suddenly, Sammy burst into the kitchen.

"There's been an accident a mile or so down the road. Daddy said to tell Mama no one was hurt. A rattler scared Brownie. The horse reared and broke the shaft. Pastor Ned was heading home from visiting Widow Cranston when he found Mrs. Landry and Miss Cristabelle stranded beside the roadway. I gotta go tell Mama!" The boy bounded toward the hallway.

"Wait! You don't want to waken Seri," Grandma Jo reasoned. "Since no one was hurt, we'll tell your mama when she lays your sister down in her cradle." The woman strode to the stove and opened the large iron kettle steaming on the burner. "The leek-potato soup for tonight's supper is simmering. I made enough to feed an army! The honey butter for our freshly baked bread is cooling in the icehouse." She pulled a watch pendant on a silver chain from a pocket in her skirt. "Your grandpa will be here by the time the men return with your folk's guests. I'd say everything is in order. Did I mention the double batch of gingersnaps I made for my favorite grandson?" She dropped the watch back into her pocket.

"Gingersnaps?" Sammy's eyes brightened. "I love your gingersnaps, Grandma."

The woman chuckled. "I thought you did."

* * * * *

When Serenity first mentioned Mrs. Landry and her daughter, Cristabelle, Becca pictured the girl to be a young child, or at the most, a preteen. Cristabelle was anything but a child. Becca gaped as Hobie entered the main entrance to the inn with an expensively dressed brunette on one arm and a fluttery blonde clinging possessively to the other.

A wide lacy collar on the older woman's teal-blue satin gown draped gracefully over her bare shoulders and upper arms. The color complimented her shiny brown hair and carefully applied makeup.

"Oh, Mr. Hobie, you're *sooo* strong. When you lifted me from the coach, I felt as light as a feather." She batted her eyelashes and cozied up to his left side. "Wasn't Mr. Hobie simply marvelous, Cristabelle?"

"Oh, my yes!" The blonde gently squeezed Hobie's bicep and batted her enormous cornflower blue eyes at him. "You are *sooo* strong and so handsome. Mr. Hobie, you leave me breathless."

Becca studied the blonde's animated face. *Lady, you are anything but breathless.* The light-blue taffeta skirt rustled as the woman, close in age to Becca, snuggled beneath the arm of the bemused man. Withdrawing a white lace fan from an unseen pocket, she waved it provocatively before her crimson lips. "I don't know what I would have done if you hadn't come along when you did to rescue me."

An uncomfortable blush crept from his neck to his forehead. "Ma'am, I am just thankful no one was injured," he mumbled as he shot a silent plea for help to his friend. A bemused smile tilted the corners of Becca's lips.

Fortunately for Hobie, Serenity came to his rescue. "What an adventure you folks had. I am grateful no one was hurt. Tell me, where are Caleb and Tavis? Didn't they come back with you?"

Hobie looked uncomfortable in the women's grasps. "No, ma'am. They stayed to repair the broken shaft. They'll be home soon, I suspect. Caleb said not to wait on supper."

The innkeeper clasped her hands before her lips in an attitude of prayer. "Willa Mae, I am sure you and Cristabelle will want to freshen up before we dine. And Hobie, I have you staying in room number four of the east wing, next door to Rebecca." She gestured in the opposite direction of the Landrys' quarters. "I filled the porcelain pitcher with hot water and set out fresh towels."

"Thank you, Mrs. Cunard." Hobie freed his arms and stepped backward.

"We'll eat in ten minutes." Serenity flashed a gracious smile at the Landrys. Slipping one arm around Hobie's arm and the other around Rebecca's, she added, "Come, sister dear. Let me show you your room. It has a large brass bed with a feather mattress Grandma Jo and I stuffed all by ourselves." The woman gave a tiny giggle at the consternation written across the Landry women's faces. "I ordered the robin-egg blue wallpaper with the hand-painted white daisies from St. Louis. I hope you'll like it."

"I'm sure I will," the girl assured her hostess. "After sleeping upright in a bouncing, swaying stagecoach for almost a month, a featherbed sounds heavenly."

"We're having potato-leek soup and freshly made bread for dinner tonight," Serenity volunteered as she opened the door to Hobie's room. "I had Ben, my husband's stable boy, bring in your luggage."

As Hobie walked past Becca, the girl teased, "Slumgullion! We're having slumgullion for supper."

Catching a part of Becca's words, Serenity turned in surprise. "Do you not like leek-potato soup? I have leftover boiled vegetables, I could reheat, if you'd prefer."

"Oh, no," Becca protested. "I am sure Grandma Jo's soup is delicious."

Later, as they gathered around the table for dinner, Cristabelle saved a place beside her for Hobie. During the meal, when the gal wasn't effusively regaling everyone with the details of the royal-blue gown she wore to her debutante ball, she spun tales about the numerous wealthy suitors she'd abandoned in New Orleans. When Cristabelle paused to catch a breath, Mama Willa Mae questioned Hobie about his family and his father's business in Placerville.

"They say men are still striking it rich in the mountains surrounding Placerville," the woman prompted.

"Not really. Most prospectors have moved on to other strikes." Hobie slathered butter on a second slice of bread. "The big mining companies have purchased the biggest and best of the veins of gold. Real money can be made supplying tools and other necessities to the working miners and the townspeople."

"And that's how your daddy made all his money, right?" Willa Mae was incorrigible. To Becca, the women's questions bordered on rudeness. "He is rich, isn't he?"

Hobie choked on the piece of bread in his mouth. "Yes, I guess you could say he's rich, but he's worked hard for his wealth."

To break the determined woman's awkward prying, Grandma Jo rose from the table. "May I refill your bowls? Or are you ready for a few gingersnaps?"

Relieved, Hobie held up his empty bowl. "I confess, I've never had a more delicious bowl of soup, Mrs. Pownell."

"It is good, of course," Willa Mae began. "Personally, I would add more butter and possibly a dollop of sour cream, don't you agree, Mrs. Cunard?"

Serenity took a deep breath. "I think Grandma Jo has found the perfect balance of smoothness and flavor. By the way, was your trip to Independence successful? You said you hoped to find a more long-term situation at one of the boarding houses."

"No, the places we visited didn't measure up to Serenity Inn's accommodations, as quaint and provincial as they may be." Willa Mae's curls danced as the woman shook her head. "I think we'll stay put until Cristabelle and I decide whether or not we wish to join a wagon train west. And you, Miss Rebecca, how long do you expect to stay here at the inn?"

The girl blinked in surprise. "I don't know. I just arrived. A while, I suspect." She stuffed another bite of jam and bread into her mouth.

* * * * *

Over the next few weeks, Rebecca felt she'd become an unwilling opponent in a tug-of-war match with Cristabelle, and Hobie was the rope. The man spent most days in the blacksmith shop with Caleb and Tavis. And in the evenings Becca avoided both Hobie and Cristabelle by helping Serenity care for the children. The girl quickly fell in love with the loquacious Sammy.

"See?" The child pointed to a wooden flume he'd constructed on his bedroom floor. "This contraption would supply water to the crops here in the valley during dry seasons. If we built a giant mill wheel along the river, like the ones that move the paddleboats, we could . . ."

She stared at the six-year-old, amazed by his logic. "You are one smart little guy, do you know that?"

"Yes, I do. Jesus gave me a good brain, and He wants me to use it to help others. By the by, Daddy says you are a sharp shooter. Could you teach me?"

Becca threw back her head and laughed. "You should really ask Hobie. He's the one who taught me."

"Yeah, I know, but Miss Cristabelle is always having Mr. Hobie take her to town or repair a latch on her humpbacked trunk or help her with some other problem." The boy wrinkled his nose. "And she's always shooing me away! Don't tell Mama, but I don't much like her!"

"I'm sure Miss Cristabelle is a very nice lady."

Sammy shook his head. "No, she's not. I heard my mama tell my daddy that Miss Cristabelle has set her cap for Mr. Hobie for his money!" The boy knitted his brow. "I'm not sure I know what that means, but it sounds real bad! You're Mr. Hobie's friend, aren't you? Why don't you tell him?"

"Maybe someday I will . . ." The boy could not understand how awkward it would be for her to broach the subject.

"This Sunday?"

The girl shook her head. "I didn't say that, but I will think about it. I promise."

"All right. Preacher Ned says, 'With God, all things are possible,' so while you think about it, I'll pray about it."

Becca smiled to herself. *Tonight, I will write to Mama and Daddy about their grandson's faith. They will be thrilled. If only I could harness a portion of his trust.* Hearing Caleb call Sammy to the parlor for family worship, Becca groaned and rose to her feet, for she knew Cristabelle Landry and her mother would attend, if only to be with Hobie.

Seated in an overstuffed chair adjacent to the sofa, Caleb opened a giant family Bible to the book of Ephesians chapter three, verse seventeen. " 'That Christ may dwell in your hearts by faith; that ye, being rooted and grounded in love . . .' "

Becca's mind wandered to her parents' home in California as he continued reading. *If I close my eyes, I can hear Papa's voice.* " 'Now unto him that is able to do exceeding abundantly above all we ask or think . . .' "

Sammy, sitting on the blue-and-white rag rug beside Becca's upholstered lady's chair, nudged his aunt's foot. "See," he whispered. "Didn't I tell you? Huh, didn't I?"

The girl chuckled at the boy's insistence "You surely did." She returned her attention to a conversation between Hobie and Caleb.

"There were times on our journey when only my faith saw me through," Hobie interjected. "I'm sure that is true for Rebecca as well. Becca, tell your family about the Apache's watering hole."

Before the girl could comply, Cristabelle interrupted. "I know what you mean. The roads between here and New Orleans are nightmarish. I

understand many stagecoaches have been robbed by highwaymen!"
Cristabelle's syrupy sweet drawl had become a major irritant for Becca.
I can always close my eyes; if only I could stop my ears as well, she thought.

CHAPTER EIGHTEEN

WOMANLY INTUITION

EVERY WEEKEND THE CUNARDS, including Becca, climbed into the family carriage to attend church. When the Landrys chose to attend as well, Hobie drove a two-seater buggy, which the ladies chose to squeeze into rather than ride in the more roomy family coach.

Seeing the little clapboard church each week produced a flood of memories for Becca. As she walked into the whitewashed sanctuary, she thought of her father and mother worshiping two thousand miles away in California.

On the way home from church one day, Becca asked her sister-in-law why the family attended Pastor Keys's church and not their friend Ned's. Serenity saddened. "We would love to, but our presence would cause trouble for Ned and Annie's congregation." The woman shook her head. "Why God's children can't worship their Father together in peace, regardless of their skin color, I do not understand!" She replaced her exasperated tone with a wistful sigh. "Maybe some day."

Before April blossomed into May, Preacher Keys had enlisted Hobie to lead the singing. His rich baritone voice counteracted the off-tune notes emitted by Widow Pendergast's heroic efforts at the wheezing pump organ. The pastor had visited his dying father in eastern Pennsylvania, and returned with a few new hymns to teach to his congregation.

Silently, Becca mouthed the words hand-printed on rag paper. " 'How happy is the pilgrim's lot, I am bound for the land of Canaan.' " Happy *is not a word I'd use to describe the pilgrim's lot, not if they traveled by the Butterfield Overland stagecoach!* While her bruises had faded, her memory still felt the pain of round-the-clock jouncing over ruts, dry creek beds, and potholes. Hobie caught her reaction to the words and grinned as he led the congregation into the second verse of the song.

The girl maintained her composure until they sang the third verse. " 'I trample on the whole delight, I am bound for the land of Canaan.' " *What does that mean anyway?* she asked herself. *"Trample on the whole delight." Was that whenever the passengers had to push the stage through a bog or up a hill?*

She tried to catch Hobie's attention a second time, only to have her smile intercepted by Cristabelle. Becca almost laughed aloud when Hobie looked their way and Cristabelle's glare blossomed into a brilliant smile. Resisting the urge to roll her eyes toward the open-beamed ceiling, Becca hid her face behind her song sheet.

Along with the new hymns, Pastor Keys preached some fresh ideas as well. "Jesus is coming soon. This is cause for rejoicing!" His face beamed with joy. "A revival is sweeping the country. You, my brother; you, my sister; we must live each day, readying our lives for our Savior's soon return."

Becca remembered the sermons her father preached on Jesus' return. The girl wondered, *Has Papa heard of this revival? Is he readying his congregation as well?* She ached to share her concerns with Hobie, but Cristabelle kept a short leash on the man.

The girl worried when Hobie appeared to be warming to Cristabelle's advances and to Willa Mae's mothering, or smothering, as Becca called the woman's actions. For a boy who'd lost his mother at an early age, the man flourished under the older woman's attention, whether it be sewing a button on his go-to-meeting shirt or patching a hole in the knee of his work britches.

"So when are you going to warn Mr. Hobie?" Sammy asked during the ride back to the inn.

She glanced back to see Hobie's carriage turn off the main road onto what Caleb called "the scenic route." "I don't know, honey. It's complicated."

"I heard Grandma Jo tell my mama that she met Mrs. Landry in New Orleans. Grandma Jo said something like, 'Willa Mae isn't the lady she pretends to be.' When they caught me listening, Mama shooed me to my room. What do you think Grandma Jo meant?"

Becca placed her arm around the boy's shoulders. "I really don't know." But she had her suspicions.

After returning home, the girl shrugged out of her go-to-meeting clothes and rushed to the kitchen to help Serenity set the table for lunch. "Will your folks be here for dinner?" Becca asked as she removed a stack of plates from the cupboard.

"No, not today. Josephine having a luncheon for the members of her book club."

The aroma of a potato-cheese casserole bubbling in the oven set Becca's taste buds to yearning. "Too bad. I had something I wanted to ask her."

"Why don't you ask Hobie to drive you into Independence tomorrow morning? You could pick up a bag of sugar and some flour for me. You and Hobie need a change of scenery."

The girl pursed her lips. "I might just do that."

Serenity opened a quart jar of green beans. "Last year, my kitchen garden yielded more green beans and corn than I could handle. Guess the Lord knew we'd have an abundant crop of guests this year. I can barely wait to see what He has in store for my humble garden this year."

Becca placed a fork beside each dinner plate. "Do you really believe God multiplies the number of green beans that grow in your garden?"

Serenity detected a note of sarcasm in her sister's voice. "Oh my, yes! Scripture says God counts the very hairs on my head." The older woman tucked a stray strand of hair into the bun at the back of her neck. "Speaking of hair, yours is certainly growing fast. By fall it will touch your shoulders."

"I hope so—about my hair growing quickly, I mean. As to the corn crop and the green bean harvest, I'm not so sure."

Serenity dumped the beans into a cast-iron pot and placed them over a flame on the stove. She turned to face her sister-in-law. "Each spring as I sow the seeds, water them, and later pull weeds determined to squeeze out my precious little plants, I pray over the sprouts. As I work, I try to visualize my best Friend Jesus digging in the soil beside me, removing pesky bugs from the leaves, and just keeping me company. Does that seem silly to you?"

Serenity continued, "Preacher Keys talks about Jesus' soon return, which is vitally important for God's people to hear, but sometimes I think we aren't to serve Him for fear of missing heaven but because we love Him." The older woman strode to the window overlooking her kitchen garden. "I'm a simple woman. I see life in simple terms. While I'm on this earth, I believe He wants me to get to know Him, to learn to trust Him, and love Him even more than I do your brother, if such a thing is possible. I guess your dad's sermons about loving God with your whole heart, soul, and mind and about loving each other as yourself stuck with me."

"I wish Papa's words stuck with me as well." Becca straightened a dinner knife beside one of the plates. A hard edge entered her voice. "On the trip across the country, I had to be resilient and strong to survive. I had no one to lean on like you can lean on my brother."

"Really? Did you ever wonder where your strength and resilience might have come from? And what about Hobie? I think you sell that young man much too short."

Becca fidgeted with the hem of the white linen tablecloth. "You don't understand. He's just Hobie. He's always been and always will be, just Hobie."

Serenity stirred the beans for a minute and then aimed the wooden spoon at her sister. "I wouldn't count on him always being there for you, sister dear. Wake up! If you keep dismissing him, one of these days, you'll awaken to find him gone, in love with another woman. Mark my words!"

"You mean a woman like Cristabelle Landry?"

"I hope not. Miss Cristabelle might not be the lady she pretends to be." Serenity removed the pot of vegetables from the burner.

"What do you mean?" the girl asked.

Serenity heaved a sigh. "It wouldn't be right for me to gossip about my guest. But I do know, gold is a rare find and difficult to keep. Trust me. The man who hurt you isn't worth losing Hobie over."

Becca whirled about, her face suffused with color. "What man?"

Serenity set her vegetables on a cold burner and walked to a cabinet where she stored her serving bowls. "The one who hardened your heart against other men."

"Who told you about Bo? Did Hobie say something? He promised he wouldn't!"

"So the man's name was Bo. *Hmm.* I've been praying that you'd tell me about him." Serenity dumped a jar of corn into a second pot and set it on the hot burner. "No one said anything to me. I knew something was eating at you the moment I laid eyes on you at the tavern in Springfield." Serenity chuckled at the astonishment revealed in the younger woman's face. "Women sense matters of the heart."

Becca recalled her talk with Sallie during the sandstorm. "And what else does your womanly intuition tell you?"

"That he hurt you deeply; that you blame yourself for falling for this Bo character, swallowing his lies. So rather than blame yourself for your lack of good judgment, you are choosing to blame God."

Onyx's barking at the kitchen door and the voices of Caleb and the other men approaching ended the conversation. Serenity removed her apron. "I'll be right back. I need to change Seri before I serve dinner. Watch that corn so it doesn't burn." At the opening to the hallway, she paused. "If you ever want to talk about it, I'm here for you, lil' sis."

When Serenity returned, everyone gathered around the table while Caleb offered a blessing. Becca and the others ate in silence while Mrs. Landry criticized the church service, the pastor's sermon, and Mrs. Keys's new cocoa-brown wool cape. "What a monstrosity! That collar looked like a groundhog had crawled onto her shoulders and died! Have you ever seen such a mangy fur piece?"

Seated across from Becca, Cristabelle fluttered her lashes and giggled like a schoolgirl. "Hobie, sweetie, you didn't say if you like my hair styled this way." The girl twisted one of the long blond ringlets that tumbled down the left side of her face. "Or do you prefer when I pin the curls atop my head? I have such thick, long hair I hardly know what to do with it all." She fluffed the ringlets and blinked innocently at Becca.

Like a deer trapped by a mountain lion, Hobie looked as if he wished he could flee. Serenity came to his rescue. "Cristabelle, may I get you another piece of the apple strudel I baked for dessert?"

"Oh, I'd love it, but we ladies must watch our figures." The girl twisted her body to give both Hobie and Caleb a better view of her slim torso.

"I'll take another piece of strudel, honey," Caleb interjected. "And by the looks of it, Hobie could use a second helping as well. So tell me, Hobie, what did you think of Pastor Keys's sermon on Ephesians chapter one, verse seven, that we make peace with God through the blood of His Son?"

Before Hobie could reply, Mrs. Landry wrinkled her nose. "Talking about blood at the dinner table. Surely there are more pleasant topics of conversations, don't you agree, Mr. Caleb?"

Becca hid her grin when the men stared at the woman in disbelief. Caleb was the first to recover. "I never thought of it like that, Mrs. Landry."

"Well, you should, Mr. Caleb. In the more refined society of New Orleans, such lapses in grace would be frowned upon." Even when scolding, Willa Mae Landry flirted with her host.

A voice from the far end of the table interrupted the awkward moment. "Papa." It was Sammy. "May I please be excused?"

"Did you finish your string beans?" The man peered the length of the table at the boy's empty plate.

"Yes, sir."

"Then, fine, you may be excused." Becca could tell by the look on her brother's face that he, too, wished he could escape. Caleb finished his second dessert in record time. As he pushed back his chair, he complimented his wife. "My, what a good meal, Serenity. As usual, you outdid yourself on the apple strudel. And, you know how I love your apple strudel!" He dotted his mouth with his napkin and rose to his feet. "If you ladies will excuse me, I need to check on Bertie. She's about to deliver her first foal. Er, excuse me, Mrs. Landry. I hope my horse's pending delivery wasn't too indelicate to your taste." He cast a condescending smile at the woman and headed out the kitchen door.

Seizing an opportune moment of escape as well, Hobie leaped to his feet. "Excuse me, ladies. Wait up, Caleb. I'll go with you."

"Oh, Hobie," Cristabelle uttered a delicate sniff. "I'll miss you."

As the door slammed behind the men, Serenity collected a handful of dishes. "My, they were in a hurry. It's unlike Caleb not to place his dirty dishes in the sink. No matter. The four of us ladies will make quick work of cleanup, won't we, Willa Mae? Rebecca, if you'll clear the dessert bowls and the silver, I'll start the water boiling. Cristabelle, would you prefer to wash or dry?"

It was Cristabelle's turn to be surprised. Both of the Landry women made a habit of slipping away whenever there was work to be done. The young woman glanced at Serenity, then at her carefully manicured nails, and then back at her hostess. "I think I prefer to dry, if it's all right with you."

"Good! Many hands make light work." Serenity filled a kettle with water and set it on the stove. At that moment, Baby Seri gave a loud wail from her room. "Oh, excuse me, ladies, the baby is awake. I need to check on her." Serenity disappeared from the kitchen.

Silently Willa Mae carried the dishes to the sink and set them on the drain board. Seizing an opportunity to pump Becca for information, she flashed a gracious smile. "So tell me, just how, er, wealthy is Mr. Masters?"

Becca blinked in surprise. "I really don't know. Mr. Masters operates a thriving mercantile in town and runs five to seven supply wagons each week to and from Sacramento. He's a nice man and a great employer."

"He is widowed, right?"

"Yes, Hobie's mom died several years ago." The kettle on the stove rescued Becca. She poured the water into the tin basin and added enough cold water to make it comfortable. "I'll wash and you dry, Cristabelle."

"Uh, all right," she answered, as Becca poured hot and then cold water into the second basin. Cristabelle stated, "Hobie and I are thinking about taking the Butterfield Overland stagecoach to California. We want to leave before the end of summer."

"Oh?" Becca swallowed hard. She swished a cotton dishrag over the top dinner plate.

"We're trying to decide if we should marry before we go or wait until we arrive in California so his father and brother can attend the ceremony." The girl tipped her head and gave Becca a catty smile. "I am sure Hobie will find it difficult to wait until we reach California to wed. You know how impatient men can be about such things."

"I don't really!" Furious, Becca rubbed the bar of lye soap into the dishcloth, wishing she could rub the caustic soap into Cristabelle's teeth. "Hobie was nothing but a gentleman to me the entire trip east."

"What can I say? You are so independent. Some men must find you intimidating. Hobie says you can shoot the head off a rattler. Why, me? I'd be a-flutter at the sight of the tiniest of reptiles, let alone stop quivering long enough to aim a gun at its head."

Becca dropped a plate in the rinsing basin, splashing water onto

Cristabelle's expensive taffeta skirt. The girl leaped back. "Hey, be careful!"

"I'm so sorry," Becca cooed. "Did I get you wet?"

Cristabelle dabbed at the water spots with the dishtowel. "You know you did!" The girl whirled about and fled the kitchen with Willa Mae in tow.

"I guess I'll finish these alone," Becca giggled. After she scrubbed the stuck-on cheese off the sides of the casserole dish, the girl clicked her tongue as she examined her nails. "Oh, dear, I've ruined my manicure."

Becca had emptied the used dishwater outside the back door when Serenity returned with Baby Seri. "So, tell me what I missed." The young mother sat down in the rocker beside the hearth to nurse Seri.

"Oh, not much, except Cristabelle's announcement that she and Hobie were getting married and moving to California. Willa Mae is accompanying them, of course. Mama has her talons out for Mr. Masters—sight unseen."

"What?"

"It's true. You were right. Hobie won't always be here for me. He's been my best friend since grade school." Becca dropped unceremoniously into the rocker opposite Serenity. "I don't know what to do. If he loves her, I can't interfere, can I?"

Baby Seri didn't seem to mind when Serenity set the chair to rocking. "If Cristabelle's claims are true, this is more serious than I thought. You definitely need to visit Josephine first thing in the morning." She adjusted the baby's blanket over her shoulder. "Tonight, when Caleb and I are alone, I will suggest that Hobie drive you to town. In the meantime, let's keep the proposed excursion between us; otherwise, you'll have an unwanted guest along for the ride."

CHAPTER NINETEEN

TRUTH TO SET ONE FREE

THE SUN HAD BARELY grazed the green hills to the east when Becca, Hobie, and the Cunard family gathered around the breakfast table. Willa Mae and Cristabelle never appeared from their rooms much before eight. Caleb opened the family Bible. "This morning I've chosen to read Proverbs three, verses five and six." He cleared his throat. " 'Trust in the LORD with all thine heart; and lean not unto thine own understanding. In all thy ways acknowledge him, and he shall direct thy paths.' " The man closed the book and folded his hands. "Let's pray."

Becca closed her eyes. Following the amen, Caleb arose from the table, grabbed his work jacket from the wall hook, and opened the kitchen door. Onyx greeted him with a loud bark. "Quiet, Onyx!" He commanded. "I'll hitch old Ben to the buckboard."

Half seated, half standing, Hobie swallowed a final spoonful of oatmeal while Serenity handed Becca her grocery list. "Thanks for doing my weekly shopping for me, Becca. With all the travelers in town purchasing supplies for the trail, it will take a lot of time rounding up everything I need. By the way, Zack's Market will give you better prices than Ross's Mercantile."

A stirring from down the hallway toward the guests' bedrooms startled Serenity to action. She grabbed Becca's shoulders and lifted the girl from her chair. "Now scoot, you two, before the morning is gone."

Serenity handed Becca her cape and bonnet, and then pushed her toward the door. "Tell Josephine to bring a couple of mincemeat pies for Sunday dinner."

Becca ran from the house with Onyx barking at her heels. Minutes later, as the supply wagon rolled past the rail fence at the edge of the property, a hand pulled back the curtain in Cristabelle's window. Becca breathed a relieved sigh. They'd made good their escape.

The wagon rolled past endless dew-laden fields of spring green. Becca gazed at Hobie's strong profile. She'd never noticed the changes in him since they had left California. *His jaw is stronger. He's lost what Mama would call his baby fat. He's become manlier, a copy of his father.*

Hobie gave her a sideways glance. "What's the matter? Why are you staring at me?"

Blushing, she glanced away. "Sorry."

During the ten-mile ride into town Becca began to have second thoughts about prying into Cristabelle's past.

"Should we do the shopping first?" Hobie asked at the edge of the city.

"Huh?" He jostled her out of her reverie. "Uh, no. I think we should see Josephine as early as possible. Mrs. Pownell has visitors for tea every Monday afternoon. The woman's a social butterfly." Becca moistened her suddenly dry lips. "She would be the center of high society regardless of where she lived."

"Didn't she once live in New Orleans before she married Serenity's father?" Hobie asked as he guided Ben down Main Street. "I wonder if she ever met Willa Mae and Cristabelle there? They would have traveled in the same social circles, right?"

"Probably so." She picked at the daisies imprinted on her yellow calico skirt. The last thing Becca wanted was for Hobie to think Josephine was bushwhacking him.

Molly, Mr. Pownell's law clerk, greeted them when they entered the office.

"Are the Pownells in?" Hobie asked.

"He is. Can I tell him who is here to see him?"

Becca frowned. She'd come to talk with Mrs. Pownell, not her husband. While they waited, the girl scanned the books on the shelves lining the walls.

"Miss Rebecca! Mr. Masters!" The gregarious lawyer bounded in the room and shook their hands. "How delightful to see you. Come into our parlor and be comfortable. My wife will be thrilled to see you."

"I understand she's not here." Becca couldn't hide her disappointment.

The lawyer held open the door to their private living quarters. "Josephine will be back from the mercantile soon. I know she needs to make a batch of thumbprint cookies to serve the ladies at her tea this afternoon. Let me get you something to drink. You must be parched."

Becca detected a note of pride in the man's voice as he spoke about his wife. "A drink would be nice. Thank you." She sat down on a needlepoint-upholstered rocker beside a marble fireplace.

"Peppermint tea? Lemonade? Ice water?" He hovered over her.

"A glass of water sounds quite refreshing, Mr. Pownell."

"Mr. Pownell?" The lawyer clicked his tongue. "We're all family, aren't we? Call me Sam, and I'll call you Rebecca. Do we have a deal?"

Try as she might Becca couldn't imagine the affable Samuel Pownell zeroing in on a lying defendant in a courtroom. Hobie stood by the long, narrow windows edged with soft gold velvet draperies.

Mr. Pownell quickly returned with two glasses of water. Behind him the front door swung open, and Josephine glided into the room carrying several bulging packages.

"I couldn't resist this pastel pink silk shawl with gold threads woven through the fibers." She unwrapped the first package and held the item up for inspection. "Mr. Courtland ordered it straight from Paris, France, can you imagine? And of course, after I bought the shawl, I absolutely had to purchase the matching parasol. But here I'm rambling on about parasols and shawls when I presume you came to speak with Samuel."

Becca shook her head. "No, I need to speak with you."

The woman arched an eyebrow and sat down on the olive-green brocade sofa across from the girl. "Me?"

"Serenity wanted me to ask you to make two mincemeat pies for Sunday dinner." Becca twisted the lace on the wrist of her cotton glove. "May I speak with you alone?"

"Oh! Of course!" Samuel gestured to Hobie. "Come, you must appraise the new mare I bought last week."

When she heard the kitchen door open and close, Becca began. "Sammy overheard you and Serenity discussing the Landrys. Last night, Serenity said she'd prefer I speak with you about it."

Josephine slowly nodded. "That little scamp. I knew my grandson heard more than he should. But, first, I'm not comfortable dishing dirt on anyone. Why do you need to know?"

"I understand you knew both women in New Orleans."

"Yes, I knew of them."

"Knew of them?" Becca cocked her head to one side. "What does that mean?"

"We didn't attend the same social functions. Let's just say we . . ." The woman hesitated.

"Cristabelle and Hobie are talking marriage. He has been my best friend since third grade. I wouldn't have survived the trip from California without him. I can't stand by and let anything bad happen to him." Becca could barely contain her anxiety. "If he and Cristabelle are in love, fine. I will back off. But if she is toying with his heart, I will scratch out her baby-blue eyes!"

"My!" A knowing grin spread across the older woman's face. "I'm glad Serenity sent you to me."

An hour later, the men announced their return by slamming the kitchen door. Josephine folded her hands in her lap. "There you have it. That is all I know firsthand."

Hobie strode into the parlor carrying his hat. "Excuse me, ladies, but Rebecca, we'd better buy the supplies on your sister's list soon, or we won't get home before dark."

"And you, Mrs. Pownell, need to bake those thumbprint cookies for your tea party this afternoon." Becca stood. Josephine rose as well. "Thank you so much. Your information explains a lot. I don't know what I will do with it, but I appreciate knowing."

Josephine hugged Becca and whispered, "Promise me you will pray before you share it with anyone. It could damage a lot of lives."

"What could damage a lot of lives?" Samuel ambled into the room behind Hobie. "What dastardly deed are you ladies cookin' up?"

Josephine withdrew a black lace fan from her skirt pocket and rapped her husband on the chest with it. "None of your business, Mr. Pownell. We ladies are entitled to our little secrets, you know."

"Speaking of secrets," the lawyer began, "two bounty hunters out of St. Louis showed up in town last week, asking about you, Rebecca. I contacted the sheriff, and he sent them packing on the next eastbound train."

* * * * *

While Hobie assembled the items on Serenity's list, Becca couldn't shake thoughts about the information she'd received from the Pownells. While her news had been good, Hobie's had not. Questions bombarded her like a swarm of angry bees. *How shall I tell him? Should I tell him? What will happen if I do tell him? Will he hate me for telling him?* The girl had never been so confused.

Hobie tapped the girl on the shoulder. "Would Serenity prefer two ten-pound bags of cornmeal or one twenty-five? Rebecca? Rebecca? Hello, are you in here?"

"Huh? Sorry, what did you say?"

The man touched her forehead with the back of his hand. "Are you feeling all right? You look flushed."

"I feel fine. Is everything loaded on the buckboard? Can we go now?" She started toward the door.

Hobie pursed his lips. "Sure. Mr. Zack charged you for the order."

"All right, whatever you say."

The man grabbed her arm as she stepped out of the store onto the boardwalk. "Wait! What is wrong?" He whirled her about to face him. "Did you hear me tell you Mr. Zack wants you to pay for the order?"

"Huh? Pay for the order? Me? Why? Serenity told me to add it to the inn's tab."

Hobie directed her toward the waiting buckboard. "I didn't think you were listening. Whatever is on your mind? You haven't been yourself since we left Pownells."

"I promise I'll tell you about it on the way back to the inn." She hiked her skirts to her ankles and climbed onto the seat before Hobie could help.

"I wish you wouldn't do that, Rebecca," he chided as he climbed aboard. "Let me be a gentleman."

An unexplained anger welled up inside her. "Don't worry, I am sure your soon-to-be bride will demand your undivided attention for years to come."

"My what?" Hobie stared at her, momentarily speechless.

Tears stung in her eyes. "Cristabelle told me about your wedding plans."

Hobie flicked the reins, inching old Ben into the jumble of covered wagons, horseback riders, and delivery carts. Tension hung between them until the road heading out of town emptied.

"We need to talk!" He shouted, "Haw!" The horse obeyed and turned off the main road onto a less used one.

Startled, Becca grabbed for the buckboard's wooden back and armrest. "Hobie, what has come over you? Where are you taking me?"

He flicked the reins a second time; the animal broke into a trot. "Don't worry, you're safe with me. I'm just a good friend, remember? Besides, according to you, I'm almost married to another woman!" The sarcasm in his voice astonished her.

If Becca had tried to reply, she would have broken a tooth as the buckboard bounced over the springtime ruts in the lightly traveled road. A gust of wind sent her bonnet into the air. It landed on a tin toolbox behind the driver's seat.

A strange combination of seething fury and stubborn determination had replaced Hobie's usual calm demeanor.

"Hobie! Have you lost your mind?" Becca gasped as the tailgate dropped open and three bags slid out of the wagon and into the road. Wheat flour flew in the air.

"Stop! Stop!" she gasped.

"What? You don't like it when someone else takes charge, do you?" he snapped, urging old Ben into a run.

Frightened, she cried out, "Hobie, you're acting crazy! We're both going to be killed!"

As suddenly as Hobie spurred the horse into a run, he pulled on the reins. The animal slowed. Becca took a deep breath and let it out slowly through her teeth. "Whatever happened back there?"

He climbed off the buckboard, turned, and offered the girl his hand. "Come! It's time we talked."

Still shaking from the wild ride, she allowed him to help her from the vehicle. The man's face remained devoid of expression when he released her hand and removed his hat. "Sorry about the flour. I'll make restitution. And I'm sorry for frightening you." He raked his fingers through his unruly hair.

Becca giggled nervously. "The ride was tame compared to the stagecoach run over the Boston Mountains." She gently rested a gloved hand on his bare forearm. "I've never seen you so angry, Hobie. What is wrong?"

"Honestly? I've never before been so angry." He ruminated a second. "For years, I've accepted your attentions like a puppy receiving scraps from his owner's table. Didn't you ever wonder why?"

She blinked in surprise. "No. I just thought you were my friend."

"Your friend? Is that all I am to you? A friend? Does a mere friend leave his home and family and travel two thousand miles across country to help his friend escape from the law?" He paused and stared at the twilight gathering over the prairie.

"Cristabelle—" she started.

"Regardless of what she led you to believe, the woman is not a part of my life—past, present, or future." He yanked a blade of grass from its stalk and nibbled on the end. "I know what you learned about the Landrys this morning. The women are con artists, swindlers. I checked them out with Sam and the sheriff when I came to town last week."

"You know? How did you come to suspect them?"

"Willa Mae asked too many questions about Pa and his money. And Cristabelle, I can't stand the way she clings to me. And can you see her battling the flies in Mariposa Wells?" he chortled, but quickly sobered. "Frankly, I want a woman with spunk—someone who challenges me out of my all-too-natural lethargy." When Becca opened her mouth to reply, he silenced her. "Let me continue. The Landry women tried their schemes on a wealthy man in New Orleans. They had to flee town in the dark of night or be jailed. That's how they found their way to Independence."

"But Cristabelle said—"

He shot Becca a sideways grin. "I can't believe you believed her. She snookered you. Why didn't you come to me? Why didn't you ask?"

Becca bit her lower lip. "After my stupid infatuation with Bo Devers, I figured that maybe I deserved to lose you to Cristabelle." She idly twisted a loose curl around her finger.

A smile flitted across the man's face. He captured the curl and spiraled it around his pinkie finger. "Do you know, in third grade, you did that whenever you missed a word in the weekly spelldown?"

"I did?" Color flooded her cheeks.

"Yup! That's when I first realized I was in love with the girl I would one day marry."

"But you were only in sixth grade. How could you know you were in love at such a young age?"

"Didn't you ever hear of puppy love?" He tipped her chin up to meet her gaze. "Puppy love is simply a love that needs time to grow. And you must admit, my love for you has certainly had time for that." He searched her eyes for several seconds. "I've laid my heart out to you, but I don't yet know how you feel about me, about us. Am I wasting my time? Is there the slightest chance you could learn to love me like I love you?"

Her breath caught in her throat.

"Tell me the truth. Don't keep me in suspense." The pleading tone in his voice broke her heart.

"All right. I've never thought of you as anything but my best friend." A wave of sadness swept across his face. He paled and turned toward the buckboard. "Wait." She grabbed his arm. "Let me finish my sentence. I said, I never thought of you as more than my best friend until I looked at you through another woman's eyes."

"Cristabelle's? I'm not sure that's a compliment. All she wants is my father's money and an escort to California."

"No, silly, through Aggie's eyes. She was right about Bo. She said he was like brass and would tarnish with time, but that you were solid gold." Becca took Hobie's hand. "I told myself that I didn't need anyone, but Sallie made me see being alone isn't such a blessing. The poor man was so lonely. Did I tell you he was going back to Visalia to court Widow Ruthie?" Her face lit up at the thought. "Isn't that amazing?"

Hobie broke into a grin. "You are something else, Rebecca Susanna Cunard."

She gave Hobie a gentle smile. "I do think I love you, Hobie."

"That's a start. We have to start somewhere, right?" Without warning he grabbed her by her arms and planted a kiss on her lips.

"Whoa! Wait a minute, cowboy." She touched her gloved hand to her lips. "I wasn't ready for that."

His forehead wrinkled with concern. "I'm going about this all wrong, aren't I?"

"Hobie, I need time to think. Everything is happening so fast between us. I feel like I'm on a whirling carousel."

He dug his toe into the earth. "I think it's time to tell you the rest of the story before we go any further."

"The rest of the story? What more can there be?"

"This is more complicated than I thought!" He rolled his eyes. "Pastor Keys is moving east to care for his aging parents. The church board has invited me to take his place."

"What? And you accepted?" Her voice scaled two octaves.

"Yes." He waited for several seconds before continuing. "I've prayed about this for several weeks. And I believe God is calling me into this. I guess I'd hoped you would join me in this mission, Rebecca, as my wife."

"Your wife?"

He ignored the note of surprise in her voice. "But I can tell, you are not ready for that level of commitment. You do need time to sort out your feelings for me, to determine if you love me enough to . . ." His words faded into the breeze. "Would you be willing for me to court you? Will you at least, give us a chance?"

A chill skittered along her spine, but she managed to nod and smile.

The next morning, Becca gazed at the face of the giant of a man conversing with her brother at the breakfast table. After Becca and Hobie made the day trip to Independence without her, Cristabelle awakened with the chickens.

Watching the gold digger sidle up to him, to see her place her hand possessively on his knee brought bile to Becca's throat.

"Anyone for seconds of French toast?" Serenity intercepted the hate-filled glares flying across the table between the two women. "How about a cup of chamomile tea? Doc says it's very calming to the spirit."

"After such a delicious meal, I could use a little exercise. Hobie, are you up to taking a walk with me? You know how much I hate snakes. And that dog hates me." Cristabelle batted her eyelashes inches from the man's face.

Hobie leaped to his feet. "Sorry, I can't, not this morning. I promised I'd help Caleb with an urgent repair. Great breakfast, Miss Serenity. Ready to go, Caleb?"

Caleb, who'd been about to ask for seconds, gulped down the last of his coffee. "Sure thing!"

Once the men left, Willa Mae and Cristabelle fled the kitchen, leaving Serenity, Sammy, and Becca to wash the dishes. Nothing could have pleased Becca more. "Serenity, can we talk?"

"Of course. What happened yesterday?"

"More than you can imagine!" Becca glanced toward Sammy who was helping clear the table, and then back at his mother.

"Sammy, I hear Seri stirring. Would you please play with her while Auntie Rebecca and I chat?"

"Aw shucks! I want to know what Grandma Jo said." He dragged his feet across the room and disappeared down the hallway.

"Keep going, Sammy. Your sister is beginning to fuss." Serenity called after him, and then whirled about, hands on her hips. "Tell me what happened."

Becca's tale took Serenity completely by surprise. "What do I do?" the girl asked. "I am so confused. I love Hobie, but I'm not sure I love him enough to become a preacher's wife. I'm not my mother. I don't have her patience."

"Your mama didn't always have patience." Serenity dried the last kettle and placed it on the shelf. "I remember." She dried her hands on the dishtowel, walked to the table, and opened Caleb's Bible. "If I were you, I'd start by reading James chapter one, verses five and six." She flipped through the onionskin pages. " 'If any of you lack wisdom, let him ask of God, that giveth to all men liberally. . . . But let him ask in faith, nothing wavering,' " she read. "Honey, you need to pray like you've never prayed before. Caleb and I will be praying as well. How soon does he expect an answer?"

Becca shrugged. "He just asked if he could court me."

"One important fact you need to remember," Serenity began, "you will not be marrying a preacher; you'll be marrying a man."

During the following week, Cristabelle and Willa Mae noted the change in Hobie. The man brought Becca a ring of daisies at breakfast. He placed a posy of violets tied with a lavender ribbon on her dinner plate. The man anticipated her every move. After each meal, Serenity shooed everyone from the kitchen to give him time alone with Becca.

By Friday the Landry women asked Caleb to take them into town. They said they heard tell of a small cottage available to rent. "Being nearer the city is more suited to our tastes than living out here in the wilderness," Willa Mae explained.

That evening, after family worship, Caleb took Seri from his sister's arms. "Here, I'll help Serenity put the children to bed this evening.

Over the last ten years, many of our guests have enjoyed taking a stroll to the top of the hill at sunset. The view is incredible. Serenity and I have discovered that the view clears the head as well as the heart."

Once outside, Hobie fell into step beside Becca. "That was awkward."

Hobie reached for her hand. "Yes, it was. Sorry. Your brother's not too subtle, is he?"

"No, I'm afraid not. I guess he took after my mother." Rebecca enjoyed the warmth of her hand in his. "Will you be moving into the parsonage after the Keyses leave?"

Their hands swung in syncopation to the rhythm of their gait. "It looks that way. They're leaving most of their furniture for me."

"That's nice of them. So it sounds like you're all set." The toe of her boot caught on a rock. She started to fall, but he steadied her. "Do you ever plan to return to California?" she asked.

"Not until they lay two thousand miles of railroad ties between Independence and Placerville. Which reminds me, my father wrote. He told me Bart had awakened from his coma. He admitted that some gambler had caught him cheating."

"Wonderful." She squealed and threw her arms around his neck. "I no longer need to look over my shoulder all the time." Instinctively, Hobie took her in his arms and lifted her off the ground. Her feet dangled twelve inches in the air. Onyx, sensing the woman's joy, barked and jumped up on Hobie's legs.

"Down, Onyx, down." The man slowly lowered the girl to her feet. His hat cast shadows across his face.

"Hobie, why haven't you kissed me this past week?" She could feel his racing heart beat through his plaid work shirt.

"Do you want me to?"

"Yes, I do. I'm so comfortable with you, I've been afraid there'll be no real spark between us." She focused her attention on the top button of his shirt.

"Don't be so sure," he whispered, his breath tickling the side of her face. His fingers caressed her shoulder and then glided slowly along her neck to gently tousle her curls. A warm sensation went along her spine. With his other hand, he drew her closer to his chest.

"Hobie." The girl found it difficult to breathe.

"Yes, Rebecca?" He tilted her head upward and kissed the tip of her nose. "Tell me again how there's no spark between us."

"Hobie, I . . ."

Soft as the flutter of a butterfly's wings, his lips brushed across hers. "Yes?"

She felt his lips arch into a smile against her cheek. The girl closed her eyes and willed him to kiss her again. He obliged, not with a flutter of butterfly wings, but with the firm kiss of a man in love. The power surge that shot through her startled her.

"Hobie, I . . ." She staggered back. "Please, I'm not ready. I need to think."

Obviously unnerved as well, the man released her. "Did I misread you? Did I presume too much?"

"No, I have no doubt but that I love you very much. But a preacher?"

He heaved a sigh. "What can I say, Rebecca? I vow to love you with my whole heart. I will be faithful to you till the day I take my dying breath. I will do whatever it takes to make you happy, anything except go against what God is asking me to do." He'd never before sounded so forceful, so determined.

She leaned her head on his chest. "I know. And I'd never ask you to go against God's will."

"I want to marry you, but not at such a high cost." He gently took her hands in his. "Ten years down the road, I want you to love me more, not less. And yet, I can't bear the thought of losing you. So it looks like you and I have some serious praying to do."

Sadness overwhelmed her as she started down the hill toward the inn.

"Wait!" He caught her arm with his hand. "We can't let this game go on much longer, as pleasant as it is. I'm preaching my first sermon this weekend. It's on Psalm thirty-seven, verses four and five."

" 'Delight thyself also in the Lord; and he shall give thee the desires of thine heart,' " Becca said from memory, remembering how she'd thrilled at the text whenever her father quoted it.

Hobie drew her back into his arms and held her fast. " 'Commit thy way unto the Lord; trust also in him; and he shall bring it to pass.' Is it God's will for us to marry? I don't know. For me, it's right. But you must be sure for both of our sakes."

Reluctantly, he released her. Side by side but not touching, they walked down the hill, lost in their own thoughts. As he unlatched the backyard gate, Hobie paused. "If you decide to refuse my hand in marriage, to refuse to marry this preacher, sleep in instead of attending church tomorrow morning. If you accept my proposal with your whole heart; if you are willing to become the wife of a simple country preacher, sit in the front pew." With that, he turned and strode toward the stables.

The next morning when Becca arrived to help Serenity fix breakfast, she asked after Hobie. "He already left for church."

Serenity set a platter of scrambled eggs and a basket of freshly baked blueberry muffins on the table. "He said he needed extra time to work on his sermon. You are going to be there to hear his first presentation, aren't you?"

Becca filled one of the cups with peppermint tea. "I guess that remains to be seen."

CHAPTER TWENTY

MARRYING THE ENTIRE PACKAGE

THE WORSHIPERS FILED INTO the church amid a bevy of kisses, hugs, and neighborly greetings. As they sought their places, the organ wheezed out a reasonably recognizable rendition of "Lo, What a Glorious Sight Appears."

Hobie's hands shook as he strode out of the pastor's study. As he crossed the platform, the young preacher noticed that while several worshipers sat on the front pew, one was missing. His heart sank. He sighed and turned to the congregation.

"Let's all stand and sing the chorus together." His eyes misted; his voice cracked with emotion as he sang, "O that will be joyful, joyful, joyful!" He looked away to clear his throat. As he did, there was a rustling of skirts in the back of the church. Caleb, holding Seri, and Serenity with Sammy in tow made their way to an empty pew.

Hobie moistened his lips and studied the song sheet on the pulpit to regain his composure. When he lifted his eyes, he gazed into the smiling face of his beloved, sitting on the aisle in the very front row. With renewed gusto he swung his arm in time to the music. "O, that will be joyful when we meet to part no more!"

Taking a deep breath, Hobie opened a brand-new Bible and removed several sheets of paper. "I had two sermons planned for this morning: one about the promises of divine leading in our lives, and the other based on a favorite verse of mine, Jeremiah thirty-three, verse one, er, I mean, Jeremiah thirty-one, verse three."

His gaze never left Becca's face as he quoted the words of the text. " 'Yea, I have loved thee with an everlasting love: therefore with loving-kindness have I drawn thee.' A second verse, though no less important, is found in the last part of Hebrews thirteen, verse five, 'I will never leave thee, nor forsake thee.' "

Becca stared transfixed as the man she loved delivered a stirring sermon on God's unchanging love. As the congregation stood to sing the closing song, Hobie stepped down from the platform, grabbed her hand, and swept her down the middle aisle to the open church doors. Graciously Rebecca stood by his side as the parishioners filed out of the building. One after another, the men shook his hand with words such as, "Good sermon, Pastor. Welcome to the pulpit." And one after another, the women, old and young, giggled and hugged Becca.

The Cunard family was the last to leave. Becca gave Serenity a knowing smile. "Don't worry. I'm marrying the man, not the preacher." Her face glowed.

"I'm so happy for you." Serenity gave Becca a squeeze. "By the quality of Hobie's delivery this morning, I'd say you're marrying the entire package, sister dear."

If you enjoyed

KAY D. RIZZO'S

Serenity Inn series,

you'll certainly be blessed by her

Chloe Mae Chronicles.

Enjoy this preview from
Book 1 in the series!

Flee
My Father's
House

THE CHLOE MAE CHRONICLES

1

Growing Pains

Tears stung my eyes as rain drummed against my bedroom window. Angry clouds belched thunder, rattling the window panes. Frightened yet fascinated, I pressed my nose against the glass to better view my cozy little world going berserk.

A boom of thunder and a charge of lightning merged into one terrifying jolt. The sound of splintering followed by a crash tingled me with fear as a massive limb from the oak tree across the road hit the ground. *Poor Patches,* I thought, *he's probably cowering under the front porch.*

I glanced about the eerie black-and-gray world inside my bedroom. Even the red-and-yellow calico quilt draped about my shoulders looked gray. I buried my face in my arms. The violence of the lightning storm mirrored the hurricane growing within me. My tumbling thoughts pushed and shoved like a batch of kids yammering for licorice sticks.

Growing up isn't fair! If I had my way, I'd stay ten years old forever. That's the year before Worley, my pesky brother, was born and before my older sister, Hattie, broke her hip by falling off the back of the wagon during a church hayride. The six years since had grown nothing but worse. I hardly noticed when my oldest brother, Riley, left home to work as foreman for Mr. Holmes, a gentleman farmer, or when my second oldest brother, Joe, got a day job at the Chamberlain stables.

However, when Hattie's twin, Myrtle, married Franklin Stone and moved into town, my childhood came to an end. Overnight, I was expected to pick up Myrtle's share of the household and farm chores while my former responsibilities moved down the line to my little sister, Orinda, Ori for short.

I learned early that being the fifth child in a large family had its advantages. At times, my rank allowed me to become almost invisible. Whenever I found the work too disagreeable or the task too boring, I'd pass it down to a younger brother or sister. If that plan failed, I'd complain until, in sheer desperation, Ma would assign the chore to one of my older siblings. And if worst came to worst, I would wait until no one was watching, then sneak away to my own special hiding place, a room in the attic of the barn where Pa dried and stored his herbs.

The sight and smell of drying mustard, parsley, and oregano plants hanging from the rafters made me feel safe. I knew better than to touch any of the containers or tamper with the assortment of tools strewn across Pa's heavy oak workbench.

Tucked under the eaves, behind a massive camelback trunk where Ma kept her treasures from Ireland, I stored my treasures, a stack of books from the town library. There I would curl up with the family mongrel, Patches, and read by the light seeping in between the wallboards until either the daylight faded, the crisis passed, or the next mealtime arrived. Other times I would sit on the floor with my arms wrapped around my knees and watch my father create his healing elixirs.

Joseph Riley Spencer's knowledge of herbs came from his Scottish grandmother, Chloe Mae McRiley, after whom I was named. Since the only other medical person, Doc Simms, lived in the town of Bradford, on the western side of Potter County, Pa assumed the responsibility of caring for our neighbors as best he could. He depended on Auntie Gert, the local midwife, to take charge of the birthings.

In addition to his medical practice and the small herd of Jerseys he milked, Pa worked for the Standard Oil Company as a pipeline inspector. His job was to check the pipes for leaks and damage. Whenever I wasn't in school, he would take me with him.

On these excursions, Pa loved to talk politics, from the Indian uprisings out West to President Cleveland's money policy, from voting rights for women to Japan's war on China. He ranted against the railway strike in Chicago and praised the president for breaking it. He applauded the Woman's Christian Temperance Union's battle to destroy demon whiskey and cursed William Jennings Bryan for wanting to cheapen the nation's gold standard with silver. My father knew everything there was to know in the whole wide world. Whenever my enthusiasm bubbled over and I told him so, he would chuckle and tug one of my waist-length, flame-red braids.

"Chloe Mae, you're good for me," he would say. And I would tuck away the praise for the days I didn't feel quite so special. We shared something else—fiery red hair, freckles, and green eyes. The other children in the family inherited Ma's sandy brown hair. With the birth of each new baby, I secretly prayed that my specialness would remain intact.

The day my mother went into labor with Dorothy, my sister Hattie, Ma, and I spent the entire day in the backyard doing the family wash. Scrubbing canvas breeches and linsey-woolsey shirts was hard work. Good old Patches dodged between our feet, thinking the three of us were there for his pleasure. I had pinned the last sheet to the clothesline when I spotted Pa and my older brothers coming up the road.

I hurried around to the back of the house, where Ma and Hattie were dumping the rinse water. "Pa's comin' home."

Exhausted, Ma straightened and stroked her lower back. The bulge produced by the unborn baby threatened to topple her forward. The men'll be wantin' supper right away, I suppose."

Hattie limped to Ma's side and guided her toward the house. "Now don't you worry about supper, Ma. Chloe and I can take care of everything."

I glared at Hattie. *Thank you very much for volunteering my services!* After all, I was tired too. My glare passed unheeded. Hattie wrapped an arm about Ma's shoulders and led her toward the back door. "Chloe, you finish up out here while I help Ma inside and get the johnnycake bakin'."

Grumbling about the unfairness of life, I dried out the washtubs and returned the laundry supplies to the storage shed. The aroma of bubbling hot vegetable stew erased all thoughts of mistreatment from my mind as I stepped inside the kitchen pantry. I could hear my seventeen-year-old brother, Joe, telling Hattie and the younger children about his first day of work at the Chamberlain stables.

Cyrus Chamberlain, Jr., the manager of Standard Oil Company's interests in Shinglehouse, as well as Pa's supervisor, owned the finest stables in Potter County. So when Mr. Chamberlain wanted to hire the finest groom in the county, neighbors recommended my brother Joe. Joe had a knack with horses. Pa said Joe spoke their language.

"How did it go today, Joe?" I called as I breezed into the kitchen through the pantry door. Amby, Jesse, and Worley sat at the table, eagerly listening to Joe, while my little sister Ori carried steaming bowls of stew to the table for Hattie.

"Oh, Chloe Mae, you should see those horses—every one of 'em a thoroughbred." For some reason, Joe and I always sought one another's approval. Now I was a bit jealous that he was being paid to do just what he wanted while I stayed at home, scrubbing dirty work pants on a washboard and chasing bratty little brothers and sisters out of the pantry.

"Humph!" I snorted. "Seems to me that a horse is a horse is a horse, regardless of its folks."

Pa stepped into the kitchen, closing my parents' bedroom door behind him. "Hardly! Bloodlines will tell in a quality horse or a quality human being. Look at all of you children-every one of you a thoroughbred."

We laughed as Pa sat down at the head of the table and opened the family Bible. "John 6:13: Therefore they gathered them together, and filled twelve baskets with the fragments of the five barley loaves, which remained over and above unto them that had eaten. Then those men . . .' "

As Pa read the story of Jesus feeding the five thousand, Amby's stomach growled in protest. Pa glanced his way and smiled. "Guess we have a few hungry stomachs of our own here tonight. What do you say we have the blessing?"

It didn't take long after Pa's amen to empty our bowls and to clean every crumb of corn bread from the platter in the center of the table. Hattie looked at our pitiful faces and laughed. "Don't worry; I made an extra pan of johnny cake."

While I dished up seconds of the stew, Hattie removed the second pan of corn bread from the oven. She turned to set the hot pan on the breadboard at the same moment I whirled about to place a bowl of stew in front of my nine-year-old brother, Jesse. Instinctively, I squealed and leapt back.

Hattie's limp prevented her from moving as quickly. The pan thumped to the floor as she lifted her hands to protect herself from the stew. The scalding liquid splashed across the palms of her hands and her bodice. She screamed in pain.

Pa leapt from the table and rushed her to the wet sink Thrusting her hands under the spout of the pump, he grabbed the handle and began pumping. Well water gushed out onto her hands. "Hattie, keep your hands under the cool water. Joe, take over the pumping while I run to the barn for some burn ointment."

The younger children and I scrambled to clean up the food that spilled on the floor. Before Pa could return with the ointment, Patches started barking at the front door. Jesse looked out the hall window, then opened the door before the visitor could begin knocking. Pa entered the back door as George Neff, a farmer from over Sunnyside way, burst in through the front. "My son Merton fell off the roof of the barn. He's hurtin' real bad!"

"I'll get my doctorin' bag." Pa shoved the jar of ointment into Jesse's hand and ran into the bedroom. "Annie, will you be all right while I . . ."

I didn't hear my mother's reply, but within seconds, Pa reappeared. Grabbing his hunting jacket from the peg behind the door, he shouted orders at each of us. "Hattie, apply the ointment to your burns. Chloe, after you clean up here, get the little ones settled down for the night. Joe, you help her, especially with the boys." He shook his finger at six-year-old Worley. "And, you, young man, don't give Joe or Chloe a rough time, you hear?" Pa handed his medicine bag to Mr. Neff and hauled on his jacket.

"Chloe, keep checking on your mother. She's actin' like it's her time, but she has a good three weeks to go." Joe and I assured him we could take care of everything.

Joe put ointment on Hattie's burns while I heated a kettle of water on the stove for the supper dishes. He appointed twelve-year-old Amby to oversee the dishwashing crew before he helped Hattie upstairs to her room. When I finished cleaning the kitchen, I hurried upstairs. I found Hattie sitting on the edge of the bed, rocking back and forth and moaning.

"Oh, Hattie, I am so sorry. Honest, I didn't know you were right behind me." I wept as I guided the sleeves of her dress over her bandaged hands.

She smiled through her tears. "It was an accident. I should have looked where I was going."

By the time I tucked her in her bed, Ori appeared, her lower lip quivering with disappointment. "Joe says I'm supposed to go to bed, and without my story too!"

I scooped my little sister into my arms and carried her to the massive bed she and I shared. "If you hurry and get into your nightdress, I'll tell you a story while I brush out your braids, all right?"

The little girl nodded eagerly. She scurried about the room getting ready for bed. The sounds of my younger brothers' griping filled the stairwell as Joe herded them up to their room across the hall. *Thank goodness for Joe!* I thought. At least I didn't have to settle the boys down for the night.

When Ori finished dressing for bed, I unwound her braids and drew the hairbrush through her brown, shoulder-length mane. "Once upon a time there was a beautiful queen . . ." My imagination soared as I described my favorite Bible character. "Of course, Queen Esther had shimmering red hair."

"Oh, Chloe," Ori groaned. "The beautiful ladies in your stories always have to have red hair like yours."

"Because I'm the one telling the story. When you tell the story, you can make them have black hair or golden hair." I tickled her stomach. "Or no hair, for that matter!" She giggled. I guided my sister to the bed and tucked the covers up around her chin.

"Where was I? Oh, yes, the beautiful queen had long, fiery-red hair. That's what the handsome king fell in love with-her hair!" Ori snuggled down and closed her eyes. My story grew far beyond anything the Bible writers intended. Long before I executed the dastardly, evil Haman on his own gallows, my little sister was sound asleep. I brushed a stray curl from the sleeping child's face, kissed her forehead, then stood up. Tiptoeing to the side of Hattie's bed, I asked, "Are you going to be all right? Can I get you anything before I go downstairs to see about Ma?"

She shook her head. "I'll be fine."

I stole one last glimpse at the sleeping Ori and stepped out of the room. Joe met me in the hall. "Ma needs you. I think that baby isn't going to wait any three weeks to be born."

My eyes widened in horror. Pa was gone. Hattie couldn't deliver the baby with her burned hands. Myrtle was in town. So was Auntie Gert. Neither Joe nor I knew anything about birthing. I grabbed my skirt and petticoats and descended the stairs three at a time. Joe bounded after me, shushing my every step. "You're going to wake Worley!"

At that moment, I didn't particularly care as I rushed into my parents' bedroom. My mother lay on her side, moaning. Sweat beaded on her frighteningly pale face. Sweat drenched the pillowslip beneath her head. I pushed aside the locks of heavy brown hair pasted to her forehead.

Why would any woman in her right mind be willing go through such torture? I remembered Pa reading from Genesis about Eve's being cursed to bear children in pain. Right then and there, standing beside my parents' bed, I decided marriage and babies were absolutely not for me. And when I got to heaven, I'd have a thing or two to tell Mother Eve too.

Gathering my courage about me, I inched closer. Suddenly Ma's eyes flew open. She gasped, "Chloe, the baby's coming. Get Auntie Gert!"

"Oh, right—get Auntie Gert!" I bolted from the room, colliding with Joe in the doorway, his eyes bulging with fear.

"What are we going to do? Should I go for Pa?"

Terrified, I shouted in his face, "No, go get Auntie Gert!" As he ran to saddle Dulcie, a cry came from the bedroom. I whirled about and rushed back to my mother.

"Chloe! Forget Auntie Gert! The baby . . . just do as I . . ."

I leapt away from the cast-iron bedstead. "I can't! No! Joe's getting Auntie Gert."

My mother rolled her head from side to side and panted as if she'd run all the way to Haney's Mercantile without stopping. "No! I need you. Listen, do everything I say . . ." Her words crumbled into a grimace. When the contraction subsided, she moaned, "Get the birthing linens out of the chest at the foot of the bed. Go boil some water."

Step by step, she explained everything I would need to do throughout the delivery. Determined to carry out her instructions, I argued with myself all the way to the hand pump. *I can do this; I can do this! No, you can't; no, you can't!*

Standing in the middle of the kitchen, I threw my hands up in the air and wailed, "Oh, dear Father, I can't do this. I just can't. Please help me help Ma." After my cry for help, I can't say I felt filled with a sudden surge of confidence, but I did sense a flicker of hope. While I didn't really know Pa's God very well, I figured my father had established a strong enough relationship over the years that He would at least help me for Pa's sake. *Yes, God, Ma and I will get through this ordeal. It wouldn't hurt if the baby helped a little too,* I decided.

As I dashed about the kitchen, I could hear Hattie upstairs quieting the younger children, whose sleep had been disturbed. I grabbed a clean washcloth, filled Ma's porcelain wash basin with cool water, and carried it to the bedside. I found her writhing in pain. I couldn't bear to see my mother suffering. Tears streamed down my face as I rinsed the sweat from her forehead and face. "Don't worry, Ma. Joe will be back with Auntie Gert in no time at all, you'll see." My words sounded hollow, even to me.

"It's too late!" she cried out in agony. "It's too late!"

I wanted to run, to hide, but I couldn't. For the first time in my life, Pa, Riley, Myrtle, Hattie, and Joe couldn't help her. My mother had only me. She needed me; she depended on me. Terrified I'd make some irreversible mistake, I recited aloud the directions she'd given me, all the while trying to comfort Ma. In spite of my fear, at some point in the delivery, my actions seemed to feel almost instinctive, natural.

Finally lusty squalls filled the air as I held my slippery newborn sister in my hands. Indignation filled her scrunched-up face. I laughed as she waved her arms and kicked strong little legs. The more she kicked, the harder I laughed, all the while sniffing back tears of relief. She was alive, and so was my mother. Shouting above the infant's squalls, I lifted her heavenward.

"A healthy baby girl—thank You, Father, thank You!"

When I heard Ma's weak laughter, I remembered that my task was not yet completed. I don't know how she did it, but Ma patiently guided me through the rest of the birthing process. As I carried out her instructions, my attention kept wandering to the tiny, flannel-wrapped bundle by her side. I was sure I'd never seen anything so beautiful, so perfectly formed as that precious girl-child.

"What are you going to call her, Ma?" I asked as I gathered up the soiled linen to take to the back porch.

"Your pa and I chose the name Dorothy Estelle, after his great aunt." My mother glanced down and held out a pinkie finger to the infant.

The baby wrapped her little fist around her finger and tried to draw it into her mouth. "However, if it's all right with him," Ma looked up at me, her eyes glistening with tears, "I'd like to name her Dorothy, after his aunt and Mae, after you."

I bit my lip and nodded. "I'd like that, Ma." I'd never felt as close to my mother as I did at that moment. Maybe our natures were too different—maybe too similar, I didn't know which—but we always seemed to be at odds. Pa said I'd inherited Ma's Irish temper and his Scottish stubbornness.

I deposited the bundle of linens on the canning shelf on the back porch and hurried upstairs. Hattie would be waiting to hear the news. I tiptoed up to our bedroom. "It's a girl, a baby girl," I whispered. "Her name is Dorothy Mae. She's beautiful, utterly beautiful. She has big blue eyes and a shock of bright red—"

I stopped midsentence. For the first time I realized I hadn't even considered the color of the baby's hair. I put my hand to my mouth to suppress my laughter. "Dorothy has red hair. Isn't that amazing?"

Delighted with my discovery, I hugged Hattie and hurried back downstairs. My mother had drifted off to sleep. Her lips curved upward into a gentle smile, replacing the earlier lines of agony. A hint of blush highlighted her delicately carved cheekbones. For the first time in my sixteen years, I saw her as a young girl instead of an overworked housewife and mother.

The infant squirmed in the crook of her arm. As I reached for the baby, my mother's eyes opened slowly. "Would you like me to hold Dorothy so you can rest?"

Ma smiled and nodded. Reverently, I took the baby into my arms, walked over to Ma's mahogany rocker, and sat down.

The sleeping infant nestled against me. I couldn't believe how perfectly the tiny bundle fit in my arms. As natural as breathing, I began to rock and hum a lullaby. The words soon followed.

"Hush, little baby, don't say a word; Papa's gonna buy you a mockingbird . . ." The lullaby affected me in the same way it did my newborn sister. I closed my eyes for a moment and felt someone lifting Dorothy out of my arms. My eyes flew open. "No."

"Shh, it's all right, Chloe Mae. It's just me." Pa's six-foot frame towered over me. Joe stood behind him in the doorway. Auntie Gert stood on the opposite side of the bed, her face flushed with happiness. Suddenly I realized my work was done. Grown-ups were there to take over. I sighed with relief. "Oh, Pa, I'm so glad you're home. I was so scared—"

"*Shh,* your mama needs her sleep. Why don't you come out to the kitchen and tell us all about it? Auntie Gert says you did a fine job."

I followed the three of them from the room. Before my parents' bedroom door had closed behind me, Auntie Gert clapped her gnarled hands with delight. "Praise God! He has answered my prayer! Now I can rest in peace."

Pa nodded. "Yes, it looks like He has answered your prayer, old friend." My father went on to explain that arthritis made midwifery increasingly difficult for the seventy-five-year-old woman. He paused and eyed me curiously, then turned to Auntie Gert. "Would you be willing to train Chloe, kind of as an apprentice? The child's got a good head on her shoulders."

The woman's eyes danced with enthusiasm. "If she is willing to learn."

Everyone looked my way. "I-I-I guess so . . ." I went to bed that night uncertain of what I might have gotten myself into.

A few days later, when Pa discussed Auntie Gert's offer with Ma, she demurred. She believed that a girl my age shouldn't be delivering babies or even be knowledgeable of the process of childbirth until after marriage. Yet, she freely admitted that I had a genuine gift of comfort and healing. After thinking about it a couple of weeks, Ma reluctantly gave her permission.

I began accompanying Auntie Gert when she attended deliveries, and found I enjoyed being her assistant.

When school opened in the fall, my mother decided it would be best if I didn't attend. As Ma explained, mothers would feel it unseemly for me to attend classes with their sons and daughters during the day and deliver their "young-uns" at night.

I missed my friends. Pa tried to make up for my loss by allowing time whenever we went into town for me to go to the library for books to read. Each day after work, he'd pick me up at Auntie Gert's. On the ride home, he not only shared his ideas on local and national events, but encouraged me to voice my own opinions too. Usually they echoed his.

Heavy gray clouds blotted out the sun as Pa and I headed home one

Monday evening. I tightened my woolen scarf about my neck and face, then burrowed deeper into my coat. Overhead, a flock of geese disappeared over the southern horizon. I sighed. "Looks like Indian summer's over for this year."

Pa grunted. "Probably so. I suppose those Yukon prospectors have given it up for winter by now." For the last several months the newspapers had reported tales of the fabulous caches of gold found in the Yukon Territory.

Pa stared off into the distance. "Yep, they called it 'Seward's folly.'" A glint of adventure flashed in his eyes. "Sure would like to get me a grubstake and head north."

I listened as he spun his dreams of life in the frozen northland. *Imagine growing up in the land of the midnight sun—living in a snow house and eating walrus blubber. Eaugh!* My imagination halted at that thought.

"Maybe next spring . . ." His voice drifted off into the silence of knowing that his roots sank too deeply in the Pennsylvania soil for him to do much more than dream.

Eager to maintain the moment of magic he'd created, I voiced my own fantasy. "Oh, Pa, when I grow up, I'm going to travel all over the world. I want to see everything there is to see."

He chuckled into his bushy red beard. "You have the heart of an explorer, Chloe Mae. Too bad you were born female."

I cocked my head to one side. "What does being a girl have to do with traveling?"

As he halted the team in front of our house, Patches bounded around the house. Pa glanced toward me and smiled sadly. "A woman was made to serve her husband and to bear his children. That's God's plan." His tone of genuine regret fueled my zeal.

"Well, it's not my plan. I don't mind delivering babies, but I sure don't intend to bear any of my own."

Twelve-year-old Amby raced from the house as Pa helped me down off the buckboard. "Unharness the team, son."

My father draped his arm over my shoulders and sighed. His sigh rankled me further. I pulled away from his touch.

"How can you be so out of date? We're living on the brink of the twentieth century. Four states already have granted women the right to vote. In no time at all, the rest of the country will follow suit—you said so yourself."

He shook his head and walked up the steps to the porch. "Chloe Mae, it's going to take more than the right to vote to change the course of history."

I stormed past him into the house. Tugging my bonnet off my crown of braids, I tossed it onto an empty peg behind the door. I thundered up the stairs with a parting prophecy. "You wait; you'll see. I'm not going to spend the rest of my life chasing after a passel of kids—female or not!"

"Chloe?" Hattie stood beside the table, slicing a loaf of fresh bread for supper. By the stove Ma dished out the boiled potatoes onto a platter.

I threw myself onto my bed and buried my face in a down pillow. In spite of the pillow, I heard the front door slam and my mother greet my father. "What bee got into Chloe's bonnet?"

I thought, *Ah, she'll understand. She's a woman; she'll set him straight.*

Instead, when she heard his answer, she snapped at him. "Serves you right, Joseph Riley Spencer. I've been telling you all along not to fill her head with world events and—and all that man stuff. How did you expect her to react?" Ma continued to sputter. "You've allowed her to read and to learn things far beyond her station in life. You've applauded the appalling behavior of those insufferable suffragettes." I could hear dishes slamming and cooking utensils clanging about the kitchen.

My father's soothing tones drifted up the stairs. "Now, Annie, don't get your Irish up. When the time comes, she'll know her God-given place and fill it admirably."

"*Humph!* Well, that time isn't so far off, you know! Remember, she turns seventeen in August. And if your rule was good enough for Riley and good enough for Myrtle, and now for Joe, it must apply to your precious Chloe as well!" The back door slammed. My brothers thundered in from doing the evening chores, ending my parents' discussion.

The aroma of gravy simmering on the back burner coaxed me back downstairs. The look of defiance on my face went unnoticed when Joe burst into the house. He shed his coat and hung it on the empty peg beside my bonnet. "Looks like a storm's brewin'. Could have snow by mornin'. Hey, what's up?"

Ma set the platter of potatoes in the center of the table with a thud and narrowed her eyes toward Pa. "Nothing! Absolutely nothing!"

Clearing his throat, Pa strode over to Ma and planted a kiss on her cheek. "Remember what the Pennsylvania Dutch say, son. 'Kissin' don't last; cookin' do.' And your ma sure knows a lot about good cookin'! So let's say we enjoy some of it while it's hot."

We took our places about the table. Pa opened the Spencer family Bible that his parents had brought from Scotland. The mantel clock ticked off the minutes while Pa searched for a verse to read. When he finally began to read, I recognized the passage instantly and sank lower into my chair, my arms tightly folded across my chest.

"Who can find a virtuous woman? for her price is far above rubies." He read all the rest of Proverbs 31. Out of the corner of my eye, I could see determination on my mother's face. While my younger brothers and little sister wriggled with impatience and Hattie fidgeted with her fork, Joe frowned, his face wreathed with confusion.

After the blessing, the usual banter of the dinner table replaced the earlier tension. The storm inside the farmhouse subsided, while outside, the first snowflakes of the season drifted past the kitchen window. By the time we'd each devoured a serving of apple cobbler, the topic was forgotten.

2

Babies Aplenty

Once the force of winter set in, so did Auntie Gert's arthritis, making it difficult for her to leave the warmth of her kitchen. I would sit beside her as she described some of the problems in a difficult delivery.

"Your biggest problem, Chloe, is going to be dealing with your losses. Perhaps that's where your mother is right. You are too young to face the fact that, sooner or later, you will face death." The old woman sighed and rubbed the fingers of her left hand. "The mystery of life is seldom far from the reality of death. And I have no easy answers except for what I find in the Good Book. If you search them out for yourself, God's promises will mean more to you."

I smiled and nodded, knowing that's what Auntie Gert expected of me. My parents had always taught me to respect my elders. The first week of December, Auntie Gert announced that my midwifery training was over. I was on my own.

I soon learned that the worse the weather or the more tired I felt, the more likely it would be that some baby in the county would insist on being born. When a call for help came, Pa would hitch the horses to the wagon, or the cutter, if the roads were covered with snow, and we would head for the neighbors' farmhouse to bring a new life into the world. Our patients paid Pa with sacks of potatoes, chickens, eggs, occasionally a side of beef—whatever they could afford. I liked knowing that my efforts contributed to the family food supply.

While I missed Auntie Gert, there was so much to learn about the entire healing process. I spent each evening with Pa, learning which herbs cured which ailments and which ones eased the symptoms. We worked side by side, grinding up herbs for potions and elixirs. Up in the herb room and while on house calls, he treated me differently—more as an adult than a child. Soon he took me along on all his medical calls.

The biting winds of January increased the bouts with sheet colds and pneumonia throughout the community. As the winter intensified, we talked less about politics and more about our patients and their problems.

The subzero temperatures in February didn't limit the community's need to socialize. Our recreation centered around the school and the county grange hall. When the town's only church, the Community Methodist church, burned down in 1895, a few of the families took to meeting in the grange hall. My parents attended whenever a circuit-riding preacher arrived because Pa didn't appreciate Mr. Haney's long-winded sermons. My favorite was the Baptist preacher. He really knew how to sing.

Each winter the people of Shinglehouse talked about building another, but with the country in the middle of a depression, most families lacked the necessary funds to keep food on the table and the mortgages paid on the farms. So building a new church stalled at the discussion stage.

Taffy pulls, sledding, and ice-skating parties filled our social calendars. At these parties, a predictable social pattern could be expected. The men stood at one end of the hall discussing the best seed for field corn or the coming threat of war with Spain, while the women gathered beside the refreshment table and gossiped, sharing recipes and sure-fire methods of toilet training a toddler. The teenage boys posed and strutted for the teenage girls from opposite sides of the room, and the younger children ran about the hall, screaming and tripping up the older folks.

Due to my newly acquired adult status as a midwife, the girls I'd grown up with were in awe of me, and the boys my own age shied away from me. They were replaced by Riley's friends, who kept my mug filled with hot apple cider and my hands with butter cookies. While Hattie always started out by my side, I didn't notice at what point she would drift away from our group to join the older women. But I heard about it the moment we reached home.

"Sashaying about like that in front of those boys! Chloe, what could you have been thinking?" Sashaying was one of Ma's favorite words. In her vocabulary it could be applied to a male's actions as well as to a female's. Once she used it to describe Patches' behavior.

By the time Ma got to, "You don't see Hattie strutting about like that," all of my siblings had disappeared upstairs to their beds. After the first or second such lecture, I stopped trying to defend myself, because I had no idea what I might have done to upset her so.

Ma's sermon on the proper decorum for young ladies always included my father. "Joseph, you must do something—soon. I realize we are living in a different age. But, remember, by the time I was Chloe's age, I already had Riley, and the twins were on the way."

An early thaw postponed our socializing for more than a month and spared me a few lectures. When the roads became long quagmires, Mr. Hennessey, the town blacksmith, lent Pa his sturdy plow horses, Hans and Franz, to pull our wagon so we could continue to treat the sick.

The winter of '98 took a heavy toll on the citizens of Potter County. A number of older people didn't survive the season. Pa called the dreaded pneumonia the old man's angel of mercy. I could accept the fact that the elderly must die, but when death touched young children, I rebelled.

Though I hadn't yet lost any babies or mothers in childbirth, pneumonia claimed one of my first babies, Jeb and Mary Blackburn's infant son, Jeb junior. Harry and Lucinda Conners' baby girl died a week later. A woman over Coudersport way contracted consumption and had to go to a sanitarium in Springfield. Her husband was left with four children to raise alone.

I began to see what Auntie Gert meant about the fine line between life and death. One moment a patient would be thrashing around from a raging fever, and the next minute, stone silent. Too often, as I held a patient erect so he or she could gasp for another breath, I would pray in vain. My prayers couldn't seem to penetrate the heavy clouds hovering over our valley.

When Pa told me, "We were lucky this winter, what with the influenza epidemic running rampant in Pittsburgh and Harrisburg," I thought to myself, *Lucky? Tell that to the Conners or the Blackburns.*

At night, as my sisters slept, I would stare into the shrouded world beyond my bedroom window and demand answers. Yet, for all of my demands, no voice spoke to me, no answers came.

The day after four-year-old Corey Hanson died with whooping

cough, I confronted my parents with my doubts. Pa looked up from his newspaper and frowned. "Like it or not, death's a part of life, my child."

Ma's knitting needles clicked as she rattled off her reply. "The Lord gave, and the Lord hath taken away; blessed be the name of the Lord." The words rolled off her tongue in what seemed to me to be careless abandon.

"Ma, how can you say that? What if we were talking about Dorothy instead of Corey Hanson?" I shuddered. Of the infants I'd delivered, none was more beautiful or more precious to me than my little sister Dorothy.

Ma glanced up from the blue sweater she was knitting and tapped her thickening waist. "You'll learn. There'll always be another."

Horrified, I whirled about and ran up the stairs to my room. How could she imply that one child could take the place of another? Did she think so little about each of us, her children? I pushed the frightening thoughts from my mind. A few minutes later, Pa called me out to the herb room to help him make a new potion for Auntie Gert's arthritis.

As I stood beside him, grinding the garlic cloves with his marble pestle, Pa measured out the dried herbs he would need for the potion. Only after he scraped the herbs into the small marble bowl did he refer to my mother's words.

"Don't be too hard on her, Chloe. Remember, she's miscarried three times. She laid a boy child in the grave before ever having held him in her arms. And with each loss, she grieved."

I shook my head. "Then how can she be so cold about the death of another woman's child?"

"Some things in life you have to learn to accept. Death is one of them." Tears filled his eyes. Silently, he wrapped his arm about me and pulled me to him. He held me close for some time. Finally, he spoke. "It's just your ma's way of dealing with her own demons." His voice grew heavy with emotion. "This young-un she's carrying—it came along too soon after Dorothy. Something's not right, and your ma's afraid."

A cold draft blew through the cracks in the wall. I wrapped my arms about myself to ward off a sudden, icy chill. *Will this winter never end?*

I went to bed one night in the cold of winter and awoke in the morning to the magic of spring green. In a matter of days, my drab little world of gray and brown sprang to life. Whenever possible, I escaped the confines of the house to discover springtime's latest surprise. A gentle green carpet covered the hillside beyond the swollen creek. Warm breezes forced the redbud and dogwood trees to compete for attention.

It was on such a day that I first encountered Emmett Sawyer. Though we'd never met, I'd overheard the town gossips talking about him and his fourteen-year-old son Charley in Haney's Mercantile. He was said to be from over Wellsville way; his wife, Sadie, was said to have died of influenza.

One glance out the window on the sunny May afternoon, and I knew it was a perfect day to wash my hair. Washing a head of hair as thick and as long as mine was a major undertaking. The drying process took hours; and the hair had to be dry by bedtime.

After rinsing my hair a second time, I wrapped a towel about my head, grabbed my hairbrush, and went out onto the front porch. A black-and-white blur raced around the corner of the house and leaped up on my skirt.

"Patches! Get down. Your paws are muddy." The dog slunk away to the barnyard. I removed the towel and shook my hair free. A long, tangled mass of burnished curls tumbled down over my shoulders and back. I flipped my hair from side to side to hasten the drying process. The wet strands responded to my persistence and to the warm afternoon sun as I brushed out the snarls. Tired of sitting, I skipped down the porch steps and whirled about on the small patch of grass in front of our house. The breeze rippling through my untamed mane felt lovely. I seemed so free, so alive—like a little girl. My skirts tangled about my ankles in protest.

I don't know whether it was the sunshine or my own impish nature that lured me down to the creek. But once I gazed into the crystal water of the creek bed, I knew what I must do. Strands of hair, unaccustomed to the freedom, swirled about my face as I sat down on the exposed elm root and undid my high-button shoes. I didn't want to think about the tangle I would later have to brush. I pushed my hair back over my shoulders and removed my black woolen stockings.

Lifting my skirts to my knees, I stepped off the bank into the shoals. The icy waters inched up to my ankles, then to my calves. I squealed with delight. Mud squished between my toes. Within seconds, I was splashing about in total abandon. Ma would have been horrified.

Suddenly, as if the sun had dipped behind a cloud, a chill skittered up my spine. Sensing I wasn't alone, I whirled about. A lone rider on horseback sat by the road, watching and laughing. My hands flew to my flushed face, then back to my now sodden skirts. Indignant, I leaped from the water and hid behind the trunk of the elm. The stranger laughed again and headed down the road.

Of all the nerve, I thought. *A gentleman would have pretended not to see me.* One of Ma's reprimands came to mind: "A lady would not have allowed herself to be caught in such a compromising situation."

Once I was certain he'd gone, I came out of hiding. I snaked my fingers through my tangled locks and tried to weave them into a semblance of braids. Tying a sprig of grass around the ends of the braids to keep them from unraveling, I danced about the moss at the base of the tree, scrubbing the mud from my toes. If I hurried home in time to help Ma prepare supper, no one would ever need to know how foolish I'd been.

I dashed across the grassy slope and into the backyard. Pausing at the slat fence, I wrung out the hem of my skirt and petticoats, adjusted the apron over my skirt, opened the gate, and ran into the house.

The door to the pantry had barely closed behind me when I realized it was later than I imagined. I heard Pa's voice and that of a stranger. A sense of foreboding nibbled at the corners of my mind. Ma must have heard the back door slam. "Chloe, is that you? Please bring me two spuds from the bin."

I chose two potatoes and squared my shoulders before entering the kitchen. *This is my home,* I thought. *I will not enter it like a stray field mouse!* I pushed the dividing door open and crossed to the stove, where Ma stood slicing a large russet potato into a frying pan. "Here, Ma, will these two do?"

My hands shook as I handed her the potatoes.

"Whatever happened to you? Your hair is a mess," she hissed. Composing myself as best I could, I smiled and walked over to where Hattie sat rocking Dorothy. "She's fast asleep. Would you like me to carry her to her cradle?"

"Wait, Chloe." Pa strode to my side and wrapped his arm about my shoulders. "I would like to introduce you to Emmett Sawyer. Emmett, this is my daughter, Chloe Mae. And Chloe Mae, this is Mr. Sawyer."

Our eyes met, and I knew my life was over. For a couple of seconds I thought I would die of humiliation right there in front of my parents. But my discomfort quickly switched to anger. My right hand itched to wipe that smug little grin from his face. Clutching his hat in both hands, the middle-aged farmer tipped his head toward me and pursed his lips.

"How nice to meet you, Miss Chloe. I look forward to getting to know you better in the days to come—if and when our paths cross."

I smiled the smile of a dutiful daughter, nodded my head in polite deference, then glared. The man took a step backward in surprise.

"If and when our paths cross, of course, Mr. Sawyer. Now, if you'll excuse me, I need to help Ma finish supper."

Over the next three weeks, I ran into the man everywhere I went—at the mercantile, at grange meetings, in front of Minnie Perkins' dress shop. Even when I stayed home, he showed up at our door, asking to see my father.

While I noticed the curious glances passing between my parents, I failed to see any significance until the all-day meeting at the grange. For weeks, posters announcing the visit of Pastor and Mrs. Victor Van Dorn, missionaries from China, appeared in every storefront in town. The advertisement said that the Van Dorn's were touring the United States to raise money for their mission work in Canton. They would have genuine Chinese artifacts, including photographs of the people and their country.

In the remote hamlet of Shinglehouse, where all entertainment was home-grown, a visiting missionary ranked right up there with a religious revival meeting or a traveling circus. Everyone would be there, from Hector, the town drunk, to the Chamberlains, the town royalty.

On the appointed Sunday, Ma had a bout of morning sickness and decided not to go. Pa agreed to take us only after Hattie and I promised to manage the younger children. After morning chores, we packed a picnic lunch and headed for town. Hattie led the way into the grange while I herded the children from the rear.

Mr. Haney, owner of the mercantile, introduced the speaker. From his first words, Pastor Van Dorn held all of us spellbound. His tales of the exotic Orient and the devastating needs of the people there wrenched tears from our eyes and coins from our pocketbooks. Even Josiah Goodwin, the town atheist, who trumpeted the teachings of the French philosopher Voltaire, dropped a coin into the offering plate.

At noon, the women of the community unpacked their choicest casseroles, pies, and cakes from their picnic baskets onto the sawhorse tables on the front lawn of the grange. As I stood looking for a place to set Ma's Dutch oven of chicken 'n' dumplings, Emmett Sawyer stepped up to my side. "My, you sure look purty in that blue gingham dress, Miss Chloe. And those dumplings smell somethin' good."

I smiled a weak smile and inched away. He pursued. In desperation, I insinuated myself between two of the women standing near the center of the table.

"Excuse me, please, got a hot kettle here." They made room for me. I placed the pot and the hot pad on the table. "Thank you," I murmured, "mighty heavy."

Turning toward the woman on my left, I smiled. "Mrs. Peterson, what a lovely gabardine frock. The rose tone accentuates your natural ivory complexion so beautifully. You must have ordered it from New York City."

The young woman twisted her head from side to side and patted her Gibson girl hairdo. Then as if confiding a choice bit of gossip, she leaned forward. "Why, Chloe Mae, I must be honest with you. I copied it from one I saw in the Monkey Ward catalog. I used the fabric from one of my mother's hoop-skirted dresses, rest her soul."

I peered over her shoulder at the retiring figure of Mr. Sawyer and returned my attention to the dress. "Well, I am impressed. Before we know it, you'll be giving poor Minnie Perkins a little competition."

Mrs. Peterson giggled behind her hand, then waved me away. "Oh, no, dear, I could never . . ."

I patted her arm. "Well, it is a lovely dress, Mrs. Peterson." I glanced over her shoulder once more to be certain Mr. Sawyer had disappeared from view. "Oh, no, will you excuse me? My little brother Worley is giving Hattie fits and commotions."

I slipped between two of the men waiting in the food line and ran to the far side of the lawn, where Hattie had spread out a blanket. Worley sat with legs crossed and lips pouting while his baby sister lay asleep on one corner of the blanket. "Hattie, let me take Worley over to Amby and Jesse. It won't hurt them to watch him for a while, at least while we eat. I'll watch Dorothy while you get yourself a plate of food."

When I returned from my errand and dropped onto the blanket, Hattie struggled to her feet and limped over to the food line. I closed my eyes. The sounds of laughter and the warmth of sunlight filled my mind with peace.

In sharp contrast to the euphoria I felt, lurid pictures of starving, diseased people paraded through my mind. Mothers and newborns dying without medical help. Children suffering from blood poisoning. I could hear Mr. Van Dorn's booming bass voice relating the physical and spiritual needs of these forgotten people.

"And the Master said unto them, 'Go ye into all the world, and preach the gospel to every creature.' That, my friends, includes the untold millions of Chinese who live and die without hearing the very name of Jesus."

With the suddenness of a lightning bolt, I knew. An icy tingle ran up my spine. *China—God wants me to go as a missionary to China. I had never been particularly religious.* For all the books I'd read, I'd never considered reading the Bible. Pa was the one who read the Bible at the table and offered a blessing before each meal. Sometimes I'd seen him late in the evening, sitting beside the kitchen stove, reading from God's Word. No, religion was Pa's job, not mine.

I'd never heard of God directing anyone to go to a foreign land. I tried to shake the conviction growing inside me. But the more I denied it, the stronger it grew. When Hattie returned with her food, I made my way over to the group of women surrounding Annabelle Van Dorn. They were asking questions. When the missionary finished answering one of the women's question, I interrupted.

"Excuse me, Mrs. Van Dorn, but what do I have to do to become a missionary to China?" The woman smiled at me as she would at a precocious ten-year-old. I continued, hoping I could convince her that I was serious. "God just told me He wants me to go to China, and I have no idea how to go about it." I knew I sounded petulant, but I refused to waver.

The surrounding women stared at me as if I'd just arrived from China instead of having proposed going. Mrs. Van Dorn cleared her throat. "Well, child, it would be very difficult for a young woman like yourself to travel alone to China. My advice to you would be, find a good man who shares your conviction."

"I-I-I don't want—"

The missionary patted me gently on the shoulder and suggested, "Make it a matter of prayer, dear."

"But-I-I—"

Sensing my frustration, she added, "Mark my words, child. If God wants you to go as a missionary to China, He will work it out."

I don't know exactly what I'd expected her to say, but that was hardly it. I wanted specific directions. I turned and walked away. I needed time to think, to be alone. I strolled over to a grassy knoll behind the grange hall and sat down. In the distance, I could hear Mr. Haney announce the beginning of the afternoon session. I knew I should go back and help Hattie round up the boys, but at that moment, I didn't care. I hugged my knees and rested my chin on my forearm.

"Dear heavenly Father, I'm so confused." I hoped I was doing it right, talking so directly, but it had worked the evening Dorothy was born. "I really did believe You spoke to me back there on the lawn. Now, I'm not so sure."

I didn't hear footsteps approaching until the intruder spoke. "Is this a private party, or may I join you?"

I twisted about, fire leaping from my eyes. "Mr. Sawyer, what do I have to do to convince you—" I stopped midsentence and blushed.

Shock filled Phillip Chamberlain's face. "I-I-I truly am sorry. I-I-I didn't mean to interrupt anything."

I reached up toward him. "Oh, no. I'm so sorry. I thought you were someone else."

He breathed a low whistle and shook his head. "I'm mighty glad I'm not whoever you thought I was. The fire in your eyes could slay a mountain lion."

I laughed. "Please, sit down if you'd like. I really don't mind."

He dropped onto the knoll beside me, allowing a comfortable space between us. "So what do you think of this Van Dorn person?"

After the women's reaction to my announcement, I wondered how honest I should be. Should I play the coquette, flirt, say all the right things—or should I risk being me? I chose to be me.

"I can't imagine a greater commission than to be sent as a missionary." My voice was heavy with emotion.

"Really?" He acted pleasantly surprised. My words tumbled over one another as I tried to explain myself, but he stopped me.

"Don't apologize, I know how you feel. Last fall, I attended similar lectures at Harvard and decided to become a missionary to Africa. I was serious enough to change my major from law to theology." He paused and inhaled slowly. "When my father came East to bail Cy, my older brother, out of trouble, Dad exploded all over the back bay. And as a result, he brought us both back to Shinglehouse with him."

Sympathy welled up inside me. I glanced over at him. But he didn't notice. His attention was focused on some distant point along the horizon. I waited for him to continue speaking. When he remained silent, I wondered if I should say something. Since I'd never been good at small talk, I waited. Five minutes or more passed. Suddenly, he shook his head as if drawing himself back to the present. The painful smile he gave me conveyed more than any words he could have spoken.

"I don't know why I'm telling you this. I hardly know you." He picked a blade of grass and nibbled it. "Sometimes I think I disappointed my parents more for wanting to be a minister than my brother did for being expelled from school for cheating."

"And what now?"

He shrugged his shoulders. "Mr. Rockefeller promised my father he would find positions for both Cy and me. Railroads, oil, banking—I don't know. And I guess I really don't care." Suddenly his face brightened. "Enough of my woes; tell me, what's there to do in a small town like Shinglehouse?"

I rolled my eyes heavenward. "We have a nice little library. And there's always the latest gossip, both local and national."

"Oh?"

"Why, yes, did you know that George, the town barber, is courting Miss Bladkin? She lives in Coudersport. And did you hear about the assistant secretary of the United States Navy's slur against President McKinley? Mr. Roosevelt said the president has as much backbone as a chocolate eclair! By the way, what's a chocolate eclair?"

Phillip tipped his head back and laughed. "A French pastry filled with air and whipped cream." I asked him questions about the cities he'd visited—Boston, Philadelphia, and Pittsburgh. I'd never enjoyed an afternoon so much in my life. When the pump organ inside the grange hall wheezed out the opening chords of "Rescue the Perishing," we stared at one another. The afternoon meeting wasn't beginning, it was over.

Phillip leaped up, took my hands in his, and helped me to my feet. He stared down at my hands still trapped in his. Reluctantly, he released them. I felt an immediate loss. "You are so easy to talk to, Miss Spencer. I hate to let you go." He brushed invisible specks from his trousers. "I hope I haven't upset your father by keeping you out here like this during the meeting."

I groaned and rolled my eyes heavenward. "I'll hear about it, I'm sure. But you didn't keep me out here. I was here first, remember?"

He glanced first one direction, then the other. A group of young boys stood talking over by the wagons. With a dimpled smile and a teasing wink, he suggested, "If I head around the other side of the building and slip into the back row of the hall, no one will need to know we played hooky from the afternoon meeting."

He disappeared around the corner of the gray stone building. I waited until the congregation started the last verse of the hymn, then strolled over to a bench in the side yard and sat down.

In a few minutes, people began emerging from the hall and hurrying to their wagons. Because most were farmers, they had cows to milk before the daylight disappeared. Hattie looked at me questioningly as I joined our family and helped her herd the children into the wagon. Pa strode over to the wagon and climbed into the driver's seat. "Hattie! Joe! You two ride in back with the young-uns. Chloe Mae, you sit up here with me!"

At the edge of town, the back wheels of the wagon cleared the bridge's surface before Pa spoke. "Chloe Mae, I have never been as angry with you as I am at this moment. If you were a few years younger, I'd give you the strapping of your life. I might anyway!" He snapped the reins across the team's back. The wagon lurched forward.

I swallowed hard. "Pa—"

He held up one finger before my face. "Don't say anything. If I had known you were out there with the Chamberlain boy . . ." Tears sprang up in my eyes. The last thing I would ever want to do was disappoint my father.

"Pa, we were just talking, honest." I hastened on before he could reply. "Did you know that Phillip wants to be a minister and go as a missionary to Africa? Isn't that exciting?"

"*Humph!* The day his parents allow him to do that!"

We rode for a few minutes without speaking. If I were going to share my newfound conviction with my father, I knew I'd better do it while I had him alone. Besides, if I could get him talking about the day's events, he might forget his anger at me.

"And, Pa, that's not all. After listening to Pastor Van Dorn describe the desperate conditions in China today, I would love to go too."

"Huh?" My father glanced toward me. He hadn't heard what I said. "Where was that you want to go, Chloe Mae?"

I sucked in my breath. "I want to become a missionary to China. I honestly believe that God . . ."

My father shook his head. "Chloe Mae, you come up with the wildest ideas sometimes. Most girls your age dream of riding off into the sunset with their knight in shining armor." He frowned. "I think your mother may be right. I've treated you too much like a son instead of a daughter—perhaps, it's not too late to rectify the situation."

I scowled as I replied, "I-I-I don't understand."

The worry lines on his face deepened. "We'll finish this conversation this evening after the young-uns are asleep."

"But, Pa . . ." My protests failed to penetrate the wall of silence he'd constructed between us.